UMP

UMP

A Dark Comedy

James Cohen

Walker and Company
New York

First published in the United States of America in 1991 by
Walker Publishing Company, Inc.

Published simultaneously in Canada by Thomas Allen & Son
Canada, Limited, Markham, Ontario.

Library of Congress Cataloging-in-Publication Data

Cohen, James.
Ump: a dark comedy / James Cohen.
p. cm.
ISBN 0-8027-1182-0
I. Title.
PS3553.042428U47   1991
813'.54—dc20   91-23588
CIP

Printed in the United States of America

2 4 6 8 10 9 7 5 3 1

To Mary McCann Cohen

Who taught her sons to bend and feel the rocks,
Who sat by the bed so fingers could run through her
* hair,*
Who tickled a frog to life, and combed a puppy into a
* ball of panting adoration,*
Who crafted her family with the attention of an artist,
* which she is.*

To my mother, who makes the thought of eternal love
* believable.*

PART I

UMP

ONE

The Golla brothers—Joey, Tony, and Sal—had to die.

For months, they had been forcing their way into Tommy Lucci's drug market. First, they tried buying off the drivers who did Tommy's weekly shipments from Miami; then the Gollas went down to Florida and nosed into his flotilla; and now they had flown to Costa Rica and actually offered Tommy's supplier a deal that would have shaved forty percent of his goods.

It was a stupid move, the sort of thing that could easily lead to a mob war. So Tommy wrote a letter telling the Gollas to rethink their corporate strategy.

The next day, the Gollas blew up Tommy Lucci's Pizza Palace.

Tommy learned of the hit around midnight. Within an hour he was at the scene, walking through the wreckage, looking for anything worth salvaging.

"Freido, Freido, Freido," Tommy lamented, calling for his "right arm," kicking at the steel door of a fallen oven. "Freido, how could this happen?"

Freido walked out of the rear kitchen. Physically, the two men were similar. They were both heavy, but in the way of aging football tackles—basic muscle that had been padded with too many good years. The main differences were in their faces. Freido's forehead ridged back a bit farther, and he had a neck scar from the time the Gambinos tried cutting his throat. Tommy had never been touched, which said a lot about how carefully he handled business. "Both cooks are dead," Freido said. "There are bullet holes all over the back wall. Looks like they were killed with a repeat .22."

Tommy couldn't believe it. He found the bodies folded under a wooden counter, bent execution-style, with mozzarella sprinkled on their heads. Dough and blood were everywhere.

"You're telling me . . ." He swallowed deeply, his anger almost painful. "You mean," he said, "the Gollas not only blew up my restaurant, they walked back here, dressed my cooks in cheese, and massacred them?"

Tommy covered his eyes, his head aching from the catastrophe.

"Talk to me, Freido," Tommy said. "Why my parlor? Why my cooks?"

When Freido still didn't answer, Tommy looked up. He saw Freido sucking his fingers, the sauce dripping from his hands. Freido sucked away until he realized Tommy was watching. Then he closed the tub and wiped his hands.

"Sorry, Mr. Lucci," Freido said. "It really was the best."

Freido was nervous. He expected Tommy to snap—to slap his face, or pour the sauce over his head, or kick him in the balls, or something much, much worse.

But Tommy Lucci only turned away. He couldn't get angry. In his own way, Freido had answered Tommy's question. The Gollas had sought revenge and had hit Tony where it hurt most: in the ego.

TWO

It wasn't meant to be a big deal. Tommy Lucci opened the Pizza Palace in 1983 as part of a general scheme for laundering drug money. The idea was to run a legitimate business that could routinely and inconspicuously process the cash Lucci acquired from the sale of cocaine. Thus, while money was changed in the cash registers, Lucci promised quality pizza dining, with only the finest whole-milk mozzarella cheese, fresh dough, and freshly simmered tomato sauce.

Tommy wasn't thinking of good food; he just wanted to avoid any complications with food inspectors. He wanted an operation so clean it would hide his real dirt.

Imagine his surprise when the crowds started coming.

"Without a doubt, the Pizza Palace is the best pizza in New York City," declared *New York* magazine.

"Good-bye, Ray's," read a *Times* review. "So long John's and Pizzeria Uno and all other pretenders to the pizza throne. There's a new pie in town. It's called the Pizza Palace and it's going to turn this city into a one-pizza town."

Six months after the Pizza Palace opened, Tommy Lucci's pies were being rated the very best in the city. Tommy Lucci—mob boss, extortionist, drug runner, embezzler, whore master, racketeer, murderer—was suddenly pizza king of Manhattan.

"Once you have a slice, you want another, another, another, another. . . ." said the *Daily News.*

"This is not a meal," said the *New York Post,* "it's food from the gods."

The city declared Tommy Lucci a king, and at last he held a title in public without the threat of indictment. Even more important, people—famous people—suddenly couldn't get enough of him. He was chic. They wanted him and his pizza at parties, at discos. . . . After a lifetime avoiding the media, Tommy Lucci had to hire a publicist.

"Mr. Lucci?" his secretary would call, her hand over the phone's mouthpiece. "Mr. Stallone wants to know if we can send five pies to his house in L.A."

Tommy would take the call himself. "Hello, Sly? How about I jet them out? . . . No, my treat. I mean it," all the time staring at a wall of photographs. Tommy Lucci and Tony Bennett. Tommy Lucci and Frank Sinatra. Tommy Lucci and Woody Allen. Tommy Lucci and anyone he wanted.

"I'll have them on the coast by four. How's that, Sly?" hanging up and buzzing his secretary. "Angela, get five from the parlor and have them on my plane in an hour. They can ride with that Vegas coke shipment."

How sweet it was. People were talking to him about franchises. The mayor called about having him cater charities. As for Tommy's mob connections, they began packaging their deals differently. "That's five kilos of coke plus a month's worth of pizza."

Tommy found himself arguing over toppings instead of cash. Work couldn't have been better.

And now this.

He left the restaurant, shaking his head, fighting the frustration.

This, he thought again, the rear door of his limousine already open. Tommy slid onto the back seat and Freido sat beside him. Christ, it hurt more than losing a kid.

Freido saw the pain. He sat with his hands folded, letting Tommy suffer quietly, thinking ahead. Tonight, Freido would start making phone calls—lining up the assignments, picking the right men for the right jobs, making all the necessary arrangements. . . . It would be a busy evening, that was certain. Despite what some said, it was work killing people, especially protected people like the Gollas. But that was Freido's specialty, and as always, he was determined not to disappoint.

"Mr. Lucci," Freido said, looking at his boss, hoping for direction. "Mr. Lucci, I need to know something."

Tommy didn't answer, and Freido edged about, waiting for a chance to ask his question.

"Mr. Lucci, I was wondering how bad you want the Gollas hurt?"

Tommy stared at Freido as if he was the world's biggest idiot. "How bad?" he said. "You want me to *show* you?"

"No," Freido said—steady, the determined professional. "I know you want them dead. I didn't ask that. I just asked how bad you want them hurt."

Tommy considered the difference.

"They blew up my parlor and killed my cooks," he said. "The best pizza in New York—the best in the goddamn country." He wiped the sweat off his brow. "The Gollas humiliated me. How do you think I feel?"

Freido tried to appreciate Tommy's pain, but it was impossible. Tommy talked pizza, but the explosion hadn't just taken away a storefront. The Gollas had buried Tommy in the celebrity graveyard. Without the pizzas—because of a single explosion—Tommy had been blasted off the society page and back into metro crimes.

"You feel the Gollas should die in great pain," Freido said.

"The greatest."

"No mercy?"

"None."

Freido nodded. "Then I got one more question," he said. "Marty and Eddie. They weren't taking anything on the side, were they?"

Tommy didn't understand.

"The cooks," said Freido. "They weren't in on the laundering?"

"The only thing they knew was how to make sauce," said Tommy.

"How about the other rackets?" Freido said. "I'm asking, Mr. Lucci, because you want the Gollas hurt bad, and I got lots of people who can do it, but only one's the best."

Tommy put a hand on Freido's shoulder. "You're losing me, Freido. What's this got to do with the cooks?"

"Well, the cooks were just cooks, and the guy I have in mind, I don't think he'd normally do this kind of job, but with the cooks dead, I may be able to make a case."

[7]

Tommy wasn't sure he followed Freido, and what he did follow Tommy didn't like. "Do I understand that you got someone for the hit, but he won't do it unless you convince him?"

"Sort of," said Freido.

"Someone who's on my payroll? Someone who works under me?"

"It's nothing to get sore about," Freido said. "It's just one guy."

"One guy who can tell me to fuck off."

"But he's the best," Freido said. "The Petrolli family? He did them. And the Rossi thing? Remember when they wired the car? This is the guy who wiped them out—four Rossis, three lieutenants, and ten soldiers. Single-handed, in under an hour."

Tommy turned away from Freido, not swayed.

"Believe me, Mr. Lucci," said Freido, "it's just the one guy. I stretch the rules for him, that's all. Everyone else knows it's just him. Shit, they were the ones who asked for it. They didn't want him working for the competition."

Tommy seemed to listen.

"The other guys pushed for him?" Tommy said.

"Practically begged me," said Freido.

Tommy thought a moment and considered what that meant. "He's that good?" he asked.

"He's better," said Freido. "It's just that, like I said, he's particular about what he'll do."

"You mean he wants more money," he said.

"I mean he needs the right kind of motivation," said Freido. "I try to look at it as a religious thing."

Tommy calmed down, wondering why he hadn't heard more of this man before. Of course he had, but Freido wasn't going to tell him now.

"And you think the dead cooks'll make the difference?"

"Don't ask me why, but yes," Freido said.

Tommy nodded, satisfied. "I hope so," he said. "For everyone's sake."

Freido tried smiling and, finally, so did Tommy, starting to appreciate how crazy it all sounded.

"You get us the weirdest fucking help, Freido," Tommy said. "What's this guy's name, anyway?"

"His real name's Frank Brady."

"Yeah?" Tommy said. "And what do you call him?"

Freido said, "I call him Ump."

THREE

There was nothing superhuman about Ump.

Bullets didn't bounce off his chest, he didn't jump over buildings, he didn't have X-ray vision.

But if you did the right thing enough times, people started to get ideas. Instead of wondering what they were doing wrong, they worried about why you did things right. And so the stories started, and so did the crazy ideas, and before long, people were saying things that didn't make sense.

Like Ump was unstoppable. That once he was given a job, no one and nothing could get in his way. He'd crash through doors, turn over cars, powerhouse his way through cement walls. . . . One way or another, Ump always finished a job.

And the reason he couldn't be stopped, they said, was he couldn't feel pain. You could bop him with a lead pipe or pop him with teflon-coated bullets; it didn't matter, because Ump kept coming until the pipe bent or the gun overheated. Some said he wore a protective vest, others said it was luck, a few thought it had to do with special training—that Ump had served in a top-secret branch of the military and had been *trained* for pain.

But then another rumor started. Someone said he had once seen Ump take several rounds and then painlessly dig the slugs out of his body. This in itself was amazing, but what made the story was the condition of the slugs. They were not only blunted, as if they had smacked into concrete instead of flesh, they were clean of blood.

Which meant Ump was not only powerful and unstoppable, he was a zombie. How else could you be shot and not bleed?

There were a ton of stories and Ump had heard most of them. The truth, however, was that much of Ump's life could be explained; you simply had to appreciate his pursuit of perfection.

For instance, Ump *could* be stopped; it was just that no one had done it. Still, the real pros credited Ump's success less to miracles and more to simpler things, such as concentration. Ump's true colleagues knew that no matter what the job—no matter how many bullets were flying—while others ducked, Ump could always be trusted to keep his head down and his body in motion. Even when he faced an army, he was focused.

As for bleeding, of course he bled. But he took more precautions than most people—padding his skin, guarding his vitals, making sure that if he did take a bullet, it would be in the fat of an arm, not an artery. Some marveled at his durability, but the truth was most people, if hit in the right places, could stand their share of bullets. Since it was his business, Ump knew what could get hit and what had to be protected.

Besides, if there was one thing about Ump, he was built for punishment. While not especially large—maybe six two and two hundred forty pounds—somehow the pounds of fat and muscle layered themselves like a protective skin. On a work day, by the time he pulled on a jacket, he was a rhinoceros.

Ump appreciated this. In the morning, when he stood naked in front of the mirror, he didn't see a man, he saw a mold of fat and muscle. Some parts were scratched, some scarred, but all of it was solid and whenever he took a deep breath, none fit comfortably in his clothes. It was as if someone had taken Ump's measurements, then subtracted two inches off his shirt, pants, and underwear. He'd pull on a T-shirt, then turn and waver back and forth just so he could see all his reflection. What he'd give if only his proportions could be rearranged—if his muscles could shrink, or if everything in the world could expand a few billion atoms.

"Frank?" his wife called. "Frank, I'm heading out. You want your breakfast?"

Ump was soon dressed and downstairs. He wrapped his

arms about Nan and for several seconds his wife completely disappeared; then, as if pulling free of a pillow, she reemerged and was back at the counter. She was a slight woman, as breakable as a match stick, but after twenty-five years of marriage, Ump's hugs hadn't come close to snapping her.

"I have to run," Nan said. "I gotta pick up the kids at Freida's." She reached for her coat and ran for the door. "I left a shopping list for you on the table, so you take care of that, okay?"

Ump nodded and settled before his eggs.

"I need fruit, but mostly I need a new plunger. We also got dry cleaning, you have to pick up the fan, and I got books for the library." She opened the door, checked her purse a last time, then dug for her car keys. "And watch how you drive," she said. "There was an accident last night on Atlantic. Two people got killed. One of the cars was driving seventy miles an hour."

Ump stretched for the salt.

"Frank?" Nan said, wanting an answer.

"I always watch out for the other guy, Nan," he said. "You know that."

"Just be extra careful," she said. "There are people who don't give a damn about anything. Some of them are lunatics. They do whatever the hell they want."

"I won't take my eyes off the road," he promised.

Nan stared until she believed him, then let Ump kiss her. "You better not," she said. "There are only three people in the world I trust. One of them is you, the others are the kids."

A half hour later, Ump had finished breakfast and was off to do the shopping. Just as he promised, Ump drove carefully. First, he went to the library, then to the dry cleaners, then to the hardware. . . . The entire time, he never drove over thirty, and the entire time, he never broke his concentration, not even when most people would have screeched off the road.

The first moment came just blocks from his house, when Ump witnessed a mugging—a woman with a fur, walking down the sidewalk, was suddenly on her knees while a kid grabbed her purse and tore across the street. She lay on the sidewalk, pleading as much to Ump as God, desperate for help.

But divine intervention wasn't Ump's thing. Besides, what

sense was there flaunting your goods while walking alone in a city? A minnow doesn't swim near a shark unless it's ready to be eaten.

He slowed to let the kid run by, then made a right at the corner and continued his drive.

A tough day in the city. He hadn't gone a mile before a cop waved him to a stop. A jumper stood on a ledge and the police were detouring traffic. Meanwhile, across the street, a crowd of teenagers shouted for the man to leap. It was disgusting. It was infuriating. Every one of these people deserved a smack across the head, and that was just for starters. Begging a man to kill himself? Nudging him over the edge?

But, if a man's gonna jump, and then not jump, then change his mind again, only to flip back and cry for help. . . .

Ump followed the detour and continued to the store.

The groceries took forty minutes. It might have gone quicker, except he kept forgetting things like Nan's nylons. He couldn't remember if he was looking for control tops or stretch tops or any other kind of top. Instead, he picked up an assortment, then went looking for the apples. But did she want Macs or Delicious or Grannies?

He finally took his grab bag to the front, emptying his basket, laying down his items. . . .

And then he saw it. While he was standing in line to pay for a cart full of crap, he saw eleven items on the ten-item express line.

It wasn't even his line. Ump was at another cashier when he saw this bodybuilder in shorts and a tank top throw a pack of gum on the conveyor belt. Without the gum, the bodybuilder was inside the limit. With it, he was over.

Ump leaned across the counter and talked to the man.

"Excuse me, but I think you're on the wrong line."

The bodybuilder tried ignoring him. Rather than face Ump, he reached in a wallet and paid the bill. Ump, however, only leaned closer to him.

"I said you got too much stuff," Ump said again.

The man still ignored him. So did the cashier and everyone else, probably because no one cared. But Ump cared. And after paying for his groceries, Ump followed the man back to the parking lot. He watched the man put his shopping bag into a

Porsche, then waited for him to run into a liquor store. When Ump was alone in the parking lot, he reached in his shopping bag and pulled out Nan's new electric iron. He walked up to the Porsche, circled the car, admired its shine, ran a finger across the smooth finish. . . .

Finally, he went to work.

He started with the front window. He came down hard, striking again and again until the glass shattered. That was his warm up. Then he broke off both side mirrors, tore off the windshield wipers, and smashed the rear window. This got him in stride, and he hammered away at the top and sides of the car until there wasn't a panel without a bend. He hammered until the casing of the iron split, then he put it back in the bag and bent down, grabbing the undercarriage and rocking the car. He rocked it twice, then heaved with all his strength. His face tightened and turned red, his muscles swelled, his fingers locked tighter to the car than a lug nut.

With a last surge, he flipped the Porsche on its side.

The bodybuilder showed up about the time Ump was cleaning his hands. First the man looked stunned, then he looked furious. By the time he faced Ump, he was ready to kill.

Or so it seemed. Because the bodybuilder only thought he was ready to kill. The truth was, he knew nothing about death.

Ump, however, knew what killing meant, and it showed. Ump was in his mood, and you didn't need to be a professional to recognize it.

The bodybuilder took a step backward. "You're crazy," he said.

"I may be crazy, but at least I can count," Ump answered.

"I'm phoning the police," the bodybuilder shouted. "I got your license number. I'll—"

Ump tore the license plates off his own car and tossed him the plates. "Keep them," he said. "I got plenty more."

The man watched as Ump settled in his station wagon and drove out of the lot.

Ump took the long way home so he'd have time to cool down. When he finally opened the front door, Nan was back and greeted him with a kiss. She also took the bag of groceries, not getting angry until she saw the broken iron.

"Shit, Frank, what good is this?"

Ump avoided facing her. "It broke in the back seat," he said.

"It broke all by itself?"

Ump looked embarrassed. "It's dry outside. That's what happens in dry heat."

Nan stared at Ump, not believing him but not sure the truth was worth hearing.

"Cheap piece of shit," she said finally, throwing it in the garbage.

Ump loved it when Nan talked dirty. He sneaked up and kissed her on the neck.

"I met this guy down at the store," Ump told her. "Absolute idiot. I mean, here's this sign staring him in the face, says express line, ten items or less, and what does he do? He puts down eleven things. I mean, with the goddamn rules right in his face."

"Someone should set him straight," Nan said. "That's why I warned you, Frank. This city's filled with lunatics."

"Yeah, well, thank God for people who can read," said Ump. "Is it asking so much for people to follow a few simple rules?"

"Not if it includes kissing me," Nan said, turning to hug him back.

"That's my number one rule," Ump said, and he gave her a kiss.

They were in each other's arms when the phone rang.

FOUR

Ump's philosophy was simple—people, more times than not, got what they deserved.

He himself was a good example. He ate steaks and french fries, drank lots of beer, and the end result was a man thick with bulk. Also, he didn't wear a hat, so the sun had started blotching his skin and had tinted his black, curly hair. The facts went on and on. Since he lifted weights, his arms were strong; since he didn't run, his legs were weak. In comparison, Nan liked to jog, so she had strong legs but weak arms. And his two kids, a pair of sons, had weak arms, legs, and heads because all they did was watch television.

It was the one true truism he believed and accepted.

But when people got more than they deserved . . . Or when people gave too much shit . . . Well, that was something different. That wasn't fine, and Ump got angry.

And this was where a lot of Ump's colleagues lost him. They could appreciate the ground rules of his thinking. Some even admired him for them. He had quite a reputation among killers, and if Ump needed personal motivation before a hit, maybe they all did.

But no one could quite make out how he applied his logic. Why was it okay to kill someone like Frank Glecco—a nobody who made his money in the numbers—but it wasn't right putting the twist on Theo Papillardi, who ran a child prostitution ring? Or why was it wrong to kill Angie Bigolo in a taxi, but it was okay slicing Billy "Crackers" Callahan during his daughter's baptism?

They knew it wasn't a matter of courage. Ump didn't

[15]

think twice about taking on ten men solo. Hell, sometimes he didn't think at all; he just heard what he needed to hear and did business. No arguments, no questions. That was how his mind worked. That was why they called him Ump.

Still, this didn't explain *why* Ump said yes or no, or why, without warning, for no obvious reason, he sometimes snapped into a rage. What made him do the things he did? Was it genetic? For that matter, what made anyone do what they did?

"Sit down, Ump," said Freido. "Have a slice of pizza."

Ump walked into Tommy Lucci's office and sat beside Freido. Tommy was also in the room, sitting in his own leather seat, but Freido normally did the talking for contract work. For one, you never knew when someone was taping a conversation, so it was safer for Tommy to have Freido act as the mouth. More important, though, was that Tommy Lucci didn't like hit men. It had nothing to do with their line of work; people with weak stomachs didn't get jobs like Tommy's. The problem was one of smell. Hit men—fixers—always stank of death, and the worst part was that you couldn't tell whose death you smelled. Was it someone they were going to kill, or someone they had killed yesterday? Or maybe it was time for the killer to die, or maybe you smelled your own death? Maybe, but who knew?

Rather than get too close to the conversation, he listened while Freido eased into his talk. This in itself was a show. For one guy, Freido might sit on the sofa, talk about the kids, give a name and address, and then call it a day. With another, he'd turn the lamp into the man's face and slap him around like he was starting an interrogation. Freido had a feel for people. That's why Tommy hung around now, to see how Freido handled Ump, to see how Freido made this fickle hit man take on a job that mattered more to Tommy than half his empire.

"Come on, Ump," Freido said. "You like plain or pepperoni?"

At first, Ump said nothing. He felt uncomfortable in the room, which only made sense. The chair Tommy had offered wasn't designed for someone Ump's size. Ump filled it to the point where his arms hung over the sides.

There was something else, though, and Freido couldn't figure it. Ump wasn't angry, but he also wasn't moving or talking. He looked from the pizza to Tommy Lucci, then back to the pizza.

Finally, Tommy understood. He waved a hand and said, "No thanks, I'm not hungry."

Ump turned back to Freido. "Pepperoni, please."

Freido slid the piece to his hit man. He watched as Ump carefully chewed, then swallowed and wiped his mouth. A minute passed before Ump gave his verdict. "Pretty good," he said.

"More than good, Ump: the best," Freido said. "That's homemade sauce."

Ump nodded, approving.

"Stewed daily," Freido said.

Ump slowed his chewing to clean a tooth. "The dough's a bit tough," he said.

"Sure it is," Freido said. "The pie's a day old. It was the only pie left from the explosion."

This time, Ump stopped eating and looked at the slice. "You giving me day-old pizza?"

"That's special pizza," Freido said. "Legendary. Sylvester Stallone ate that pizza."

"Not this one," said Ump.

"One just like it," Freido said. "Except there aren't gonna be any more slices because of the explosion."

Ump thought a moment, uncertain whether to keep eating.

He shrugged and bit in.

"A big explosion," Freido continued. "Took out the whole front window."

"I heard," Ump said. "Tough luck."

"It wasn't tough luck, Ump," Freido said. "Tough luck is when someone forgets to turn off the gas and you light a match. That's not what happened here. Someone made a hit against us. They went for Mr. Lucci by going after the restaurant."

Ump bit, chewed, wiped his mouth.

"The people who did this—the Gollas—they've been trying for months to break into Mr. Lucci's business," said Freido. "First they tried buying off our drivers. When that didn't work,

[17]

they went after our boats. And when that flopped, they went after our sources."

"The Gollas have been busy," Ump said, not meaning to be so offhand, but he just wasn't interested. He looked at Tommy, certain there was something else he had to do, then remembered his package. Ump reached under his chair for a bag and presented Tommy Lucci with a jar of tomato sauce. "Mr. Lucci, my wife asked me to bring this for you. She cooked it herself. Said bring it along, maybe it'll get you in good with the boss."

Ump put the jar on the desk and Tommy took it. He stared at the sauce, not quite sure what to make of the gift. Here they were, trying to talk murder, and suddenly Freido's ace hit man was cluttering his desk with presents. He didn't know what to do, aside from saying thank you and glaring at Freido.

"Ump, pay attention," Freido said. "The Gollas are trying to make us bleed. We don't like bleeding. We want to take out at least one of the Gollas and straighten things out. Sal Golla. All these problems have been his idea. If we take out Sal, then the other brothers will leave us alone. Hell, maybe the two of them will fight over Sal's third."

"Yeah?" said Ump, leaning forward, letting Freido know he was listening.

Freido tried rephrasing what he had said. "The Gollas are trying to squeeze us. They've tried taking our business, and now they've blown up our restaurant."

"Yeah?" said Ump, still listening.

"We can't let that go unanswered. We want you to take care of Sal."

Ump considered what Freido had said. He seemed to think real hard, his eyebrows crunching down, his mouth frowning. Tommy and Freido stared at him, waiting for Ump to comprehend the situation.

When Ump did, he leaned back. "No, Freido," he said. "I don't think so."

Freido glanced at Tommy so they could share the frustration. "Listen carefully, all right?" Freido told Ump. "We're not the bad guys here; we're the good guys. We didn't go looking for trouble. Every week, business was fine, we did our jobs, we let other people do theirs. The *Gollas*, though. The *bad* guys.

They tried hurting us. And if we don't do something soon, they may kill everyone here, including you."

Ump again considered what he had heard, then studied his slice of pizza. Freido hoped that Ump was thinking about Sal Golla and how right they were in taking him out of the life cycle. He hoped that something in the story gave Ump the push necessary for taking the assignment.

"Don't tell Nan, Freido, but I think this sauce is better than hers."

"Jesus," Tommy said.

Freido knew it was time to play the trump card. He pulled the slice of pizza away from Ump and held him by the shoulders. "Well, before you take another bite, my friend, think about this. Two men died for this pie. Two men that had nothing to do with anything. Just a couple of guys who tossed dough for a living. Both of them, shot in the head execution style, just because they happened to get in the way of Sal Golla."

Ump shrugged. "Those things happen," he said. "Maybe if I knew them, I could say different, but as far as I know, there isn't no one who gets it that probably doesn't deserve it."

Tommy slammed down a fist. "Yeah?" he shouted. "That include me? You think I should die?"

"I'm not saying anyone should die," said Ump. "I'm just saying it's part of the ball game. You can't fight life; that's what Nan says."

Tommy rolled his eyes. "I don't believe this." He turned his attention completely away from Ump, focusing on Freido. "Look, he's going to do it, right? When all this bullshit is done, he's going to take the job?"

Freido wanted to say yes, but couldn't. He knew, as of this moment, if he asked Ump, the answer would be no. And if he ordered Ump, the answer would still be no. Freido moved closer to Ump, his eyes pleading for understanding, trying to figure out some way to break through the barrier.

Ump reached for a second slice of pie. "This is great sauce. You got to give me the recipe."

"Forget about the sauce," Freido said. "Tommy Lucci is asking you to do a job for him. He's asking you because he respects your work. He could give this job to anyone. *Anyone.*

But his honor's at stake and he wants the best. That's you, Ump. You appreciate honor, don't you?"

"Honor is a very personal thing," Ump answered.

"Exactly," said Freido. "And Mr. Lucci has been personally insulted, which is why this job is so important to him."

Ump tried to put his thoughts together. "Except honor isn't something you can save, is it? I mean, if my wife is walking down the beach in a bikini, and someone makes a crack about her great knockers, and I break the guy's neck, she's still got great knockers. I haven't changed anything, have I?"

Freido stared back, making no sense of what Ump said, except that he was still refusing the job.

Ump shook his head, put down the slice, and stood up. "I just don't get it, Freido. I mean, I respect Mr. Lucci." To Lucci, he said, "I've done some good work for you, sir," then to Freido, "but I don't see what's broken here. You do one thing, he does another. . . . That's what the business is about."

"You don't understand," Freido said. "Mr. Lucci *wants* you to do it."

"The job doesn't interest me. I can't work if the job doesn't interest me."

Tommy covered his face. "This is too much," he muttered.

"Ump?" Freido pleaded one last time. He leaned closer to Ump, whispering, "It's my job on the line, Ump. Don't do this to me, *please.*"

"I'm really sorry, Freido," Ump answered. "You should know I'm no good for this kind of thing. I've told you a hundred times what I can and can't do."

"Yeah, I know," Freido said, exhausted. "And I still don't understand."

Ump nodded good-bye and turned for the door. He was almost out when he stopped.

"Incidentally, my wife's sauce?" Ump said to Tommy.

Tommy stared at him.

"Try it on sausage tortellini," Ump said. "I hope you enjoy it."

"Sure," Tommy said. "Great. Thanks."

"And if you can get the recipe for that pizza sauce, I know my wife would appreciate it."

Freido laughed at him. "Right, Ump," he said. "If I stop by the morgue, I'll ask."

Ump looked confused. "Morgue?"

"That's where the cooks are," Freido said. "In the morgue."

Ump still didn't understand.

"The guys Sal Golla killed were the cooks," Freido explained. "They were the only ones who knew how to make the sauce. The recipe died with them."

Ump listened, digested, comprehended.

He walked back into the room and sat in his chair.

"No more sauce," Ump said.

"No more sauce," Freido said.

"No more sauce," Tommy said.

Ump shook his head.

"Now that," he said, "is a different story."

FIVE

It wasn't going to be easy killing Sal Golla.

Of the three Golla brothers, Sal was the one reputed to be careful and ruthless. In contrast, Tony Golla was little more than a financial whiz, a kind of unacclaimed Wall Street trader, respected by his brothers for buying the sort of reliable insider information that guaranteed no matter what else happened, Tony's end would bring a profit.

Likewise, Joey Golla was known less as a cutthroat and more for certain lower-management skills. Joey enjoyed supervising the day-to-day operations of the family, in fact, enjoyed it so much he didn't bother with an office. Instead, after meeting once in the morning with his brothers, Joey spent most of the day in his limousine, personally overseeing the pimping, drug sales, and extortion. It was Joey who had made the trips to Miami and Central America. Joey also arranged the Pizza Palace bombing, taking care of everything with the same efficiency he used for organizing their parents' fiftieth anniversary.

Not once did it occur to Joey or Tony to seek a more influential position in the Golla hierarchy. In part, this was because they enjoyed their jobs, an enjoyment reinforced by a family bond. Another reason, however, was that both Joey and Tony Golla knew better than to risk angering Sal. There were few things worse in the world than Sal Golla angry, and usually, by the time he stopped being angry, there were fewer things left for comparison.

Sal simply had no control over his temper. He wasn't impulsive—he didn't grab a bat and start smashing cars like some people in the business—but once the anger simmered, it simmered until it boiled, then it kept boiling until his anger evaporated and the world was left scalded. Sal could stay angry for days, weeks, months . . . however long it took not only to even the score, but to finish with a lopsided victory.

That was why he had initiated his attack against Lucci by blowing apart the restaurant and killing a pair of innocent cooks. It was a signal that no one associated with Lucci would be safe. No matter how weak the tie—even if you just shined Tommy Lucci's shoes—you'd better be careful, because for the Gollas, any solution was a final one.

No wonder his brothers regarded Sal as their strength and protector. They depended completely on him. If someone told a joke, they turned to Sal to see if it was funny. If someone had an idea, they asked Sal if it was any good.

Without Sal, there simply was no Golla organization; Joey and Tony would be little more than two kid brothers over their heads in crime. There was only one problem with Tommy Lucci's plan—figuring out how to catch Sal off guard, because Sal didn't leave much to chance. First, there was the place where he lived, a mansion in New Jersey, surrounded by dogs and alarms and every conceivable security gizmo. Second, there were Sal's bodyguards, each one a death machine, armed or unarmed.

Most important was Sal himself. Besides being a damn good fighter and a better marksman, he never made himself available for target practice. He kept his appointments secret, traveled different routes each day, and often sent out decoys, just to make certain a road was safe. There was only one sure place to catch Sal, and that was at his home, behind the alarms, dogs, and killers. And even then you couldn't be sure, because Sal also had a little genetic security: something that could confuse even the most determined assassin.

The Gollas were identical triplets.

Sal, Tony, Joey . . . Aside from differences in dress, physically there was simply no telling them apart. And if Tony and Joey looked up to Sal as a big brother, it was because Sal had been born three minutes before Tony, and nine before Joey.

It made things hell for people who met the Gollas, and it also didn't do much good for the people working for them. Of course, once you said hello, you soon knew who it was; Tony would talk dividends, Joey would bitch about labor relations, and Sal wouldn't talk at all, he'd just stare at you, wondering why the hell you were wasting his time. But until then—if, for instance, it was a formal dress evening and a Golla passed you in a hallway—you couldn't begin guessing his identity.

There was another quirk about the brothers; they had a knack for knowing things about each other. Like other triplets, they had been born with a kind of psychic bond that almost let them talk without saying a word. They could be miles apart and know instantly that someone in the family had eaten bad fish. It was discomforting to see, especially when they gathered for a family meal. The Gollas told jokes, talked business, asked for second helpings, and all the time barely said a word. It was through this bond that Sal first learned the bombing of the Pizza Palace had been a success. He had been sitting in his office, waiting for the phone call, when a satisfied feeling swept over him. Five minutes later, Joey called to confirm the good news.

"It's taken care of," Joey told him.

"Yeah, I know," Sal said.

"I know you know," Joey answered, hanging up.

It was also how Tony and Joey realized Sal was in danger. No one knew exactly why they had to collect in the mansion; there was simply an instinct that sometime soon the brothers would be needed. Tony left his office, and Joey turned his car around and headed back to the mansion. Sal had been struck by the same feeling, and soon they were all sitting in the study, waiting for something to happen.

Finally, something did.

"There's a car at the front gate," said one of Sal's guards, staring out the front window.

"Who is it?" Sal said. He wasn't nervous, just alert to trouble.

The guard spoke into a walkie-talkie, then turned again to Sal. "He says he's from Tommy Lucci."

Sal turned to his brothers, who also looked calm. Why not? They had been expecting trouble, and if the best Lucci could do was send a car to the front gate . . . Sal left his seat and pressed the intercom button.

"This is Sal Golla," he said. "Who am I talking to?"

"Tommy Lucci sent me," the man answered.

"Yeah? And what's Tommy got to tell me?"

"Nothing," the man said.

"Not a thing?"

"No, sir."

Sal thought a moment, trying to figure out what the visit was about, wanting to keep a step in front of his guest.

"You came all the way out here, alone, and you don't have a message?"

"No, sir."

"Well, that's very sociable of you," Sal said. "So why did Tommy send you."

"To do something."

"Yeah? And what's that?" Sal asked.

"To kill you," the man said.

SIX

Ump had barely driven onto the gravel driveway when several men stepped in front of him. One stopped the car and took the keys; another nodded Ump out and pressed him over the hood for a body search. Finding nothing on Ump, the first man drove the car from the mansion to a distant garage, just in case it had been loaded with explosives. Only one of the bodyguards made real conversation. When the others weren't looking, the man moved closer to him and said, "Are you really Ump Brady?"

Ump looked at the guard. The man glanced about, made sure no one heard, then whispered, "I've heard stories about you."

Before the guard could say anything else, the others surrounded Ump and turned him toward a wall. "Okay, let's do it again," one of them said. Ump was again frisked.

Ump endured the inconvenience by thinking less about the job and more about what to get his kid for graduation. Ump's boy, Frank Jr., nineteen years old, was graduating high school. He had been held back one grade, which explained the extra year in his graduating age, and Ump wasn't certain if a prsent was appropriate. On the one hand, he was glad his son had graduated; on the other hand, Frank Jr. had been suspended a year for beating the crap out of his gym instructor. This happened after the instructor miscounted Frank's push-ups. Frank Jr., like the rest of his class, had just finished the mandatory ten, but the instructor only saw him do nine. "Don't cheat on me, Brady," the instructor shouted. "I want to see one more."

Fifteen minutes later, the instructor was on his way to the

hospital. As for Frank Jr., he was in the principal's office. The principal demanded to know what had happened. Frank Jr. said only, "A person should know how to count."

Now Ump had to make his own decision. Frank Jr. was too young to be beating up people just because they couldn't count. At the same time, there was something wonderful about a son who would take a year's suspension rather than face an extra push-up. So what to do? And what would Nan allow? Because she hadn't forgiven her son, and no matter how much Ump loved Frank Jr., he wouldn't do anything to cross Nan.

It was a lot to think about, and Ump had to be tapped twice before he moved.

"I said you can go inside," Ump was again told.

Ump followed a small army into the foyer and through another check. Finally, twenty minutes from the time of his arrival, he reached the main hallway, where more men stared at him through a one-way mirror, taking his picture and trying to figure out how this legend planned to make his kill. It seemed a joke—Ump sitting there like a schoolboy, his hands carefully folded, without a weapon on his body, showing nothing but patience, perhaps aware he was being watched. They waited for him to flinch or scratch or give away some little secret of what he planned to do. Ump, meanwhile, gave away nothing, because he had no secrets.

When they were ready, an escort rounded the hall and directed Ump through an open doorway. Ump followed the man into an office. Inside, sitting behind the desk, were all three of the Golla brothers.

"Good afternoon," Ump said.

"The same," each of the brothers said.

A man nudged Ump forward, then stripped him of his jacket and turned his pants pockets inside out. "Put your hands between your legs and sit," the man said, and Ump did, sitting on a chair that would leave a normal man several inches below Sal Golla's eye level. In Ump's case, it simply made things even.

"Is this it?" Sal asked, looking at a bodyguard but indicating Ump. The guard nodded. "And he's clean?" The guard nodded again.

Sal turned to his brothers. "It's okay. I can handle this."

The other brothers hesitated, but Sal led them out of the office and closed the door. Sal was now alone with Ump and two of his famous Golla bodyguards, both stationed behind his guest and armed. Sal also had a pistol, which he kept on top of his desk.

"So," said Sal, "you really came to kill me?"

"I wouldn't lie about a thing like that," said Ump.

"Just me or also my brothers?"

"Just you."

"And was there any particular way you were going to do this?"

"Any way I wanted, except for one thing," said Ump. He hesitated, almost embarrassed to answer.

"It's all right. Tell me," said Sal.

"Just that I'm supposed to make it hurt real bad."

"Really," Sal said, not surprised, perhaps approving. "So what happened? You came driving up here, you saw how secure the place was, you got to maybe thinking, 'Hey, instead of hitting this guy, I should make a deal'?"

Ump didn't answer, but that was okay; Sal was busy figuring out the scenario.

"So," Sal thought aloud, "you come up to the door, ring the bell, not a thing on your body or in the car. . . ." Sal eyed Ump, trying to make sure he understood the situation. "That's right, isn't it? You're not going to fart a gun out your ass and kill me now, are you?"

Ump shook his head.

"Good," Sal said. "So I got it right? I mean, instead of making the hit, you're here to do a little business? Maybe take some money from me and do a job on Lucci, huh? Straddle the fence?"

Sal made a pouring motion to a bodyguard, and soon Ump and Sal were drinking scotch.

"How much money are we talking about?" Sal asked. He sipped his drink and leaned back, getting comfortable in his chair. "If you're going to take care of Tommy Lucci for me—I mean permanently take care of him—I'd say a hit like that is worth at least twenty thousand, maybe even thirty, if you can make him beg first."

[28]

Ump still didn't say anything; on the other hand, he seemed to enjoy his drink.

Sal watched him carefully, impressed with how Ump conducted business. "But those are just my figures," he said. "You must've had something in mind, right? So why don't I listen to your offer and see if it wets my whistle."

Sal put down his drink and folded his hands, waiting for Ump to talk. Ump, aware of the extra attention, also put down his drink and wondered where he should begin.

"Mr. Golla," Ump said, "have you ever wondered why mankind has lasted as long as it has?"

Sal looked perplexed.

Ump talked slowly, wanting to be clear. "We live by rules," he said. "I don't mean the horseshit laws thrown together by courts; I mean universal rules. Things that have to do with . . ." Ump struggled for the right thought. "I don't know, with physics."

Sal struggled to keep up with Ump. "Is this something religious?" he asked.

"No," said Ump. "Those are more horseshit rules. The kind of thing I'm talking about has to do with survival, except it's more than that; I mean things that don't make a difference where you are, because they're always right. Absolutes that'll follow you to the grave. Right?"

"Rules," Sal said, repeating Ump.

"Rules," Ump agreed, pleased.

"What's this got to do with money?"

"It has to do with everything," Ump said. "It's why I'm here to kill you."

Sal looked uncertain.

"See," Ump continued, "it's when people break these rules that we get all kinds of shit hitting the fan. And one of the rules is you don't extinct nothing, because when you extinct something, you don't have it anymore. It's a pattern. You don't have water, you don't have food, you don't have family. . . ."

"What the fuck are you talking about?" Sal said.

"The sauce," Ump said. "You extincted it."

Now Sal was completely lost.

"Just answer me one thing," Sal said, "are you or are you not going to kill Tommy Lucci for me?"

[29]

"I can't do that," Ump said.

"Why not?"

"Because of another rule," Ump said. "Rule number two, right after loving the wife."

"And what's that?" Sal asked.

"Never breaking your word," Ump said.

Sal finally understood. "This means you really think you're going to kill me?"

Ump answered with actions. He had already wedged his body into the chair. He tilted forward, lifting the front end of Sal's desk and tumbling it on top of the mob boss. Sal's guards fired immediately, but with Ump's ass in the air and the seat wedged tight, the back of the chair made a decent shield. Ump ran backwards, ramming one of the bodyguards, then picking him up and using the body to guard his vitals, which meant his head, chest and groin. Ump didn't care about the rest of his body. He could take bullets all day in his arms and legs, provided the arteries were kept clean.

So the second guard fired away, not caring at all that he was killing his partner, popping bullets until Ump charged into him as well, throwing the guard against the bar, then breaking both of the man's hands.

Ump heaved the man into a corner and returned to business—taking out Sal. He walked around the overturned desk and found him underneath the marble top of his desk. By the look of things, Sal's back had been broken.

Ump kneeled next to Sal and asked, "You dead yet?"

Sal couldn't help groaning.

"Painful, huh?" Ump said.

Sal groaned again.

"Tell you what," Ump said. "Instead of making things worse, I'll hang out until you die and then leave. That sound okay?"

Sal wanted to kill Ump, but Ump had taken his gun. All Sal could do was watch while Ump checked his own body for bullet holes, which, considering that Sal usually used the high-powered megaguns, wasn't too likely. When a slug from one of those guns hit the body it didn't just make a hole; it made a manhole. Since Ump was still a hundred percent Ump, the most that could have popped him was a revolver slug.

And that's what he found, in the fat of his upper arm. He could barely feel it; still, he understood infections, and reached for his jacket. In one pocket he found a penknife and tweezers, and in another a box of Band-Aids. He pulled back the sleeve, then dug into the skin until he found the slug. It was bearable, so long as you kept your mind elsewhere. Ump compared it to taking out bad splinters.

"How you doing, Sal?" Ump said. "You want a pillow? I don't think Mr. Lucci would mind a little bit of comfort."

Sal didn't answer and when Ump was done with the slug, he took a closer look.

"Sal?" he tried again, squeezing the man's cheeks.

Sal was wide-eyed and dead.

Ump got down to business, patting the body, as always wanting to bring back evidence that the job was finished. He took Sal's wallet, then searched it for a driver's license. He found the license between credit cards. Ump stared at it a long time, satisfied that the face matched, bothered by one little detail: The name on the license was Anthony Lorenzo Golla. It fact, it was the same name on all the credit cards. Anthony Lorenzo Golla, Anthony Lorenzo Golla . . .

Fuck.

Ump wiped his face.

He had killed the wrong Golla.

SEVEN

Joey stopped playing pool, rubbed his back, and said, "You feel that?"

Sal nodded.

"Couldn't be Tony," Joey said. "Tony doesn't have back problems."

"Who else could it be?" Sal said.

Joey considered a couple of ideas, but nothing seemed right. "Maybe we should check up on him."

"Except Tony hates interruptions," Sal said. "We should wait. He wanted to handle this, he's in there with two top guns and a guy too fat to fit in a chair. What's gonna happen?"

Five minutes later, they heard an explosion.

Sal and Joey ran out of the game room and into the hall. Smoke was coming out of Sal's office. They peeked inside and found the whole damn place on fire.

"Holy shit," Joey said.

Sal ducked into the room and stumbled on a pile of dead guards—the two who had been inside the office, and another pair Sal had stationed outside the door. He also found Tony lying with the desk on top of him.

"That guy Lucci sent," Joey shouted to his brother. "He axed Tony and put a match to the liquor."

"Get some help," Sal said.

Joey gave a thumbs up and ran down the hall. Meanwhile, more of Sal's men came into action, one with a fire extinguisher, the others with guns.

A minute later came a second explosion.

It came from the second floor. Sal ran to the landing and

found bodies littering the staircase. Whoever the hell Lucci had sent, he was killing left and right while blowing apart the most secure mob palace in existence. Sal fought through the flames only to find himself in the middle of a gunfight. He dropped down and crawled forward, his own gun raised, taking potshots into the smoke. But the only things he found, no matter where he crawled, were more dead guards—at least until he heard someone shout to him. He couldn't tell where the voice came from—left or right, up or down—but it was clear, calm, and businesslike. It was also to the point.

"Anyone see Sal?"

For a moment, there was no shooting and, aside from the fires, there was no noise at all. Finally, Sal himself answered. "Sal's gone for the day," he said.

There was another moment of quiet, of thought. Then, "If Sal left, how come his car's outside?"

Sal nudged the man next to him. "If he can see my car," he whispered, "he's in the upstairs office."

"He sounds downstairs to me," the man told Sal.

"Did I ask you?" Sal said. "Get some people and shoot into that fucking window."

The man crawled off while Sal tried keeping Ump busy. "Hey, upstairs," he called. "Sal left, so maybe you should come back tomorrow? Give us a chance to clean up a little and clear out the smoke?"

Sal was sure he had him pinned. Meanwhile, downstairs, Joey Golla gagged as Ump reached around the kitchen door and wrapped his throat with the phone cord.

"You're one of the Gollas, aren't you?" Ump said.

He dragged Joey against the counter and tightened the knot. Joey could barely breathe.

"Which one are you? Are you Sal?"

Joey shook his head.

"Come on," Ump said. "You look like Sal."

Joey kept shaking his head.

Ump sighed, hoping Joey was lying. "Let's see the wallet."

Joey fumbled in his pocket until a wallet fell to the floor. He then tried bending for it, but Ump reached for it himself, which was fine with Joey. The moment Ump bent down, Joey stretched for a nearby butcher knife. Joey gripped the blade and lifted it high, ready to drive it deep into Ump's back. He would have Ump cold. There Joey was, holding nine inches of razor-sharp steel, faced with a wall of flesh easier to strike than a barn. The knife was already in motion. A split second of time, that was all it took. Down went the knife, its target impossible to miss, Joey's weight behind the blade.

Then Ump tugged on the phone cord and Joey swung to the floor, landing face first on the linoleum. Joey rolled over, and in the center of his gut was the knife, sunk deep between the bones of his rib cage.

Ump kept going through the wallet. Joseph Golla, read the driver's license. Joseph Golla, read the credit card. "This is really getting fucked," he said, disgusted with himself, sneaking away to look out the kitchen window. His car was parked about fifty yards away, and whatever guards had been watching it were probably now inside the mansion.

Ump didn't know what to do. Things were definitely out of hand, and with so much smoke and so many people running around, he'd be lucky finding Sal Golla.

But then again, Sal was also looking for him.

"Joey?" Sal shouted. "Joey, come on. We got him upstairs!"

Sal reached the kitchen doorway before seeing his brother on the floor. He looked past Joey to his brothers' killer.

"Sal," Ump said, satisfied.

Sal froze. The two men stared at each other and at first neither moved. Then Ump stepped forward, and the moment he did, Sal stepped back. He braced against the doorjamb, pointed his gun, and fired. He pulled on the trigger once, twice. . . .

The clip was empty.

Sal threw the gun and ran into the dining room, slamming shut the sliding doors and locking them. "He's here!" he shouted. "He's here! He's—"

With one heave of his shoulder, Ump rammed open the doors.

Sal ran from the dining room to the living room, slamming shut another set of doors, dashing out of the living room and into the den. He headed for the foyer, feeling in his pocket for the key to the outside lock.

Ump followed, slamming into the room while Sal was still digging in his pants.

"It'll be easier if you tilt your head down," Ump said. "That way I can hit you across the temple."

Sal didn't know what he was talking about, but then he saw the chair leg in Ump's hand.

"He's here!" Sal shouted again. "For Chrissake, where the fuck is everybody? He's here!"

Ump moved closer and Sal backed away, now desperate, looking anywhere for rescue, finally seeing a window. He ran to it and struggled with the lock. Jammed. He hammered at the pane, heaving up and up and . . .

And without another thought, Sal threw himself into the glass.

Another alarm went off, but it didn't matter. Sal lay on the porch, free of danger, while all hell broke loose inside the mansion. He kept his head bent, huddled beneath the window-sill, while above him a blast of bullets smashed away the remainder of the glass. His bodyguards had cornered Ump and it was a massacre, with his men letting go with every damn weapon Sal had ever bought. The place was literally being blown apart, and for three minutes the gun blasts were the only sound Sal could hear.

Then Sal heard another sound—the grind and roar of a car engine.

Sal raised himself enough to see Ump's car turning onto the driveway and heading for the gate. He couldn't believe it. "He's out here!" he shouted. "Fucking idiots, he's getting away!"

The car triggered an electric eye, and the gate automatically swung open. Ump drove onto the main road and idled a moment, looking in Sal's direction.

Sal stared back. His head was bruised, his arms were bleeding, his legs were sliced by shards of glass. . . .

None of it mattered. So long as he saw Ump, he only felt rage. He only saw unfinished business.

Ump felt the same, but he also felt something else—a sore in the middle of his stomach. He looked down and saw the blood staining his shirt.

Hit in the vitals, he thought. Never think twice when hit in the vitals.

Ump looked away. Before he could suffer the temptation of finishing Sal, he headed for the hospital.

EIGHT

"So, how you feeling, Ump?" Freido asked.

Ump grunted, as much from annoyance as pain. He was in bed, his stomach wrapped in bandages, with an IV feeding one of his arms. His clothes were off, and he wore a thin cotton gown that barely covered his body. Fortunately, most of his body had been tucked beneath a sheet, so Ump had at least been spared the humiliation of being seen naked. But the humiliation of losing . . . Of not doing his job . . .

"What?" said Freido. "Are you feeling some pain?"

Ump turned away and Freido walked around the bed so he could again face him.

"Talk to me, Ump. If you're worried about your family, don't be. We're taking care of them."

Ump still wouldn't answer.

"If that's not it, what's on your mind? Is it the job? Because if it is, I'm telling you again; considering you buried both brothers and burned down half Sal's house—"

"What I have to say I'll say to Mr. Lucci," said Ump. He stared at Freido, angry. "I'd like to talk with him, Freido."

Freido shrugged and walked out of the room, leaving Ump to his glucose and his thoughts. Ump stirred, uncomfortable, and with Freido out of the room, turned his anger on himself. This was a new experience, being shot in the vitals. So was being in the hospital. After all these years, Ump had not only kept the wounds superficial, he rarely needed anything more than an occasional checkup. Now he was laid up in the hospital with nurses twittering about how he was lucky to be alive, when all he could think of was how lucky Sal had been.

When all he could think of was screwing up his job. . . .

"Frank?" said Nan.

Ump looked up and groaned from embarrassment. Nan rushed to his bedside and held his face until she had smothered it with kisses. Ump kept cursing and turning left and right, but Nan held tight all the time, saying, "Oh, God, Frank, I can't believe this. Are you feeling all right? You look awful. What are the doctors saying? You should be sleeping, you shouldn't be up. Frank, what is this? You have a temperature?"

"Let go, Nan," Ump said. The exertion tightened his stomach muscles, and Ump winced.

"You're in pain," she said. "I'm getting the nurse."

"Don't get the nurse."

"She's in the hall. I'm—"

"Nan, will you stop it?"

Nan quieted. After taking a steady, calming breath, she pulled up a chair, sat next to the bed, and held Ump's hand. Ump watched her, the whole time dreading what came next. Questions. Hard questions. Questions that he hadn't figured out how to answer.

"I want to know exactly what happened, Frank."

Christ, she didn't waste any time. Ump's mind worked hard, not only concerned about exposing Nan to the truth, but also hurting her with it. Because he had a secret from Nan that dated back to when they first met, and it was that Nan didn't know what he really did for a living. After all the years and all the kids, Nan still believed Ump was in the security business, working as a private bodyguard. Now Ump wondered what she would think if he told her he was a professional killer. He worried less about her reaction to the work than the fact that he had lied. How much less would she think of him? What would happen when they got home, provided she let him come home?

"Frank, tell me what happened."

Ump glanced at her, then said, "I had an accident."

"What kind of accident?"

"I got beat up."

"You were *attacked*?"

"I wasn't looking," he said. "The man had a gun and—"

She squeezed his hand impossibly tight.

[37]

"Nan, you're hurting my fingers."

"Someone tried killing you?" she said.

"It happens all the time in this city," Ump said. "Besides, I know who did it."

"Jesus Christ," Nan said.

"It wasn't exactly a mugging," Ump said. "The whole thing isn't that important, except that until things clear up a bit, it may be a good idea for you and the kids to leave town. Maybe stay with your cousins."

"Why?"

"Because I hurt this guy bad too, so there may be more trouble."

"You think he'll come after you?"

"I don't know what he's going to do," Ump said, "but it's better playing it safe, right? I mean, until I patch up, I'm not exactly your neighborhood bouncer."

"Oh, Frank," she said, crying.

Ump brushed her cheek. Nan was still crying when Freido knocked on the door and walked inside. Tommy Lucci followed, and Freido deferred to his boss.

"Mrs. Brady," said Tommy. "Thank you so much for your sauce. It's delicious."

Nan wiped her eyes.

"You've got one brave husband," Tommy said. "I don't know how much he's told you, but he's done me a great service today."

Nan didn't trust Tommy. She didn't trust anyone who could let such a thing happen to her husband. "I don't mean any disrespect, Mr. Lucci, but I don't want Frank dying for anyone but his children."

Tommy Lucci proved patient. "I'm not just saying this for me, Mrs. Brady. I'm talking for the country. Frank has us on the verge of busting one of the city's biggest crime families."

Now Nan looked totally confused. "You work for the government?"

"Let's just say we all work for the country, Mrs. Brady. And what this country would now like to do is protect you and your children until we manage to take care of a few loose ends. You will let us help, won't you?"

Nan didn't know what to say. She looked to Ump for an answer, and Ump gave a gentle nod.

Nan looked back at Tommy. The moment he sensed her willingness to bend, he turned to Freido. "Take Mrs. Brady outside, all right?" Tommy said. "Get her and the kids on the road."

"What about Frank?" Nan asked.

"He'll be fine," Tommy said.

"I'll be okay," Ump said. "Just do what he says."

Nan hesitated, then threw her arms about her husband, at first refusing to go, then refusing to leave until Ump kissed her.

"It's only for a few weeks, Nan," Ump whispered, kissing and pulling free.

Nan stopped crying. She stood, straightened her clothes, and gave Ump a last, loving look.

"You'll call me tonight, Frank."

"I'll call."

"We'll all take care of him, Mrs. Brady," said Freido.

She glared at Freido, walked to the door, then turned to her husband a last time. "Frank, don't you take crap from anyone."

"Don't talk dirty to me, Nan. I can't stand the excitement."

Before she could cry again, Nan left the room. Satisfied that matters were under control, Tommy took a seat and allowed himself a smile. "She really don't know what's up?"

"I never found the right time to tell her," Ump said.

"That's one hell of a double life," Tommy said. "I'm glad you're used to it, because we're taking you a few states west. Let you get well and keep you hidden from Sal. He's going bananas. I love it."

"I don't have to go anywhere," Ump said.

"Believe me, it's better," Tommy said. "It's my own private relocation program. You'll stay with Freido's sister and brother-in-law. After I finish Sal, you can come back."

Ump didn't like what he heard. "No," he said.

Tommy Lucci looked perplexed. He wasn't particularly familiar with the word, especially when someone directed it at him.

"As long as Sal's alive, I've got a job to do."

"But Sal's hiding," Tommy said. "You can't kill him if you can't find him."

Ump thought a moment, then said, "Then I'll go, but only if I'm brought back once you find Sal."

Tommy was, once again, incredulous. "You got to tell me what to do again, huh? You always got to shovel shit up my ass."

"Just bring me back," Ump said. "It's my job and I'll do it."

"Don't worry about it, Ump. Just get better and—"

"No."

Tommy stared hard at him. "Stop saying that," he said.

"You got to bring me back for the job," said Ump. "It's fundamental. If I don't, I break one of the top rules of life."

"Which one's that?" Tommy said, as if Ump made sense.

"Never," Ump said, "*never* break your word."

Tommy thought for a moment, then patted Ump's hand and left the room. He would abide by Ump's wishes.

It was one of the few rules Ump lived by that Tommy understood.

PART II

WAYLIN

NINE

The town of Waylin was a town without pity.

Darlene Maye was a good example. She had just found out that her husband, George Maye, was not only having an affair, he was sleeping with Darlene's boss. This meant if Darlene threw him out of the house, she wouldn't only lose a husband, she'd probably also lose her job. And no matter what she thought of George, it was a damn good job.

They were more complications than anyone deserved, and Darlene decided to bring her problems to the church. She entered the confessional, dropped to her knees and said, "Bless me, Father, for I married scum."

She told the priest everything: how the affair had begun, how her husband continued cheating, how she had come this close to taking matters in her own hands—of actually clubbing him while he slept in bed.

"Those two bastards," Darlene said. "If I say anything, I'll lose my work, and if I don't, then I'm no better off unless I cheat on him, but that's only good if I want him jealous, and I don't—I want him dead. What do I do, Father? What do you do when the only thing you want from your husband is having him dead?"

Father Carroll listened, but didn't answer. On a day like today, he had a hard time concentrating. It wasn't lack of interest; his thoughts were simply on his own villain. In Carroll's case, this was the chairman of the town council, a man who threatened to tear apart the priest's neighborhood; a man so callous, so driven by the dollar, he was not only prepared to develop the town's few parklands, but also the town cemetery, a small plot of grass and monuments that ran adjacent to Carroll's church.

Why waste prime town property on the dead? Farber asked. Why not sell the land and move the bodies? What can they do, complain?

It infuriated Father Carroll. How could Farber forget the dead were also God's children? How could he forget they were Waylin's ancestry? How could he forget that their topsoil made a buffer between the church and the sidewalk.

Dig them out, Farber declared. Tear up the ground, sell the land, and build a Hardee's.

"Father, what should I do?" Darlene asked. "Why has God cursed me with such a shit?"

Carroll didn't know. All he knew was for the first time in his life, he wanted more than peace on earth; he wanted to administer pain. Indeed, he wanted Farber to know what it was like to be dead, and then to have his everlasting peace disturbed by a hydraulic crane.

"Join me in prayer," Carroll suggested, and together Darlene and the priest prayed. Neither, however, prayed for redemption; they prayed for revenge. They prayed for vengeance against their enemies, and wished hard for the sort of thing that neither dared say out loud, because it was all too frightening to hear.

"This is helping," Darlene said.

Carroll said nothing, his own eyes closed, his hands firmly clasped. Darlene started to stand, but the priest sensed her movement and rested a hand on her shoulder.

"No," he said. "A moment longer."

Darlene agreed and again kneeled. They prayed for blood; they prayed as, elsewhere in Waylin, others joined the swell of hatred.

Bill Conley, for instance, wanted nothing but the worst for Shirley Anderson, the town treasurer. For a decade he had run the town, and for a decade he had felt secure. Now, instead of sleepwalking to an upcoming election victory, Conley found himself making retractions, followed by apologies, followed by a desperate effort to fight the slipping polls. In less than a week, Bill Conley had become the campaign underdog. All because of one little comment, all because Conley had made

an offhand suggestion that Shirley Anderson, the sole chal-
lenger to his seat, should worry more about menopause than
politics.

It's not fair, Conley thought. How could his years of
service be so easily ignored? How could a few words undermine
so much of his life?

He wanted Shirley Anderson at his feet, holding tight to
his ankles, begging for every remaining second of her life. He
wanted her in pain; he wanted her feeling the kind of agony
Father Carroll imagined for Farber, or Darlene imagined for her
husband.

And while Bill Conley hated Shirley Anderson, Shirley
Anderson hated Walter Fleming.

Fleming was the bank president, and as the mayoral race
closed on the final weeks, Fleming was in possession of what
Anderson needed most—campaign money.

So she had written him.

Dear Walter,
I do hate pressing matters, but as we reach the
closing weeks of the primary, time is of the essence.
As I have said before, my campaign desperately needs
the help of your bank. Your assistance in this matter
would be *greatly* appreciated. Please phone me ASAP
so my wheels can again turn.
Your friend, Shirley Anderson.

Only Fleming could clear the funds to finance the rest of
Anderson's campaign. But the bank wouldn't so much as
answer her calls. Anderson knew why, too—Fleming and the
mayor were too deep in each other's debt. It was the old-boy's
game, and Anderson wasn't being allowed to take her chips.
About the only way she could get her money was if Fleming
resigned or was fired or died.

It was a despicable situation. In a better world, Anderson
would have refused their help and concentrated on the best
grassroots campaign the county had ever seen. But there was
another reason she needed a loan. Anderson not only had to
finance the end of her campaign; she had to cover several
unconventional expenses, including a private "loan" she had

taken from the town treasury. She had to replace the cash before anyone discovered her liberal use of local funds. Every day she didn't was another day of risk.

Fleming, she thought. What she'd do for the keys to his bank. What she'd do to get him out of the picture—forced to resign, or even better, forced into the hospital—his ulcer perforated, his heart so clogged with fat it could be spooned from his body and fried.

Fleming . . . There was so much to hate about him; that's what came of too much power. The amazing thing was how infrequently he returned the hatred, unless that's what came of being a complete success. He owned Waylin's biggest home, had the biggest cars, pocketed the biggest salary. He could retire at will, and without a doubt, retirement was overdue. For health reasons alone, he needed time to relax, a chance to let his body take care of itself. He had to cut back his schedule, open his days, and learn, once again, how to enjoy himself.

But for all he had, and how infrequently he let the world bother him, somehow, throughout his career, there was always someone or something keeping him at the bank. One little job that kept him at his desk, one nagging responsibility that forbade him from giving up his office.

For the past year, that someone was a man who had turned Fleming into a local joke: the one resident of the county to whom Fleming should never have given a loan, and the one man whom Fleming had personally approved, despite the advice of his board.

It had been a weak moment. Fleming had pitied the man—or, more precisely, the man's family. Now, since that day of approval, rather than repay the loan, Fleming's personally approved client waved the money about town and bragged he could always get more; all he had to do was squirrel another thirty thousand from the local bank. "Isn't a trick at all," the man told everyone. "Not when the goddamn bank president's a fat-ass idiot."

Fleming had been a sucker and still was. With all the real accounts aching for his attention, he spent the day brooding over a paltry loan. All because pride was on the line, all because some no-name was grinding his name in the ashtray.

He turned in the direction of Joseph Gratton's house and

concentrated. Fleming tried willing his hatred into a powerful, supernatural force that would swirl into a ball and careen through town, punching through walls until it struck Gratton's house, blasting and billowing into a mushroom of fire.

He concentrated and concentrated. . . . And something was felt. Not by Joseph, and not as a ball of explosive flames. Francine, Joseph's wife, however, knew something bad was coming in her direction and she faced the window, staring outside, wondering when matters would become out of hand and they would be forced to hand over the house.

Finally, desperate for advice, she decided to discuss the problem with her big-city brother.

"I don't know what to do," Francine told him. "I really think they mean it this time. I think they're going to take the house."

Her brother listened, then said, "Why doesn't Joseph get a job?"

"He's got a job," Francine said. "It's just not enough, that's all."

"Not the way he spends the money, you mean," her brother said. Then, reconsidering, "Why don't you take in a boarder?"

"Very funny," she answered. "Waylin doesn't get visitors. We don't even have a motel."

"I can have someone there by the weekend," her brother said.

"Oh, really? And for how much?"

"How about a hundred a day?"

Francine turned angry. "Don't fool with me, because I really need money."

"I'm not fooling. There's just one thing: I don't know how long this guy will need a place, and he may also need some nursing."

"Is he an invalid?"

"He's recovering from an accident, that's all."

Francine wondered what to say, knowing she couldn't say anything, not before talking with her husband, Joseph. "Let me think about it," she told her brother, and hung up.

An hour later, Joseph came home. First, she heard the door open; then, when she went in the living room, she found

Joseph standing by the doorway, thumbing through the day's mail. "Look at all this," he said, waving a pile of sweepstakes. "Francine, how we ever gonna win if you don't start entering?"

Francine took away the mail and faced him.

"The bank called," she said. "They're going to foreclose. They want to take the house."

Joseph looked more amused than worried. "Oh, yeah?" he said. "Then what are they going to do with it?"

"This is serious, Joseph," she said. "I wasn't sure what to do, so I talked to my brother, and—"

Joseph shook his head.

"—and he had a suggestion."

Joseph refused to listen. Rather than face Francine, he walked to the kitchen. Francine followed him.

"It doesn't cost anything and could bring in some good money," she said. "He has a friend that needs a place to stay. If we want, he can stay with us and pay rent."

"And when did we become a hotel?" said Joseph.

"I don't see the problem."

"The problem is your brother," he said. "If he's the hot-shot city businessman, let his friend stay with him."

"His friend wants to stay in Waylin," said Francine.

Joseph took a swig of milk, then wiped his mouth and straddled a kitchen chair. When he again talked, he spoke slowly, deliberately. "You tell your brother," Joseph said, "that if his friend wants to stay here, it's going to cost him good money."

"He knows that," Francine said.

"I mean *good* money," said Joseph. "A hundred, maybe one fifty a week."

"He's already agreed to pay a hundred a day," Francine said.

Joseph stopped drinking his milk and listened.

TEN

They wanted to put Ump into deep cover, at least until they figured out a new way for finishing Sal Golla. And finishing Sal was absolutely necessary. Sal wanted revenge for his brothers' deaths, but before he killed Tommy Lucci, he wanted Ump. Ump hadn't been out of the hospital a half hour before an explosive went off beneath his former bed.

"We need to send him somewhere safe, Freido," Tommy had said. "Some backwoods place so that he can patch up. You got any ideas?"

Freido didn't think twice. When anyone said backwoods, he immediately thought of his idiot brother-in-law a hundred miles west in a shit hole called Waylin. And while Waylin couldn't guarantee Ump the kind of armed protection Tommy Lucci expected, why would Ump need it? Tommy used body-guards because his enemies knew where to find him; if no one knew where to find Ump, theoretically no one could find him.

Tommy Lucci liked the idea. The only thing that caused him trouble was the town itself. He didn't know anything about it.

"Are you sure about this, Freido?" Tommy said. "I never heard of the place."

But that, of course, was the point. There was a time when Waylin had been home to a smelting industry; today, ever since the black smoke and the blue collars had disappeared, the town lived off commuters and a momentum that, in a few decades, would probably completely die out. Waylin was so quiet, he couldn't even imagine his sister getting in trouble.

They turned a corner and parked shy of Francine's house.

On Freido's nod, the driver, Leon, and a second muscle, Teddy, did a quick patrol of the street—an unnecessary but routine security step. Leon checked the neighbor's bushes while Teddy walked the sidewalk, Teddy unnerved by a town where people didn't think twice about leaving their valuables unguarded. A bicycle, a mower, a toy swimming pool . . . They were all on the lawns, waiting to be taken. He bet the doors were also unlocked.

"This is a strange place, Freido," Teddy reported.

"I don't like it," said Leon.

"You don't have to," said Freido. "I just wanna know if it's safe."

"Plenty safe," said Teddy. "Too safe."

Leon agreed.

Freido looked at them as if they were crazy. "How can a place be too safe?" he said.

Neither could answer.

"You two don't get out of the city enough," Freido said, leaving the car and walking to his sister's front door.

Considering how little Joseph did, it wasn't a bad house: two stories, three bedrooms. . . . Maybe the outside looked crappy because of the cinder block, but in a pinch Freido would always pick cinder block over siding. The government made fallout shelters out of cinder block. Freido bet that if Sal pasted an explosive against one of these walls, one room might go, but the house would hold.

Francine opened the door and Freido stopped thinking like a businessman. "Freido," Francine said.

"Hi, sweetheart," Freido said. He kissed his sister, then looked past her to his brother-in-law. Freido gave him the usual cursory nod. "Francine, Joseph—I'd like you to meet your house guest." He stepped aside and opened an arm. "Ump?"

Ump, balanced on crutches, limped into the living room.

On behalf of Waylin residents everywhere, Joseph took Ump's hand and smiled.

"I'm pleased to meet you," Joseph said. "Welcome to our happy town."

Freido, Ump, Leon, and Teddy moved into the hallway. The promise of a hundred a day had Joseph in a good mood, and he offered everyone a drink.

"How about something for the throat," Joseph said. "We got juice, we got beer. . . . I think we got beer. Francine, what we got?"

Francine went to the kitchen while Joseph stretched on a sofa. Freido rested a hand on Ump and helped him into the living room.

"So," Joseph said to Ump, "this your first time in Waylin?"

Ump leaned on his crutches and swung his body toward a chair. Every time Ump moved, they heard the floor moan from the press of his weight.

Joseph turned his attention on his brother-in-law. "Freido," he said, "we don't see you much anymore. New York move farther away, or what?"

"New York's still there," Freido said.

"So then what's your problem?" Joseph said. "Why don't you visit? Why don't you invite us down?"

Freido struggled to maintain his best behavior. He looked to Francine, who came back with a tray of open beers. Everyone took one, and Joseph again waved to a set of chairs.

"Sit down," he said. "Come on, I hate looking up."

Freido considered the offer and decided it was one he'd accept. After seating himself, he motioned Ump toward a chair. Only when he was settled did he notice; Ump hadn't moved. Freido looked at him, trying to understand, but all he saw was a kind of brooding anxiety. Something had got under Ump's skin, and Freido couldn't tell what. Was it the way Joseph talked? Was it the house? Freido wasn't sure, and this was bad, because if Ump was troubled, and Freido had no idea why, Freido couldn't fix things. And if he didn't fix things, then there was no telling what would happen. Cinder block or no cinder block, Freido worried whether Ump was about to lose control and start punching holes in the bombproof walls.

Thank God he suddenly understood. Freido left his seat and made room for his sister.

"Please, Sis," he said. "Why don't you sit first?"

Francine settled on the couch, and Ump relaxed. Slowly, he turned and approached a chair.

"Wonderful," Freido sighed. He looked to the hallway, where Leon gave a nod, assuring Freido all was secure. "Perfect," he said again, looking to Ump for reassurance. "Everything's fine, right Ump?"

Ump adjusted in his seat. Freido watched the chair sag, expecting the support to buckle. "You have a nice home, Mrs. Gratton," Ump finally said.

"Why, thank you, Mr. Brady."

"You must be very happy here," Ump said. "I hope my visit's not an inconvenience."

"Not at all," she said.

"Stay as long as you want," Joseph said. Then, to Freido, "What about you? Staying for supper?"

Freido directed his answer to Francine. "I wanted to spend the night, Franny, if you don't mind. Just to make sure everything's okay."

Francine looked concerned. "What about your friends? I don't have any place for—"

"Don't worry, they can sleep in the car."

"Freido, that wouldn't be right."

"Are you kidding?" he said. "With my boss paying overtime, they'd love it."

To prove the point, Freido called Leon in the room and told him the news. Leon didn't even look surprised. He simply waved his okay and left the house.

"See?" Freido said to his sister. "Francine, don't worry so much about other people. They can take care of themselves."

"I tell her that all the time," Joseph said.

Freido still wouldn't look at him. "You know what I'm talking about," he said. "You gotta take control of things."

Francine looked embarrassed by her brother, less by what he said than for saying it in front of a guest.

"Freido, not now," she whispered.

"I don't care if Joseph hears," Freido said. "I *want* him to hear."

"This is family business," Francine said.

"So, I'm family. Are you saying I'm not family?"

"Of course you're family, but not everyone is," she said.

Freido didn't understand, but then he realized she was talking about Ump. It didn't make any sense to Freido. After discussing murders in front of Ump, talking about Joseph seemed like nothing.

Ump, however, understood. "I think I should lie down," he said to Freido. Then, to Francine, "If you don't mind, Mrs. Gratton, I'd like to go upstairs."

"I don't mind at all, Mr. Brady," Francine said.

Freido watched as his sister guided Ump up the staircase. Ump was being given one of the children's rooms, which, despite her efforts, was still the room of a nine-year-old. Ump, however, showed no discomfort. He used his crutches to reach the bed, then sat heavily on the mattress. The mattress sagged until Ump spread his body weight. Then, with a tired, relieved breath, he leaned back on the pillow and stretched out, his feet extending over the edge.

"Oh, God," Francine said, embarrassed. "I didn't even think. . . ."

"I'm fine," Ump said.

"No, you're not," she said.

"Believe me," he said, "I've had bigger problems than this." With that, he shut his eyes.

Francine refused to let her guest suffer. "Please," she said. I've got a portable bed that's longer."

Ump didn't answer.

"It's in the closet," she said. "I can bring it in right away and—"

Freido knocked on the open door. "Don't worry," he said. "If Ump says it's okay, it's okay. You couldn't have a better guest."

Francine still objected, but Ump played dead until his hostess left the room. Then, satisfied he was alone, he began taking account of himself. He started by unwrapping his bandage. There were about six layers of gauze wrapped about his chest and beneath the gauze was a wad of cotton. He took it all off, then fingered the bullet wound. While the bullet had made only a quarter-inch hole, removing it had left an itchy twelve-stitch scar. The entire region had been shaved of body hair and looked deeply bruised. The worst part, however, was still feeling drained of blood. Well, the doctors had told him he'd be tired, and if he didn't rest, they told him to expect a lot worse. Ump believed them, too. He knew that if you didn't take care of your vitals you'd be out of work and out of life. He wiped the wound with a fresh piece of cotton and taped a new bandage to his body. With that finished, he turned his attention to the room, staring at the toys cluttering the shelves and the baseball posters pasted to the walls. He also bent over the bed to open a foot locker. Inside were more toys, including an arsenal of plastic guns.

Ump reached inside his pocket for a real gun.

Freido had insisted Ump take it. Freido pushed the weapon in his hands, saying better safe than sorry, but Ump didn't see what was safe about having a real gun maybe getting mixed up with all these toys. He pulled the clip from his automatic, emptied it of bullets, then threw the clip and gun into the trash. He then put the toy gun in his pocket, just in case Freido asked him to show his piece. With that part of his life back to normal, he pulled himself carefully off the bed and searched for a more practical weapon. He lumbered about—every step a careful one, moving on his toes so he made only a little sound—picking up objects and weighing them in his hands. A lamp, a stapler, a telephone . . .

There it was. In the corner of the room, leaning against a wall, hiding behind a hockey stick, mitt, and pair of knee pads. His absolute favorite weapon, ever since he was old enough to break down a door—a baseball bat. He picked it up now. It was a child's bat—only thirty inches long, he guessed, with maybe a three-inch diameter at the meat—but it felt good. The stick balanced cleanly, and when Ump gave it a test swing, he could still master the momentum, pulling short of impact by a fraction, the bat's barrel frozen over the bedspread.

He slid the bat under his bed, then reached again for the telephone, dialing his wife.

"Nan?"

"Frank, darling," Nan said. "You getting rest? What's your room like? Where do they have you?"

"Everything's fine," Ump said. "How about you?"

"We're settled," Nan said.

"What did you tell the kids?"

"I said their dad's a hero and we've got to hide out while he serves our country."

"And what did you tell your cousins?"

"That you were off on business and the house got robbed, so I didn't feel safe."

[54]

"That's a good one, Nan," Ump said, satisfied, wishing he were good at manufacturing stories. "I'm really sorry about all this. I wish it wasn't so much trouble."

"Sorry?" Nan said. "Ump, I'm proud of you. You're a hero."

Ump didn't like hearing that. The last thing he felt like was a hero, and the suggestion embarrassed him. Still, he let Nan talk, knowing it helped her, all the time looking elsewhere for relief. He stared out the window and watched a number of children play in a nearby yard. He watched them, not as a romantic, but like the new neighborhood cop learning a beat. He stared down, almost satisfied that, at the very least, he was in a town with some sense of order.

Then a cab raced through the intersection.

Ump couldn't believe it. He had seen the car approach the corner, but presumed it would stop. Instead, the driver gunned forward, speeding through the light and by the playing children.

Ump was stunned. Not only had the car raced a light, it was being driven by a cabbie. A fucking driver for hire . . . someone who *knew the rules.*

It was more than Ump could take. He pushed off the chair, his face red, wanting nothing less than to chase after the son of a bitch. He lunged for his crutches and almost made it past the bed, but then his right crutch gave way and his stomach tensed, the pain hitting him hard. Ump slumped to the side, somehow managing to fall on the bed.

"Frank?" he heard Nan calling. "Frank, you still there?"

"I'm here," he said, the heart out of him.

"Are you all right, Frank?"

Ump shook his head. "I don't know, Nan," he said.

"You don't know what?"

Ump wondered how to answer. He stared out the window and said, "I'm out here with a strange family, no one to talk to. . . . It doesn't feel like home."

"Good," she said. "It shouldn't."

"I got a feeling these people are going to drive me crazy."

"Then ignore them," she said. "Don't talk to them."

"It's not that easy," he said.

"Then do whatever you have to," she said. "I don't care, so long as you get better."

Five minutes later, they said good-bye and Ump lay down, trying to sleep, in fact thinking about that damn cabbie breaking one of life's simplest rules. Christ, how much else was wrong with this town?

He shook his head.

No doubt about it; a man like Ump would be busy no matter where he went.

Waylin would be no exception.

ELEVEN

"Come on, sit up straight for our guest," Joseph told his children. "For a hundred bucks a day, that's the least we should do."

His children—Jennifer, nine, and Michael, four—obeyed and sat straighter at the table. They also stared at their father, not so much from what he had said, but that he had said anything. It had been a long time since Joseph was home for dinner.

"Delicious steaks," Joseph told Freido. Then, to everyone, "Wasn't it nice of your Uncle Freido to bring these big, juicy steaks all the way from—" Joseph fought for the name of the restaurant.

"Delmonico's," Freido said. "It's nothing. The cook owed a favor."

"Don't say 'nothing,'" Joseph said. "It's impressive. You're an impressive guy. People sleep in cars for you." Joseph turned to Ump, who sat beside him. "So is Freido this impressive at work?"

Ump looked from his food and stared at Joseph. There was no approval or disapproval in his look; he simply listened, chewed, and swallowed . . . a silent observer. "Freido's okay at his job," Ump said.

Freido tried changing topics.

"Let's not talk about work, Joseph," Freido said. "You're probably not too comfortable with the idea."

Joseph feigned a smile. "That's funny," he said. "Kids, you hear how your Uncle Freido makes fun of your father? That's because your father doesn't eat at Delmonico's. Your father's not as good as Freido."

"That's one reason," Freido said.

Joseph turned back to his other guest. "What do you do, Ump? Is Freido your boss?"

Ump nodded.

"Then maybe you wouldn't mind telling me what the hell he does for a living."

"Joseph!" Francine said.

"Freido brought up work, not me," Joseph said. "I've known him ten years and I still don't know what the fuck he does. Christ, for all I know, he's a goddamn mobster."

"He's in the supply-and-demand business. He's told you," said Francine.

"And what the hell does that mean?"

Freido chuckled, as if Joseph had proven his point. "You see?" Freido said. "He doesn't know what I'm talking about. You know, Joseph, maybe if you learned a bit about business, you'd understand. Maybe if I thought you had a chance of understanding, I'd tell you more."

Joseph looked annoyed. To Ump, he said, "What do you do?"

Ump finished chewing, put down his fork and knife, wiped his mouth, refolded the napkin, and glanced at Freido. Finally, he said, "I'm in security."

"Security?"

Ump nodded and returned to eating. Joseph, however, wasn't put off so easily. "Ump," he said, switching thoughts. "That's not your real name."

Ump kept eating.

"Who calls you Ump?" Joseph said. To the children, he said, "Anyone else hear the name Ump?"

"At the ballpark," said Jennifer.

Joseph ignored his daughter, but Freido picked up on the remark.

"He used to be a professional umpire," Freido said.

Ump again needed a moment to activate. He looked up from his food and, after checking with Freido, approved the story.

"Really," said Joseph, "I've never met an umpire before." It sounded like a joke, but Joseph was genuinely impressed.

Ump could tell. He wiped his mouth and extended a hand. "Nice to meet you," he said.

This pleased Joseph. Earlier, when first meeting Ump, he had only shaken hands with a lodger; now he was meeting a celebrity.

"An *umpire*," Joseph said. "I'm gonna have to hear all about it."

"Later," Freido said. "Let the man rest, all right? That's why he's here: to get away from people and—"

Ump stood up. "If you'll excuse me."

The talking stopped.

"I need some air." Ump reached for his crutches and left the table. The conversation didn't begin again until Ump had hobbled out the front door; then Francine leaned close to her brother.

"Did we embarrass him?" she whispered.

"*We?*" said Freido, staring at Joseph.

Ump, meanwhile, walked outside and leaned against a porch beam. He wondered where Sal Golla was hiding. Hell, for all Ump knew, they were neighbors.

"Hey, Ump," called Teddy. He was sitting on the limo's hood and smoking a cigarette. Beside him was Leon, a bucket of fried chicken on his lap. "How's it going in there?"

Ump shrugged. Teddy nudged Leon, and together they walked over.

"Freido has us spending the night in the car," Teddy said.

"Should be good money," said Ump.

"Leon and me saw this whole friggin' town in fifteen minutes," said Teddy. "You're gonna go crazy here, Ump."

Leon offered the bucket. "You want some chicken?"

"I ate inside, thanks," Ump said.

Teddy reached for another drumstick. "I swear, you're gonna be wishing you were back home with Sal snapping at your heels."

"Yeah, well, maybe I didn't want to come here in the first place," Ump said.

Leon caught the tone. He smiled and tried smoothing things. "Good thing for Sal you are."

[59]

"That's right," said Teddy. "Hey Ump, we were talking about that time you took care of the Petrolli family. We were trying to remember how many you whacked."

"We couldn't remember," said Leon. "Was it fifteen or sixteen?"

"Sixteen," said Teddy. "That's right, isn't it? Sixteen?"

Ump shrugged, not especially interested.

"Wait a minute," said Leon. "*Nineteen.* Nineteen, including Mike Petrolli."

"No," said Ump. "I went through nineteen to reach Mike Petrolli. I whacked twenty."

Teddy looked awestruck. "I never whacked more than four at a time, and that was with explosives."

"I did nine once, but they were asleep," said Leon.

"Nothing wrong with that," Ump said. "Petrolli was almost asleep."

"Petrolli never slept, everyone knows that," said Leon. "You got him wide awake."

"I forget, Ump," said Teddy. "That was in L.A., right?"

Ump nodded.

"And how'd you get to Petrolli?"

"Same as I always do it—through the front door."

Leon grinned, remembering the whole story but still loving to hear it. "That's right," he said. "Meanwhile, I bust my chops crawling on rooftops and squeezing through vents."

Ump smiled. "I haven't whacked a person yet who didn't let me in through the door."

Teddy wanted to hear more about Petrolli. "How'd you get by the bodyguards? With a repeat? A bomb?"

Ump again shrugged.

Leon, turning serious, said, "It don't matter what you use, so long as it does the job."

"I guess you can kill anyone with anything," Teddy said.

Ump agreed. "The trick," he said, "isn't figuring how to kill someone; it's figuring who to kill."

Neither Leon nor Teddy said it, but this was what they really wanted to hear: the secrets of Ump's success. Both listened, afraid of pulling Ump off the track, anxious for him to get over the hump and into the conversation. Ump relaxed, tilting his head in the evening air and letting the mood sweep over him.

"There's a lot of good and a lot of bad in this world." Ump said. "If you think about it, and if you care, the easiest thing for anyone to do is decide what's good and what's bad, and then spend your days cutting down the bad. Except there's a problem. Who knows what's good or bad? You can't tell from laws, because laws change every day of the week. You can't tell from your gut either, because your gut changes with each meal.

"So you gotta dig underneath all the crap, dig down to the good and bad, and not even then look at the good and bad, because that's more crap," said Ump. "Instead, you gotta figure out what it is that keeps the world going. What are the basic rules that make it possible for even the dumbest shits to get along. And then, once you figure out those rules, you protect them."

"The basic rules of life," said Leon, remembering earlier conversations.

"So far, I got nine of them," said Ump. "But that doesn't mean I got them all; I just got the ones which smacked me on the head."

"Like never breaking your word," said Leon.

"Or counting wrong," said Ump. "How many fights have started because some asshole thought he had more soldiers than someone else? Or how many football games have been lost because the fucking quarterback lost count of the clock? Or how much money has disappeared because a teller carries the wrong zero?"

"Or how many cars have been racked up because some dick in a grocery store tries buying a pack of gum?"

Teddy was making a joke, but Ump didn't laugh. Neither did Leon, who wished Teddy would shut up. But the damage was done. Ump brought the conversation to a close.

"The main point," he finished, "is if I'm gonna be asked to kill anyone—*anyone*—then I have to know where he stands on the rules. And once I figure that out, and if he stands wrong, I don't care how many people I go through; the rules are gonna be obeyed."

"What are some other rules, Ump?" Leon asked. "How do I know when to kill?"

Ump grinned. "Come on, Leon. Everybody knows the rules."

"Just help me out," said Leon. "What else besides counting and keeping your word?"

But again Teddy interfered. He rolled up a pants leg, unsnapped a sheath, and pulled free a hunter's knife. He offered the weapon to Ump. "Would you mind signing this for me, Ump? It would mean a lot."

Ump obliged, taking the knife and signing the handle. As for Leon, he felt embarrassed. Here they were, lucky enough to get Ump alone, getting him to talk as if they were all in the same league, and Teddy had to chuck it for a goddamn autograph. He hoped to hell that one day Teddy double-crossed Mr. Lucci. Leon would take the job, gratis.

Ump stood and turned back to the house. "See you in the morning."

"Yeah," said Leon.

"Right," said Teddy. "And don't worry, Ump. We'll take care of you."

It was another wrong thing to say, but Ump understood the intent.

"Thanks," said Ump.

A moment later, he was back indoors. And outdoors, Teddy covered up as Leon slapped his head and walked back to the car.

Ump stood at his bedroom door. "What are you doing in here?"

Jennifer looked up at Ump. She had been on her knees, digging into her foot locker, pulling out toys and spreading them on the floor. "I'm looking for something," she said.

Ump walked into the room and sat on his bed. "A toy gun?"

Jennifer nodded.

"A gun like this?" he said, pulling the toy pistol from his pocket.

Jennifer stared at it. "That's mine," she said.

"I was just borrowing it," Ump said. "You want it back? Here, you can have it. It's yours."

Jennifer shook her head. "You can use it. Just don't show it to Uncle Freido. He doesn't like me playing with guns."

"I wouldn't have guessed that about your uncle," Ump said.

"That's all you know," she said, again digging in the bin.

Ump agreed, returning the gun to his pocket. "Can you keep a secret?"

The girl looked up at him, and Ump lifted his shirt, pointing at the bandage.

"I got that from a gun," he said.

Jennifer moved closer. When Ump nodded, she touched the wound. "Really?"

"Shot in the stomach," Ump said.

"That's great," she said.

"It's great if you're a kid, maybe," Ump said. "I got a couple of kids, too. Both boys. One's about your age. Maybe the two of you'll get married."

Jennifer pulled out another toy gun. She aimed it at Ump and pulled the trigger. Ump fell gently back on the bed, playing dead. Jennifer, however, turned serious, actually studying him.

"Is that what it's like?" she asked.

Ump didn't understand.

"When you get shot," Jennifer said. "Do you really roll up your eyes and drop like that?"

Ump considered what to tell her. "Can you keep another secret?"

This time, she nodded.

"Okay. Then the truth is it depends totally on where you're shot. If you're shot in the stomach, like I am, you may not feel a thing. You can be sitting for five, ten minutes bleeding before it starts acting up, but when it does, it's like the biggest guy you know slammed you in the gut."

"What about if it hits your arm?"

"That's different," Ump said. "Some parts of your arm got nothing, so you don't feel a thing. But other parts have nerves, so if you get hit wrong, the muscles kind of make you flinch." Ump pretended to get shot in the arm.

"And what if you get shot in the head?"

"That's the easiest," Ump said. He slapped his forehead, rolled his eyes up and fell backward.

Jennifer laughed.

"Come on, now," Ump said. "Get out. I gotta get some sleep."

Jennifer closed the bin and walked to the door. "See you tomorrow," she said.

"Tomorrow," Ump answered, waiting for the door to close before taking off his clothes.

The next day, Ump walked Freido to the limousine. It was a beautiful morning—the air clean, the sun out, the grass wet from dew.

"Remember," Freido said, "I want you to take care of yourself. If you have any complaints, let me know and I'll straighten them out."

"Sure," said Ump.

"You're looking better already. I wouldn't be surprised if you're out of here in a week. In the meantime, keep indoors. I'll let you know the moment we find Sal."

Ump nodded. They were almost at the car when Freido grabbed Ump by the arm and stopped him. "Now, I know you can take care of yourself, but there's one thing that still makes me nervous."

Ump waited. Freido eyed him suspiciously, looking for trouble.

"I'm thinking of your temper," Freido said. "I know how good you are, I know how professional you are. . . . *However*, you can't treat this place like the city. You understand that? You can't snap just because something rubs you the wrong way. That isn't good. It isn't low profile, *capisce?*"

Ump and Freido stared at each other, Freido hoping his warning had sunk in, and Ump giving no clue as to whether it had.

"Are you gonna be all right out here?"

"Sure," Ump said.

"You're gonna keep calm, keep your head. . . ."

"I'll be fine."

Freido still didn't trust him, but what could he do? He

patted Ump's arm and they finished their walk. "You're a class act, Ump," he said. "Enjoy the peace and quiet."

Leon opened the limousine door and Freido settled into the back seat. When the door was shut Freido pushed a button and the window rolled down. "One last thought," Freido said. "You're gonna find my brother-in-law a real pain in the ass. He may get on your nerves quick and you may want to do something about it."

Ump waited.

"I just want you to know that if he really drives you crazy—if you do get the urge to kill him—go ahead. It's perfectly fine. Francine'll love you, and I promise to take care of her kids."

Ump grinned, but Freido wasn't smiling.

"I'm not kidding," he said. "I'd consider it a personal favor." Freido finally winked and sat back in his seat. "Other than that, remember: low profile."

"Low profile," Ump repeated, holding his ground until the limousine was out of sight.

Ump returned to the house, determined to do his absolute best to keep out of the way and be discreet. He had a room, he had his meals, and he had company. How hard could it be?

TWELVE

Francine was knocking at Ump's door. She waited, swung it open, then stopped and stared at him. Ump was stripped to the waist, and it was the first time she had seen a man, other than her husband, lying on a bed and naked from the belt up.

"Excuse me," she said. "I just thought, with your injury and all, you might want a change of sheets."

"No, thanks," he said, but she moved closer anyway, staring at the bandage. It looked as if Ump was recovering from an appendix operation, except an appendix was lower than Ump's wound.

"Does it hurt?" she asked.

"Not at the moment," he said. Then, anticipating her next question, "I got mugged."

The lie hadn't worked with Nan, but Francine took it easily. She asked Ump for details, and he muttered vaguely about a fight. "I swung one way, he swung the other, that was that," Ump said. "It's nothing."

"You fought with him?"

"Just enough to get laid up," Ump said.

Francine should have left the room. She should have apologized for intruding, said good-bye, and returned to the hallway, closing the door behind her.

"I'm going shopping in a few minutes," she said. "I'm taking the kids, but if you feel like getting outside . . ."

Ump stared at her—no expression, always the professional listener.

"There's room in the car, I mean," Francine said. "I'll show you the town and you can get some sun."

Ump considered the offer, weighing his promise to Freido versus getting outside.

A half hour later, they were all in the car, Ump settling in the front passenger seat while Jennifer and Michael piled into the back. Francine smiled, fixed her hair a last time, then turned the ignition. She backed out of the driveway and headed for downtown Waylin.

Ump was waiting in the parked car when he saw the two young thugs park their motorcycles and go inside the grocery store. One even held his pocket the way Freido did when he hid a gun.

Instead of worrying, Ump enjoyed the sun while the children stretched over the front seat and stared at him.

"Can I see it?" Michael asked.

"See what?" Ump said.

"The hole."

Ump turned to Jennifer.

"I only told Michael," she said.

Ump looked serious. "I thought we had a promise. One of the worst things you can do in life is break a promise."

"I thought you meant my Mom and Dad," Jennifer said.

Ump grunted, glared at both of them, then picked up his shirt.

"Wow," Michael said.

Ump tucked in his shirt.

"What else you got?" Jennifer asked.

"I got your water pistol," Ump said.

"Besides that."

Ump thought a moment, then said, "Want to see me start a car without using a key?"

Both children said yes, and Ump got to work, reaching in his pocket for a knife, then leaning under the dashboard. A moment later, he was tapping the ignition wires.

The children screamed their delight when the engine turned.

Ump cut the engine and reconnected the wires. "Remember," he said. "Don't tell anyone. I mean it."

The children, of course, agreed, and Ump opened the side door.

"Jennifer, you take care of your brother a minute. I gotta make a phone call."

Ump left the car and hobbled to the side of the store, where he found a pay phone. His call rang almost a dozen times before it was answered, and even then, the voice sounded reluctant.

"Yeah?"

"This the Golla residence?" Ump said.

"Who are you?" the man answered.

"I'm the guy who whacked Sal's brothers."

There was a moment of silence. Ump couldn't tell if the man was passing word about the call or just thinking on his own. Finally, the man said, "Well, Mr. Whack Off, what can I do for you?"

"I understand Sal's in hiding," Ump said. "I thought you could tell me where to find him."

"And why would I do that?"

"I thought Sal and me could settle this on our own," Ump said. "See, what happened with his brothers was an accident. I didn't mean to kill them; I wanted Sal."

"Oh, so you want to apologize?"

"I just figured since Sal wants to kill me, and I gotta kill him, rather than bullshit for a month we could work things out quick."

"That's very thoughtful of you," said the man. He hesitated, then said, "You're Frank Brady, aren't you?"

"Most people call me Ump," Ump said.

"Most people call me Bagel," the man answered.

Ump grinned. "You're Bagel? Hey, I'm impressed."

"It's not so shabby on my end, either," said Bagel.

Ump relaxed some. It helped talking to a professional. "Tell me the truth, Bagel. Think Sal and me can get together?"

"I shouldn't even answer that," said Bagel. "But if you want the truth, Sal's not in the best of shape. Most doctors warn against jumping through closed windows."

"I saw that," Ump said.

"The main point is Sal can't even wang his dick. He's out at least a week. In the meantime, it's my job to kill you."

Ump frowned. "That don't sound like Sal," he said. "I thought he liked to do his own work."

"Normally he does, but it's not every day your brothers get whacked," said Bagel.

Ump, of course, knew Bagel was right. "At least do me the favor of talking to Sal," Ump said. "I can't help thinking there's a way for us to move things along. I'm not in the best shape, either. Can you talk to him?"

"Sure," Bagel said. "You want to give me your phone number?"

"I'll phone back. You just talk to him, Bagel, and see what he'd like. Okay?"

"Sounds good here."

"I'll call in about three days," Ump said. "In the meantime, don't open the door to strangers."

Bagel chuckled. "I think we learned that lesson pretty good."

Ump hung up. He wondered briefly if Freido would mind him pushing things along, but who cared? Ump was pleased just to talk with Bagel. Since they were on different sides of the fence, Bagel and Ump rarely met, but in Ump's head, Bagel was pound for pound every bit as good a hit man as himself. Ump would like to sit with him sometime and trade stories; for now, though, Ump kept his head in the present. He checked on the children, then went into the store, hoping to buy a New York paper.

That was when he saw the robbery.

Or so he figured. In fact, he didn't see any gunmen, not immediately. All he saw were customers and cashiers lying on the tiled floor, apparently under orders to stay put, even though the gunmen were busy rifling through the store safe. Ump stared at the scene, then continued into the store. He walked slowly, so as not to strain his stomach, and stopped by the newspaper rack. It was a lucky day; not only did he find the *Times*, but a *Post* and *News*. He picked up all three papers and headed to the nearest cashier.

"How much for all of them?" he asked.

The clerk looked up, terrified. Ump, annoyed, leaned closer to the boy.

"You hear me?" he said.

The cashier glanced toward the gunmen and whispered, "A dollar fifty."

Ump paid and headed for the door. He might have left, but he saw Francine on the floor. He stopped, stooped down, and lifted her. "What are you doing?" he asked. "Let's go home."

"They have guns," she said.

"So? That's their business," he said.

They had actually made it to the door when one of the gunmen saw them. "Hey, assholes," the man shouted.

Francine dragged Ump to a stop. They turned and faced the gunman, Francine waiting for the next order, Ump looking impatient.

"Back on the floor."

Francine obeyed immediately, but not Ump. He stared at the gunmen as if they were even younger than Francine's kids.

"Didn't you hear me?" the gunman said.

"I heard you," Ump answered. He looked and sounded thoroughly unimpressed. "What is this? You guys just break out of an orphanage?"

"Get on the goddamn floor," the gunman ordered.

Ump shook his head, but he remembered his promise to Freido. Slowly, he limped back toward the cash registers.

"The *floor*," the gunman said.

"My stomach's killing me," Ump said. He was disgusted with the kid's orders, but went so far as to sit on a bench. When he was comfortable, he nodded his okay, and the gunmen seemed to accept this. While Ump read one of his papers, one of them approached and fumbled through his pockets, taking his money, patting down and finding Jennifer's toy gun. He took the toy and waved it in front of Ump's face. "A little old for this, aren't you?" he asked Ump.

Ump didn't say anything, and the gunman jabbed him in the side.

"Don't you talk?" the gunman asked.

"I'm thinking," Ump said.

"About what?" the gunman said.

"About the newspapers," Ump said. He glanced again at the prices, then looked past the gunman to the cashier. "Hey," Ump called. "How much did you charge me?"

The cashier didn't answer, but he didn't have to; Ump knew the answer. He had dropped a buck fifty, and meanwhile,

Ump calculated the real cost at a buck thirty. That meant he had paid twenty cents extra.

The gunman jabbed Ump again, this time with muscle.

"I want you on the floor," the gunman said. "I want you *down*."

If he had nudged Ump anywhere else, Ump could have taken it. But in his stomach—in his *wound*—it was like jabbing a stick in a bleeding bear.

Ump faced the gunman.

"What's the matter?" the gunman said. "Can't you hear me?"

Ump stared back, his mouth tight, his rage close to unbearable. "Before I lie down," Ump said slowly, "how much is eighty plus fifty?"

The gunman thought a moment. *He* was the one with the gun—*he* was the one standing over Ump—but he felt obliged to answer. "One hundred forty," he said.

Ump listened, held it in, held against everything, held to the point of combustion. . . . It was unbearable. Either his heart was going to blow, or his temper.

Then the gunman jabbed him one last time.

Ump went berserk.

THIRTEEN

They were calling him a hero.

They were saying how amazing it was that one man could overpower two renegade gunmen. They were saying how any number of innocent people might have died except for the heroic efforts of a single stranger who, thank *God*, arrived in Waylin just in the nick of time.

And they were saying all this on the front page of the local newspaper.

At least it wasn't a good picture. The photo showed Ump frowning and rubbing his stomach. There were also pictures of the gunmen, mug shots taken at the hospital.

Ump stared at the photos, still wondering why some diddly robbery got so much attention when back in the city it wouldn't make a line in the crime section. But what could he expect in a small town? How often do a couple of wayward bikers drift off the wrong highway exit and end up pulling pistols? And how often did a town like Waylin actually catch the gunmen?

All Ump could do was sit and pretend the only thing new in his life was a little extra scab around his wound. He hoped Waylin would catch on and do the same. But, once again, there it was . . . a knock on his bedroom door. "Ump?" Francine said, "you've got another phone call."

Ump stopped his reading, said thank you, and picked up his extension.

"Mr. Brady?" the caller said. "Mr. Brady, my name's Donald Whitestone. I own a hardware store in downtown Waylin."

Ump rolled his eyes. The whole day had been like this,

[72]

people calling to say thanks or hello or welcome to our town. This time, he listened while Mr. Whitehead or Whitson or whatever told Ump about how brave he was, as if Ump hadn't been there . . . as if Ump didn't know a thing about bravery. Nonetheless, the store manager insisted on reminding him, then ended the call by saying, "I'd like to give you a hundred-dollar gift certificate for my store."

Ump looked to Francine, who waited by the door. She had been staring at Ump, perhaps believing he had saved her life. Ump covered the mouthpiece and asked her, "You need any hardware?"

She nodded and Ump said to the manager, "Sure. Just no strings, okay?"

"Of course not, Mr. Brady," the manager said. "Waylin owes you, not the other way."

Francine waited until Ump hung up the phone. Then she said, "I thought I'd have the neighbors over for dinner."

"Why?" Ump said.

"I just thought it would be nice," said Francine. "Their names are George and Darlene Maye. They can be here about six. Unless, of course, you need to rest. Do you? Do you mind?"

He knew what this was about—Francine had a hero on her hands, and she wanted to show him off. At the same time, he was a guest, so what could he do?

Instead of answering, he gave his patented blank stare, letting Francine make up her own mind. Francine seemed to find what she needed. She smiled, said, "Six o'clock, then," and left the room.

As for Ump, he tossed the paper in the trash. Christ, what would Freido say? What would Mr. Lucci say?

He worried perhaps a full minute. Then he relaxed. After all, it was Freido's fault for putting him here. If the shit was going to hit the fan, let Freido do the ducking.

"Well," said Joseph, "aren't we dolled up for the ladies."

Ump straightened his jacket and walked down the stairs. He was overdressed for the evening, but at home Nan always had him dress for company, and he honored the Gratton house accordingly, allowing Joseph his remark, just as he allowed George Maye to walk closer and offer his hand.

"You must be Mr. Brady," said George.

"He prefers Ump," Francine said.

Darlene also shook his hand. "Ump," she said, testing the name. "You're supposed to be a hero, Ump."

"He *is* a hero," George said.

Ump and Darlene stared at each other, Darlene trying to penetrate his personality, Ump sensing the effort.

A half hour later, Francine served dinner. They took their places, and while Francine passed the vegetables, George nudged Joseph and said, "That was one hell of a show Ump put on yesterday. What is he, a law officer?"

"An umpire," Joseph said. "that's why they call him Ump." Joseph tapped Ump on the arm, showing him off. "A professional big leaguer. Isn't that right?"

"That's what Freido said," Ump said.

"What was it like, Ump, catching those crooks?" George asked. "Was it scary? Ever do anything like that before?"

"I heard one of the bastards might die," Joseph said, grinning. "Wouldn't that be a shame? What did you do? Hit him on the head with a cash register?"

"Something like that," Ump said.

"They can't blame you," George told Ump. "I'm sure it was self-defense."

Darlene stopped eating. "Is that true? Was it self-defense?" she asked Ump.

Ump shrugged. "The truth is," he said, "I'd rather forget the whole thing."

"I'm sure you would," said Francine. "It was horrible."

"Very horrible," Darlene agreed. "Wasn't it, Mr. Brady? I mean, what was it like killing those men?"

"No one's dead yet," George said.

"But Mr. Brady was trying to kill them," she answered. "Please," she said to Ump. "Was it just instinct? If you had to think about it first—think about killing them—could you do it? Or if you had time to think, would you have done things differently?"

Joseph chuckled. "He'd drop two registers on their heads," he said.

Ump, however, understood the nature of the question. He

could see it in her face, the same look Leon and Teddy had when they wanted to talk about the business. And when he answered Darlene, Ump talked as if shaking off an unwanted apprentice.

"I didn't think about it," he answered carefully. "Why should I? This kind of crap happens all the time in the city."

"It doesn't happen around here," Darlene said. "But I'm wrong anyway. You're a big, strong man, Ump. You didn't mean to kill them. If you did, there wouldn't be any doubt."

Ump reached for the potatoes.

"I want to hear more about umpiring," said George. "Who've you called against? You called against Reggie? What about Yaz?"

"I've seen them," Ump said.

"Yeah?" said George. "What was it like against Reggie. He a tough call?"

"What's your favorite ballpark?" Joseph said. "You like Yankee Stadium?"

"I like it," Ump said.

"So you umped in the National and American leagues?" George asked.

Ump handled the questions as best he could, and then Francine rescued him by beginning a verbal tour of the town. She talked about the view from a local hill and the annual Thanksgiving parade . . . and all the time she talked, it was Darlene, saying absolutely nothing, who preoccupied Ump. She simply stared at him, biding her time, looking for a private moment to finish her conversation. And then she found her opening. It came while her husband bantered about Waylin's worst winter. She leaned closer to Ump and whispered, "Was it easy?"

No one else heard her, and at first, Ump ignored the question. But Darlene persisted. She discreetly touched his wrist and said, "It was easy, wasn't it?"

Ump could have pulled free. He could have tugged and left the table, and maybe he should have. Instead, he looked Darlene in the eyes, shrugged, and said, "Once you make up your mind, most things are easy."

Despite the answer, Darlene seemed uncertain. "What about if you've never done it before?" She glanced at her husband and asked, "Is it easy the first time?"

Ump thought hard. He wanted to answer, but couldn't. "I don't know," he said. And it was the truth. Because the truth was, he didn't remember. It had been awhile.

FOURTEEN

When Freido phoned Ump, he was furious. "I can't leave you alone two days, can I?" he shouted. "What the hell were you doing out of the house? Why weren't you in your bedroom?"

"I didn't plan on it happening," Ump said. "These guys were holding up a store. They were holding up your sister."

"Yeah?" said Freido. "So why didn't you let them?"

"I tried."

"Oh, really?" Freido said, an argument he found hard to believe. Freido tried calming down. Maybe things weren't so bad? After all, who cared about a robbery in some fucking little town? Who would read about it? What was the big deal? "Look," he finally said, "do you know if any other paper ran the story?"

"Freido, things are already blowing over," Ump answered.

"Yeah?"

"Yeah."

Freido took another breath. "Okay," he said, definitely calming. "How about you? You're all right?"

"I think so," said Ump. "I'm starting to adjust."

Freido sneered. "I'm glad someone's happy."

"Freido," Ump said, "don't worry so much about me. Just track down Sal. The sooner you find him, the sooner I'm out of here."

Freido couldn't argue with that. Ump and Freido shared the silence, Freido thinking about Ump, Ump thinking about Sal. "All right, I'm calm now," Freido said. "But *no more cops and robbers*. My heart can't take it."

"No more cops and robbers," Ump promised.

Freido hesitated, then said, "What about my family?"

"Nothing new here," said Ump. "Wanna talk to your sister again?"

"Naw," said Freido. He hesitated, then said, "How about Joseph?"

"What about him?"

"He still alive?"

"He's eating dinner right now," Ump said. "Wanna talk with him?"

Freido sighed. "Just say hi to the kids," he said, hanging up.

An hour later, Ump was in bed, drawing on a notepad, trying to make a layout of Sal's New Jersey mansion. Ump didn't know whether or not it would be useful, but as long as the place was fresh in his memory, he wanted to jot down everything. With the help of the calculator, he added up how many feet he walked from room to room and then used a ruler to draw the walls and doors. First the office—eight paces in, two to the left—about three body lengths across. Then out of the office and down the hall, straight nine paces to the kitchen—seven across, ten in length. . . . Then—

"Ump?"

Ump looked up from the bed and saw Jennifer.

"Mom says you got tickets for the baseball game," she said.

It was true. Word had gotten out that Frank Brady, local hero, was also a professional umpire. There was a small minor-league club in the next county, and as a token of the town's appreciation, the mayor of Waylin had delivered Ump a pass to his box seats. Ump, however, hadn't decided whether or not to use them. The tickets had come with a note: "Please stop by my office after the game and let me know who won. Your friend, Bill Conley." It was the sort of note that suggested a tangle of strings.

"You going alone?" she asked.

Ump said, "I thought I'd give the tickets to your dad. He can take you."

"He doesn't like baseball," Jennifer said.

"He might if it's free."

"I want to go with you," she said. "You can hot-wire cars."

"I just talked with your Uncle Freido," Ump said. "He's not too keen on my leaving the house."

"Uncle Freido doesn't like me playing with toy guns," said Jennifer. "Uncle Freido's a chicken shit."

"Uncle Freido is my boss," said Ump. "And he's not as much a chicken shit as you think."

Jennifer frowned and turned to leave. "What if my dad can't make it? Will you take me then?"

"I'll think about it," Ump said, "but I want to be alone now."

Jennifer backed out the door and closed it. Ump, meanwhile, returned to his calculations, trying to remember how many paces he had figured from the living room to the kitchen. He was staring at the map, his ruler ready, when from outside he heard the screech of a late-braking car.

Ump slid off the bed and looked out the window. It was the taxi again, the same one that had run the red light. Now it had dropped off a passenger, turned across two lanes, and was again running the intersection.

Ump couldn't take it. He grabbed his jacket and, in a hurried walk, left the room and trotted downstairs. No one saw him leave—Francine was too busy with dishes, Joseph was at the pub. Ump limped out the door in time to see the cab shift out of park and turn back toward the intersection. The light was still red, but the driver didn't care. For the third time, the cabbie drove through it.

"Hey!" Ump shouted. "Hey, cabbie!"

Ump waddled into the middle of the street and opened his jacket. He reached for his gun, pulled it out, took aim and squeezed the trigger.

Water squirted in the air.

The cabbie looked back and saw Ump standing there, his gun extended, the water dripping down.

He flipped his finger.

Ump watched as the taxi left him in the street. For a moment, he was furious. Then, as he turned back for the house, he realized not only was he crutchless; he could also flex his stomach muscles. No pain, no nothing.

Not bad, he thought. Not bad at all.

He went back to the house, into the living room, and knelt beside Jennifer. "Hey," he said.

Jennifer looked up at him. Ump was smiling.

"That game tomorrow," he said. "What time do we go?"

"Your attention please to section twelve, row double-A," the stadium announcer said, "where we are pleased to have in attendance former major-league umpire and local hero, Mr. Frank Brady."

Ump didn't ask for the attention, but, as with the previous days, it was thrust upon him. The only good news was that the announcement happened twenty minutes before game time, so only a handful of people applauded instead of hundreds. As for the visit from the game's umpires—well, Ump was getting good at his patter.

"Mr. Brady?" said the home-plate umpire, "my name's Harry Martin." Martin reached over the railing to shake Ump's hand. "It's a pleasure to be in the company of a real pro."

They were still shaking hands when the other umpires approached. Hank Doolen, the first-base umpire, smiled, waited, then also shook Ump's hand. Behind him, the third-base umpire, Mickey Tuttle, soon also imposed on Ump's company. For all of them, meeting Ump was like meeting their dream.

"So where you coming down from, Mr. Brady?" Hank Doolen asked. "The Nationals?"

Martin winced at the question. None of them knew Ump. But suppose they *should*? You don't ask Reggie Jackson if he ever played in the American League. Suppose you don't ask Frank Brady where he umpired?

"I heard National's the best," said Tuttle. "I've been in the rookies for two years. In another three, if I'm not in the Nationals, I'm out of here."

"You can spend a career down in the minors," Doolen told Tuttle.

"Tell me something I don't know," Tuttle answered, then to Ump, asked, "Mr. Brady, how'd you break in?"

Ump thought a moment. "I started by working under another pro. His name was Manny Santos."

"Santos?" said Martin, stung by another name he didn't know.

"Manny showed me tricks to get by anything," Ump said. "There wasn't a guy in any of the cities could touch Manny. I spent a little while under his wing, learned how to protect myself, learned how to finish a job. . . ."

"Manny Santos was also in the Nationals?" said Tuttle.

"Manny was all over the place," said Ump. "It was Manny who taught me the most important thing about life."

"Yeah?" said Tuttle, waiting.

"Principles," Ump said. "With principles and judgment, you can go anywhere."

All three of the minor-league umpires looked as if Ump had given them a jewel of information.

"And that's how you made it?" said Tuttle.

"Well, there wasn't much choice at the time," said Ump. "Not after the Alonzo family chopped him down in the Battery. But that was over twenty years ago, so who the hell remembers?"

Martin again didn't understand who Ump was talking about or what he meant, but he'd be damned to admit it. Nor would he let anyone else make the mistake. "Santos was one of the best," Martin said. If Tuttle and Doolen had been considering a dumb question, hopefully that shut them up.

"There's been better since," said Ump, "but Santos was a thinking-man's pro, and there aren't enough thinkers in my business, which is maybe why we got so many problems."

"Ain't that the truth," said Doolen. "All you hear during training is don't think, just make the call. I mean, why the hell did God give us brains if all we're supposed to do is throw up an arm?"

"Maybe because that's our job," said Tuttle.

"Maybe that's why we're still in the rookie leagues," said Doolen.

"I'm sure Mr. Brady doesn't need our pearls of wisdom," Martin told both of them. The home team's manager shouted at the umpires, and Martin turned, waving for patience. "Time to check the lineup cards. Enjoy the game, Mr. Brady. Have a beer on me."

"And me," said Doolen.

[81]

"Me, too," said Tuttle.

But there was no need for their offers. As soon as the umpires returned to work, Ump was overwhelmed with well-wishers offering everything from beer to soda to hot dogs. Always, Ump considered the obligations of the offer, then looked to Jennifer for approval. And always, Jennifer said yes, accepting the nachos and cheese, while Ump took the beer and popcorn. Only after she was full did she ask, "You're sure this is all right?"

Ump shrugged. "If someone shoves a buck in your pocket, you can do two things: you can keep the buck or shove it back. If you keep it, everyone's happy; if you shove it back, you got a shoving match. Which would you do?"

Jennifer took another sip of soda.

The game was between the Engerville Cubs and the South County Knights, and the Knights wasted no time grabbing a lead. Three of their runs came in the top of the second, and while the Cubs didn't like being dumped on, one thing the Cubs manager couldn't blame was the umpiring. Tuttle, Doolen, and Martin were out to make an impression, and they were on top of the game with Martin tightening the strike zone, Doolen getting his nose down for every first-base play, and Tuttle charging out as the balls lobbed into left field.

But in the second, things went way out of hand when the Cubs pitcher walked four straight batters. When the inning ended, the Cubs manager greeted his pitcher with a shouting barrage. "What the hell you doing? You're balancing on your heels? Why? You balance on the toes, Duncan, not the heels. . . ."

Martin used the moment to find Ump. Ump raised his beer, more than happy to compliment a professional. Ump was all comfortable when the Cubs again took the field. He sat back, ate his peanuts, and watched as the South County Knights hit their second homer, this one going dead center over a 410-foot fence.

The Cubs pitcher wiped his face, dared to glance at his manager, then to the bullpen. . . . No one was warming up. The manager saw him sneaking a peek. "You're on your fucking own," the manager shouted at him. "You can stay out there until hell freezes."

The pitcher slapped a new ball in his mitt and the next batter got into the box.

"All goddamn day, Duncan," said the manager. "I don't care *what* you do."

Duncan nodded to the catcher, rocked back on his heels and—

"Ball!" shouted Martin, the baseball hitting the dirt.

The batter stepped out of the box, stepped in, took his stance. Duncan remembered not to rock back, but his toes didn't hold his balance and . . .

"Ball two!" Martin said, this time the pitch outside.

The pitcher stepped from the mound, furious with himself. He had no control and no motion. All he was doing was heaving the ball, not pitching it. He looked again for help, but the manager was sipping a cup of water.

"Ball three!" Martin shouted, this time the ball below the knees.

"Throw your fast ball!" shouted the pitching coach. "Try your goddamn fast ball!"

The pitcher heard, but what the hell did they think he'd been throwing? Duncan wiped his hands clean of sweat, felt for the ball's seams, and stepped on the rubber. As for the batter, he couldn't be more relaxed. The pitcher hadn't thrown a strike in three pitches. Before that, he'd thrown a home-run meatball. The batter leaned back, while the catcher waited for a hanging curve and the umpire for an outside ball.

Duncan surprised them. He rocked back and fired. Again, it wasn't a pitch, it was a heave. But it was a 98-MPH heave, and the baseball rocketed from the mound, soaring past the batter's chin, over the catcher's outstretched mitt and powering into Martin's face mask.

On impact, Martin made a quarter turn and dropped on his back.

The catcher was the first at the umpire's side. He shook Martin and said, "You all right? You all right?"

Martin didn't move. Even after smelling salts, he lay still. A full five minutes passed before he opened his eyes, and then he passed out again. When he finally managed not only to regain consciousness but keep it, Martin stood, took a tentative step, and floundered. The ball players just managed to carry him to the bench. From behind the stadium came the whine of an ambulance.

Tuttle and Doolen comforted their friend. They also wanted instructions. Doolen and Tuttle talked, trying to decide how to manage the game, hoping to get advice. Should Tuttle cover the plate, or was it Doolen's turn in the rotation? Nothing like this had happened before, and none of the umpires seemed certain what to do, at least until Martin pointed toward the box seats.

A moment later, Tuttle walked over to Ump.

"Mr. Brady, I hate to impose, but we're a man short. Since you're here, and since you're professional, we wondered if you'd come on the field. Just for one night."

Ump stared at Tuttle.

"We'd consider it an honor," Tuttle said. "I'm certain both teams would agree."

Ump glanced down at Jennifer. She nodded and Ump considered the idea. "What would you want me to do?"

"Whatever you'd like, Mr. Brady," said Tuttle.

"Call me Ump," Ump said. "When I'm on a job, call me by my working name."

"Okay," said Tuttle. "You can take any position you like, Ump. We're already on the field, so why don't you take the plate?"

Ump agreed, then after getting the usher to watch Jennifer, followed a guard onto the field. It didn't take long: Martin had left behind his chest protector and mask, and with Tuttle's help, both were stretched to accommodate Ump's physique. While Ump was fitted, the announcer broadcast his entry in the game. He also identified him as the same Franklin Brady who had stopped the robbery.

The crowd gave a standing ovation.

Twenty minutes passed from the time Martin was beaned to the moment when Ump, behind the plate, shouted, "Play ball." After advancing the last batter to first base, Ump waved in the next victim, then pointed at the pitcher and settled into position. Duncan looked back and acknowledged Ump, but he still didn't have the confidence to pitch. He wiped the sweat off his forehead, nodded once to his catcher, put his foot on

[84]

the rubber, came to a stop, rocked back on his heels, prayed for a break. . . .

The ball soared a half foot over Ump's head.

Ump stared at the pitcher. When the catcher had retrieved the ball, Ump took it, examined the ball, and personally carried it to the mound. The pitcher opened his hand, but that wasn't good enough for Ump. He waved the pitcher closer—close enough so Ump could whisper in his ear.

The Cubs manager watched, wondering what the hell an umpire could be whispering to his pitcher. He might have walked out, but Duncan was nodding along, looking respectful . . . maybe even fearful.

Ump turned to the manager and said, "Ball one." Then he settled back behind the plate and waited for the pitch.

Duncan, meanwhile, dared glancing to the dugout, his eyes pleading for a relief pitcher. He fingered the baseball, knowing he had to throw it, at the same time remembering what Ump had said. He'd never before heard such talk from an umpire. If this was how things worked in the majors, he wasn't certain he wanted to be a professional.

When the batter took position, Duncan rubbed his toe against the rubber. He nodded, reared back, and followed forward, trying ever so hard to hit the strike zone. But the ball again tailed away and . . .

"Ball two," Ump said, "and that's your headlights."

The catcher glanced up at Ump, but Ump didn't bother with him. It was the pitcher who was dangerous. He stared hard at Duncan, daring him to try again. Duncan wiped his face, caught his breath, reared back, and . . .

"Ball three," Ump said, "and that's your windshield."

Duncan walked off the mound, terrified. He wasn't thinking so much of the broken headlights and windshield, but of what would happen if he threw ball four. A lot more than a car rested on that pitch. He focused hard on his target, blocking out the catcalls, thinking only of his motion. He settled, kept on his toes, shifted his weight. . . .

"Strike," Ump called.

Yes, the pitcher thought, settling down. Could he manage it again? He kept his foot on the rubber, afraid to lose the magic, then reared back and threw another fast ball. "Strike two," said Ump, and there he was, with a full count.

Duncan stepped back and struggled to keep his concentration. He touched the rubber, kept on his toes. . . . But his right foot slipped back. His arm came around too high, and the ball rose. Duncan could see it starting to sail away, a certain ball four. Jesus Christ, the pitcher thought. Please, dear God, don't do this. Not now. Please, not my—

The batter swung.

Ump sucked hard on his lower lip and so did the pitcher. They both knew what had happened. It should have been a ball. It should have been a walk. . . . "Strike three," Ump finally said.

Duncan sighed while the batter cursed. The pitcher thought it was over, but Ump walked back to the mound. Again Ump whispered, and again he went back to the plate.

Duncan stared at Ump and shook his head. "No," the pitcher begged. "Not my fingers."

But the Cubs manager had seen enough of Duncan. He called in a reliever and made his own visit to the mound. Duncan waited just long enough to drop the ball in the manager's hand, then he disappeared into the lockers.

While a new pitcher came in, Ump and his colleagues collected by the plate.

"How's it going?" Tuttle asked.

Ump nodded, satisfied with himself. "I think I'm okay."

"What was it you told him?" Doolen asked.

"I told him to pitch off his toes," said Ump. He glanced at his watch. "How much time we got between innings?"

"A minute," Tuttle said. "What's the matter?"

"I gotta do something," Ump said, walking into the home dugout, reaching in the bat rack, and heading for the parking lot.

Soon, he was again behind the plate, assuming a crouch. He eyed the new pitcher. "What's his name?" Ump asked the catcher.

"Jenkins," the catcher answered.

Ump nodded at the pitcher and yelled, "Play ball, Jenkins." Then he added, "And remember, Jenkins, I want strikes."

Jenkins didn't think twice of the comment, not until he

went into his motion and remembered that sick look on Duncan's face as he had left the mound. Jenkins reared back, rotated his foot, trying to concentrate on his catcher, but his attention drifted up to the umpire. It was like staring into the eyes of an executioner.

And while Jenkins started sweating, Ump got ready for the call.

FIFTEEN

Ump was melancholy.

It wasn't anyone's fault, because the day had been pretty good. His stomach still felt strong, the game had gone well, Jennifer was smiling. . . . But when he started feeling too good, it made him think of Nan, and when he started thinking of Nan, and then the kids, it made him homesick.

Ump just wasn't used to being away from his family. He also wasn't used to this kind of depression. He didn't know quite how to handle it, and about the only thing left to do was become sullen.

"Hey," said Doolen, "can you come out tomorrow?"

"I don't know," Ump said.

"You got to let us buy you a beer," said Tuttle.

"I don't think so," Ump said. "Maybe next time."

"*Next* time," said Doolen. "That's a promise."

"You looked terrific today, Ump," Tuttle said.

Ump accepted the compliment. Standing behind the plate, shouting balls and strikes, making the tough calls and, above all, making sure the players respected the rules . . . nothing was more natural to Ump, not even killing.

Still, he wanted to get Jennifer back to the house. When they were home, he sent her upstairs and reached for the phone. He tried calling Nan. He let the phone ring fifteen times, then tried again, letting the phone ring another two minutes.

Francine finally walked into the living room and saw him. "Something the matter?" she asked.

Ump hung up. "Trying to reach the wife," he said. "She normally stays home in the afternoons."

Francine joined Ump by the sofa. With Jennifer and Michael upstairs, and Joseph out of the house, Ump and Francine were alone. Francine seemed to like the situation, actually letting their knees touch. "You must love her a lot," she said.

Ump was still thinking about his phone call, wondering whether to phone Freido. He just couldn't remember the last time Nan had gone out during the day. On the other hand, maybe she was out at a restaurant with her cousins. Maybe her cousins always went out for dinner.

"It was thoughtful taking Jennifer to the park," Francine said.

Ump thought about other ways to reach Nan. He was still thinking when he saw Francine staring at him. He tried grinning, feeling embarrassed. "This is new to me, being without the wife."

"Not all men would take it so hard," Francine said.

Ump cradled the phone. He looked about the room for a solution to his problem. Finally, he turned back to Francine. She seemed an inch or two closer.

"Joseph used to be that way, but things haven't been so good lately."

"Freido doesn't think so much of Joseph," Ump said.

"Joseph is difficult," Francine said. "Sometimes I have a hard time remembering when things were different."

Ump studied her carefully. He thought a moment, then said, "Mind if I ask you something?"

Francine waited.

"What would you do if Joseph died? Would you be upset?"

"Of course," she said. "Joseph dead? I'd—"

"Don't just answer," Ump said. "Think about it. I mean it. Would you be upset?"

Francine again didn't answer. At first Ump didn't say anything either; then he nodded, as if she had said everything. "What would you do about money?" he said.

This made her laugh. "Freido told you to ask this, didn't he?" she said.

"Freido asked me something," Ump said.

"Tell Freido to butt out of my life."

"Freido's my boss," Ump said. "It might be smarter for you to tell him."

Francine couldn't argue, nor did it look like she was going to try. She was again moving a shade closer. Ump, however, stood up and began pacing the room. "It's stupid worrying about Nan, isn't it?"

"I'd say so," Francine said.

Ump nodded to himself, then patted his stomach. "It's feeling better."

"You look wonderful," Francine said.

The remark pleased Ump, but pleasure wasn't an expression that stayed long on his face. After glancing at his watch, he decided on an early evening walk before dinner. "I got time, don't I?" Ump asked.

"Go ahead," Francine said. "When Joseph's out, I usually don't eat until late, anyway."

Ump thanked her, left the house, and headed toward town. It was his first real look at Waylin. Yes, he had seen it from the car, but buildings and places lost dimension in a car. So much of time and space relied on speed, and even at twenty miles an hour, you lost the feel for a hill or the length of a city block.

Now, walking through downtown, Ump began to appreciate its gentleness. The bakery, the bank, the drugstore, the coffee shop . . . The town had a careful ecology of merchants that lined both sides of the street without, at any time, encroaching on one another. Even in the rare instance when there was more than one type of store—such as the two coffee shops—both were spaced to give each its own block. There was a balance here, as tender as any environment, and while it was perhaps possible for Waylin to expand, as the town council was indeed trying, it took incredible vision to imagine such a change.

Ump walked until he reached the church. Then something caught his attention.

Father Jonathan Carroll had chained himself to a mausoleum gate. Meanwhile, in front of the church, an elderly woman was marching back and forth with a coffee can. She stopped before Ump, asked for money, then recognized him.

Soon she was digging in the can and offering him cash. "Please," she said. "It's the least we can do."

Ump, however, insisted she keep the money. Curious, he also approached the priest.

Carroll was slow to notice his visitor. He had been there since early afternoon, ever since Farber had managed bending the county rules for the council to get approval for the cemetery's removal. In that time, few had noticed his protest.

Ump, however, couldn't quite make sense of it. He stood next to him and asked, "Sal do this to you?"

Carroll looked up, and Ump stared down. The thought had crossed Ump's mind that Sal was in town and maybe he had chained the priest as a message.

"I'm protecting the dead," the priest said.

Ump didn't understand, except that Father Carroll's dilemma seemed intentional.

"The town is trying to move the cemetery," the priest elaborated. "I'm stopping them."

"You must be doing a good job, because it's still here," said Ump.

"Not much longer," Carroll said. "Not unless I can get people to notice me."

Ump evaluated the situation, then did a closer examination of the chains.

"You really want attention?" he said.

"Of course," said Carroll. "The vote's this evening."

"I mean *really*," Ump said.

"I told you," Carroll said, annoyed.

Ump bent closer and readjusted the chains so they crossed the priest's neck instead of his chest. He tightened the loop, bringing Carroll's head flush against the iron mausoleum doorway.

With an extra twist, Father Carroll gasped.

Carroll rolled his eyes up and looked desperately for help. He could barely breath, let alone speak; but Ump calmed him. "Just hold still," he said. "You should do great." Then Ump walked back to the sidewalk, tapped the woman on the shoulder and pointed out the priest's dilemma.

"Dear God," she screamed.

And the crowds began collecting.

Ump didn't stay for the scene. What was there to see? Soon there'd be lots of people, and maybe a fire department truck, and after that everyone would be helping the priest, some offering sympathy and others money. At the very least, there'd be a passing curiosity over how Carroll had almost let himself be killed. And the priest really was at risk. That, however, was what good extortion was all about, and that was all Ump had done—moved Father Carroll up from begging to extortion. What Ump did wasn't even original. It was just a variant on how the Biaggi family took ten grand from the Katinskis, kidnapping the youngest Katinski and roping him to a chair, using the same strangling twist Ump used on the priest.

No, there wasn't anything here Ump hadn't seen before and in more interesting circumstances. Besides, he had already been involved with too many people. The last thing in the world he needed was someone else clapping him on the back— which was about to happen anyway.

"Crazy son of a bitch, isn't he?" said Fleming.

Ump turned and faced the banker. Fleming nodded in the direction of Father Carroll. "I've been talking to the mayor about you," said Fleming. "I wish you were living here, Mr. Brady. Waylin could use more take-charge people."

Fleming introduced himself, then said, "Do you know me, Mr. Brady?"

Ump shook his head.

"I run the local bank," Fleming explained. "I thought your host might have mentioned me, since we have certain unfinished business matters that need to be concluded."

"If you mean Joseph," Ump said, "he hasn't said a thing."

Fleming nodded. "Good," he said, "because I'm not here to talk about that." Fleming rested both hands on Ump's shoulders. "Mr. Brady, I could be a bad judge of character, but it seems to me a man like you—someone who stops a robbery and then takes charge of an entire ballgame—a man like you is an activist. Not a radical activist, but someone who can't sit on the sidelines. Someone who gets involved. Someone," said Fleming, "who likes to help people."

Ump didn't answer.

"As one volunteer soldier to another," Fleming said, "would you mind if I bought you a beer?"

The two men headed for the corner bar, in itself a triumph for Fleming. It allowed Fleming to share in the cheers as Ump was again hailed. Ump sat on a stool, then tightened against the slapping hands of more well-wishers. Pretty soon, everyone was offering him beers, with Fleming leading the pack. "You're a man's man, Mr. Brady," Fleming said. "So's our mayor, Bill Conley. That's why I'm here; I'm a friend of Bill's, and he asked me to talk with you."

"Why?" said Ump.

"No special reason," said Fleming. "The mayor simply thinks a great deal of you. Frankly, Mayor Conley would like to be associated with you."

"Associated?" Ump said.

"Publicly," Fleming explained.

Ump pulled back, already shaking his head.

"Please," Fleming said. "You haven't even heard what I said. Just give me a few minutes." He reached in his pocket, pulled out fifty dollars, and placed it on the bar. "I'd be more than happy to pay for your time."

Ump stared at the money, then settled down, letting Fleming give his five-minute pitch.

Meanwhile, outside the bar, across the street, two people stared through the pub window, both with their own interest in Ump.

One was Shirley Anderson. She sat in her second-floor office, staring down at the pub, wondering what Waylin's local hero was doing in Walter Fleming's company. Was Conley getting his endorsement? And if not, could she get it?

The other person sat patiently in a parked car. He was a stick-thin man with black hair and a gold tooth. The tooth replaced one he had lost after being sucker-punched with a steel pipe. His name was Gus "The Blade" Franco, and in his lap he held a straightedge razor.

SIXTEEN

Gus Franco was a psychopath.

Even he would admit it, since it wasn't his fault. He had been an abused child. It started from the day of conception, when, shortly after making love, Gus's mother slipped and struck her abdomen against a bed rail. As for growing up, his father was not only a professional boxer with a short temper; he was proof that punches to the head caused serious brain damage. All this made Gus's psychosis easier to understand and perhaps even sympathetic; but it didn't make him any less a psychopath, and it didn't change one basic fact:

Gus Franco loved slicing things.

Above all, he liked slicing flesh. Any kind of flesh—human, dog, cat, rat . . . He simply enjoyed nicking the skin, sliding his razor into the muscle, then slipping the blade to the bone. He liked seeing the meat split. He liked cutting through the flesh, then watching the body twitch and deaden. He enjoyed the panic on his victims' faces, and the complete terror as they realized their helplessness. But foremost, he enjoyed the blood—how it poured so freely, like water liberated from a dam. He could watch it for hours, which, of course, was impossible, since the way Gus worked, a victim was drained in under thirty minutes. Still, he had tried stretching the pleasure: first with fat victims, then with muscular ones. He decided the perfect victim needed to be a mix of fat and fitness, someone heavy enough to have a few added pints of blood, but also with the muscles to support a strong liver.

Gus could spend an afternoon thinking of his dream victim. What would he look like? Large and chunky? Short and powerful?

But those were old questions.

Now he had Ump.

He sat in the car, his eyes focused on the bar, wondering if he could dare leave and phone Sal. Gus knew he should. When he was given the assignment, Sal made Gus promise to phone twice a day and let him know how things stood.

"You think you can do that, Blade?" Sal had asked. "Think you know how to dial a telephone?"

"No problem, Mr. Golla," Gus said. "I'll phone twice a day, I promise."

Sal looked unconvinced. "I'm asking, Blade, because I know from experience you can't trust lunatics."

"No, sir, you can't."

"At the same time, I want Frank Brady hurt, and I can't think of a better guy for the job than a basket case."

"That's right," Gus answered. "That's me, Mr. Golla."

"I just wish you didn't have such a short memory."

Sal was talking about the previous day, after the Gollas managed to kidnap one of Tommy Lucci's lieutenants. Gus had been put in charge of breaking the man. Unfortunately, Gus got lost in his work and killed the lieutenant before the man had a chance to talk. Worse, only moments before Gus gave the death slice, the guy had been on his knees begging to tell everything. "I know where he is. Please! Tommy's hidden him. Frank Brady . . . He's—" Sal was watching at the door when Gus, ever the psycho, swung down with the razor, slicing the man's voice box. Sal was still staring when Gus remembered the job and, embarrassed, looked up at him. "Whoops," Blade said.

"Whoops." Blade said that all too often, and when Sal gave his instructions for Ump, it came back to him. "I swear, you can trust me, Mr. Golla," he told Sal. "It's not a problem anymore. I've learned self-restraint."

Sal shook his head, knowing better than to believe him. He circled Gus, trying to discern the truth, which was impossible; you couldn't discern anything from Blade.

"Just do your best, Blade," Sal finally said. "Find Brady, kill him, and make it very painful."

"Yes, sir, Mr. Golla."

And if you get the chance, phone. Let me know where you are and what you find out."

"Absolutely, sir."

"*Phone.* I mean it."

"Yes, sir," said Blade. "Twice a day. You can trust me, sir."

"Yeah, right," said Sal, sounding like he had already given up.

And now, here Blade was, several days and several victims later, tracking his prey. He had done it with tenacity, courage, inside sources, outside sources, pay-offs. . . . He had also done it with the help of his mother. In fact, mostly his mother, who lived in a town not far from Waylin and had sent him the clipping on Ump's heroics. She also included a note. "Some lunatics tried robbing the neighborhood store," it said. "Thinking of you."

Blade recognized Ump immediately. And now he was waiting for his victim to come outside and wondering whether to phone Sal. Sure, he *could* phone Sal, but if he waited an hour, Blade could phone with the news that Frank Brady was *dead.* And that would really make Sal happy. Besides, he hadn't phoned Sal yet—not about his mother, not about the clipping, not about Waylin. If he started talking, Blade could end up spending an hour on the phone.

No, Gus decided. Better to stay put.

He kept his eye on the pub, remarkably patient for a man about to face his lifelong fantasy made real. He watched while sliding the flat of the razor back and forth against his palm like a barber testing an edge. And with each swipe, he thought again and again about Ump, trying to decide where to put the first cut. What would cause a slow, steady bleed? What would be painful? And by painful, Gus meant absolute, complete agony, the kind of pain that only the dead could talk about.

Boy, he thought. He would owe Sal big for this one.

Inside the pub, Ump had managed to fend off Fleming's pleadings. No sooner had they finished their talk than Ump was again surrounded by people pulling him into two arguments, one about business, the other about hunting.

For the first argument, Ump made one contribution; he

said the word no. The word was uttered in the middle of a joke about whether death was too good a fate for people who made a living collecting mortgages. Some people laughed, but not Fleming. There was nothing at all funny in the way Ump had said it. In fact, Fleming soon excused himself from the bar and headed back to his office, where he privately drank his scotch.

For the second topic, Ump offered a slightly fuller account of his views. Someone mentioned deer hunting, and soon the small crowd was comparing the advantages of the rifle versus the bow and arrow. One group argued that it was pointless using a dated weapon, while the other saw no point in hunting animals with weapons so advanced there was no testing of skill.

"What about you, Mr. Brady?" someone asked. "Do you hunt?"

Ump nodded. "Sure, I hunt," he said.

"Which do you like, a gun or bow?"

Ump looked thoughtful, then said, "I never used a bow and arrow, but guns I'm not too fond of. I mean, you shoot something. . . . Big deal. You get the same thrill sinking a hole in miniature golf."

"So what do you use?"

"Whatever's around," he said. "It's not important, anyway. I just go about business and try to think of myself as a disinterested third party—kind of floating around, making sure the hunt goes right, if you understand me."

No one did, but they toasted Ump anyway. Ump finished his drink and walked to the door, and the bartender said, "If you're interested, we'll be doing a little deer hunting this weekend."

"No, thanks," Ump said.

"We'd be mighty honored," said the bartender.

Ump again thanked the man, but shook his head. "Thanks, but I don't believe in killing animals."

Ump left, and the bartender waved good-bye. Only later would he wonder what Frank Brady hunted.

As for Ump, he didn't get a half block before Blade was on him.

"Just keep walking," Gus said.

Ump felt the gun in his back and did what he was told. It

was a familiar and respected request in his business. "I know the voice, but I can't place it," he said. "Is it Pickles?"

"Me? Pickles?" Gus said. "Do I smell like Pickles?"

"Well, you're not Hammer and you're not Bagel," Ump said.

Gus, for effect, waved his razor under Ump's nose. "You know me, Ump. You cleaned up after me when Sal popped it on DeMarcos."

"Blade," Ump remembered. "Yeah, the DeMarcos thing. Shit, you left a mess."

"That's because he wouldn't stop moving," said Gus.

"Hey, you can't blame him," Ump said, more memories coming back. "What are you doing these days? You were experimenting, weren't you? Something about bleeders."

"I'm looking for long ones," Gus said. "I figure I got a good one tonight."

Ump didn't answer, instead waiting for instructions. "Where are we going?"

"I don't know yet," Gus said. "Someplace quiet and private. Looking at you, you could take an hour."

"I'm two blocks to the left," Ump said. "If you want private, I got a garage."

A few minutes later, Ump led Gus to the side of the house. He quietly raised the garage door and turned on an overhead light. When they were both inside, Ump brought down the door to ensure their privacy.

Gus relaxed. With the door closed, there was nowhere for Ump to run. The garage was a clutter of garden and automobile tools, all surrounding an old Dodge Dart. Gus nodded Ump back, and Ump moved in front of the car grille.

"You're in great shape, Ump," Gus said. "I just can't figure out where to make the cut. I've been thinking about it since I saw you."

Ump waited patiently, neither angry nor upset. He knew better, since a psycho couldn't be held responsible for his actions. The best you could do was make conversation.

"I don't want to blow this," said Gus. "You look too good."

"Have you tried the arteries lately?" Ump said.

"Arteries," Gus scoffed. "That's the first thing everyone says. They're terrible. Muscles tense, blood pumping. . . ."

"How about the heart?"

"After what I said about arteries?" Gus shook his head. "I've been thinking about the throat."

"Throat's been done a lot," Ump said. "I could be wrong, Blade, but it seems that for me to bleed slow, I got to die slow. But who's got the time for that, anymore? I mean, these days, everyone's a clock watcher."

"I don't care about everyone," Gus said.

"That's easy to say," said Ump. "But if you ask me, people today live in a fast-food society. Anything slow is a risk. If you're a cook, cook it quick. If you want death, break a skull."

"I *like* slow," said Gus. "Maybe I'll cut off your hands."

"You'd be making a mistake," said Ump.

"Or your fingers," said Gus, but still unconvinced. He struggled a moment, then saw the hedge clippers and knew the answer. The *fingertips*.

Yes, this satisfied Gus. Now the only trick was figuring out how to keep Ump in place. Gus considered using a rope or garden hose, but he knew neither would do the job. He needed a one-ton weight, something so heavy that Ump would be paralyzed. He looked about, searching for a solution, then found it.

"Lie down," Gus said.

Ump stretched on the concrete.

"Now slide under the car."

Ump tried, but stopped. "I can't fit too well."

"Then squeeze," Gus said.

Ump squeezed and managed to get his body beneath the undercarriage.'

"Perfect," Gus said. "Now stick one arm out."

Ump did what he was told, and with his victim in position, Gus circled the car, slashing all four tires. The air hissed free and the car lowered. By the time the hissing stopped, the entire weight of the Dodge Dart rested on Ump's chest.

Gus stepped back and stared at the scene, proud of himself. "You comfortable down there?" he asked.

Ump gave a groan.

Gus stared down at Ump's free hand. It was stretched open, with each of the fingers pressed against the garage floor. Gus knelt beside the hand, delighting in the sight, touching the top knuckles and admiring their size. He leaned low so he could look beneath the car. "This is going to be like popping a melon," he said, then again walked to the garden tools. He returned with the hedge clippers, thinking they'd be best for cutting through bone, and pressed Ump's fingers together, massaging them to build up the blood. "Hold still," Gus said. "This'll just take a second. Just hold still."

But Ump was disappointing him. Gus had expected Ump to be calm, patient . . . a professional. Instead, he began twitching and shifting. His hand closed into a fist, then opened again, pressing down even harder against the concrete floor, as if by pressing down, he could avoid being cut. It was ridiculous; Gus could just as easily chop them, like a chef chopping carrot sticks.

"Come on, Ump," said Gus. "Don't make me waste a blade."

Ump wouldn't stop. He was squirming now, and Gus could see the car rocking. Without wasting another word, Gus set aside the clippers and reached in his pocket for the straight-edge razor. He pressed a knee on Ump's wrist and used his own hand for keeping the fingers steady. With Ump again paralyzed, Gus positioned himself, ready to press the razor into flesh, hoping to navigate through the joint. He even got so far as to position the blade above the flesh, much like a guillotine hanging over the neck, ready to separate the head from the body.

Then Ump moved again and with him moved the car.

It happened quickly for Gus: one minute he was pinning Ump's hand, the next he was pinned down, this time wedged to the floor by an overturned Dodge Dart.

As for Ump, he sat up, took a breath, and wiped his face with a shirt sleeve. "That was tough," he said, stretching his back.

Gus couldn't answer; there was a monster of a car on top of him, and there was something else the matter. His razor blade. During the fall, it had carved his wrist. Gus could see the blade still in his flesh, the blood flowing freely.

Ump assessed the situation. He saw the blood pooling under the car, but it was going down a drain, so he didn't worry too much. He worried even less when he saw Gus half-dead.

"You comfortable?" Ump said.

Gus squirmed and settled. "Not too bad," he said.

Ump examined the bleeding wrist. Near Gus's hand was the gun. Ump took away the weapon as a precaution, then squatted beside the hit man.

"You did a good job of tracking me down," Ump said. "Do it alone?"

"All by myself," Gus said.

"I'm impressed," Ump said. "I mean, with your brain the way it is."

"Thanks," said Gus.

"Anyone else know where I am?"

"No," Gus said. "They're looking, but they don't know I'm here. I think you're okay."

Ump looked around and found a package of triple-ply garbage sacks. He unfolded two and stretched them out. "When you're dead, I'll have to drop off your body, but don't worry; I'll phone Sal and he'll pick you up."

"Thanks, again," said Gus. He talked slower and with greater difficulty. "I should have known you were figuring an escape."

"You got preoccupied, that's all," said Ump. "Anything else I can do?"

"No," said Gus, but then saying, "Yeah. Clock me."

"You mean now?"

"When else?" Gus said. "I'm betting I take twenty-five minutes. And Ump?"

"Yeah?"

"When you kill Sal?"

"Yeah?"

"Clock him, too," Gus said. "I'd guess twenty-three minutes on the wrists, or twelve on the throat. Bet money on it."

"Sure," said Ump. He looked at his watch and waited for Gus to die. "Good luck on the other side."

SEVENTEEN

Gus guessed wrong by forty-five seconds, although Ump's count wasn't notably accurate. The moment Gus lost consciousness, Ump worried less about last wishes and more about cleaning up. In particular, there was flipping back the car, then swabbing the blood, and, not least of all, disposing of the body. Ump thought about the last problem while heading back to the house, hoping to find Francine and borrow her car. Francine, however, was serving dinner. She refused to give Ump anything unless he first ate. "Sit down," she said. "Tell me about your walk."

Ump reluctantly obeyed. There was a tone to Francine's voice as if Ump had done something wrong. And, in a way, he had. When he had gone for his walk, he left Francine feeling uncertain about too many things. Francine felt she had embarrassed herself, and now she needed to make up for it.

"I went to a bar," said Ump. "I talked politics with some guy and came back here."

Francine gave him a plate. "You look dirty."

"I fell, but I'm all right."

"You should be careful with that stomach," she said. "Liquor may not be good for it, either."

"I'll watch out," he said.

Francine sat beside him, and Michael and Jennifer began eating.

"What did they have to say?" Francine asked.

Ump had no idea what she meant.

"At the bar," she said. "Politics."

Ump shrugged. "It was nothing," he said. "A guy talked to me about the mayor. He talked like I could do something."

"You probably can," she said.

"Not me. I work for Freido and Mr. Lucci," Ump said. "At least for now."

"You're thinking of quitting Freido?"

Ump considered whether to go into details. "Is this between you and me?"

"Of course," she said.

"Then between us, I wouldn't mind moving on. Before Mr. Lucci, I was a freelancer. I liked freelancing. Now I work regular hours, I commute back and forth, there's all this office politics. . . . It's just not my cup of tea. I could be back at home right now if I was freelancing, not taking orders from Freido. But I owe Freido, and I owe Mr. Lucci, so I listen."

"What do you owe?" Francine asked.

"I owe him a job I botched," Ump said.

"What kind of job?"

"Nothing special," he said. "Some contract work."

"So once you fulfill the contract, you can do what you want?"

"It'll be a weight off my chest, that's for sure," he said. "There's been a lot on my chest lately."

Francine thought about what Ump said, trying to follow, but unable to. She admitted as much, saying, "You know, Joseph's right. Freido doesn't tell us a thing about what he does. Can you tell me?"

"Not like Freido," he said.

"Why don't you try?"

"Freido works under Mr. Lucci."

"And what does he do for Mr. Lucci?"

Ump shrugged. "The truth?" he said.

"The truth."

Ump stopped eating. "Okay," he said, "The truth is, Freido talks for a living. I'm not knocking him, understand? I've known your brother for years and I like him. He talks real good when he's got something to say. He listens good, too. But I swear to God, I've never seen him do a day's work in his life."

"He just talks," said Francine, grinning at the idea.

"Yeah," Ump said. "That's New York, huh? Paid big bucks just for talking."

"You'd think Mr. Lucci would've learned how to do that himself."

"There's lots of things Mr. Lucci should do for himself," Ump said.

Francine stared at Ump, still smiling over her brother.

No, that wasn't true. She was smiling over the conversation. It had been a long time since she had enjoyed such a thing. She slipped into such a good mood she didn't think twice when Ump asked to borrow the car keys. It was as natural as giving them to her husband. Perhaps more natural, since in Joseph's case, she'd hesitate. With Ump, she felt secure.

Ump was almost out the door when Jennifer grabbed his sleeve.

"Are you gonna ump again?" she asked.

"Maybe," he said.

"Then I'm coming," she said.

"Maybe, again," Ump said. "Maybe if you bring along your dad."

Jennifer didn't take quickly to the suggestion, but Ump pushed her back toward the table. There was, after all, business to finish. He left the house, went to the car, and then drove the station wagon until it was just out of sight from the Gratton house. Then he parked and followed the shadows back to the garage.

Inside, things were much the way Ump had left them, albeit damper. Ump did his best to sponge up, then walked about to catch anything he missed. When he finished, he couldn't see a thing wrong, at least nothing that looked like murder. Reasonably satisfied, he slipped Gus into the trash bags, flipped the body on his shoulder, and turned off the overhead light. Again in total dark, he raised the garage door and walked quickly back into the shadows.

Ump was doing well, considering discretion wasn't his strong point. For him, the meaning of professional meant getting the job done quickly. Stuffing Gus in a bag, worrying the whole time over what the neighbors might see . . . That, to Ump, was nonsense. In fact, it was an embarrassment, like asking a chef to throw out the garbage. But Ump did it. He opened the rear of the station wagon, heaved Gus into the back, slammed down the hatch, and again sat behind the steering wheel. He still wasn't sure where to go, but he knew it would have to be a decent distance from Waylin. Someplace where Sal wouldn't be able to trace him. If he had had Gus's temperament, he might have chopped up the body and sent the pieces to Hawaii; instead, he did the next best thing and drove to the train station.

It was a passenger and freight depot, less than twenty miles from Waylin. It was also the only station near town, which explained why, even this late at night, it was busy.

Ump didn't know what to make of the scene. He had expected quiet, but Waylin, like the surrounding towns, only had an evening run, and there were at least a dozen people under the station roof. He decided to park in a far corner of the lot. Then, in the dark, he took Gus the long way to the freight depot, crossing the tracks, walking alongside a freight train, and grabbing hold of a steel ladder that led to the open top of a coal car. Ump carried Gus up and leaned forward.

The body slid off Ump's shoulders and onto the car.

It was good timing. No sooner was Gus off his shoulders than the entire train lurched forward. Ump made it off and waited for the train to pass. He used this time to talk with a station hand. "Where's it going?" he asked.

"Pittsburgh," the man answered.

When the train was gone, Ump retraced his steps to the car. On his way home, he stopped at a gas station, first to wash off, and after cleaning, to make his call.

"Hello?" a voice said.

Ump glanced at his watch. "It's only eleven, Bagel. Why do you sound so tired?"

"Ump?" Bagel said. "Jeez, things have been crazy around here. Every time we think Sal's safely tucked away, we got to wake up and shuffle him elsewhere."

"That doesn't make sense," Ump said. "Mr. Lucci was supposed to call me when he found Sal."

"Well, maybe you should have a talk with your boss," Bagel said. "Is that why you're calling? I didn't think we'd talk until next week."

"I'm calling about Blade," Ump said.

[105]

"Blade?" Bagel sounded amused. "I take it since you're the one calling, he's had better days."

"You can find him in Pittsburgh," Ump said. "Try their morgue late tomorrow."

"Okay," the Bagel said. "Thanks, Ump. And just to return the favor? Blade was on his own."

"I know that," Ump said.

"Good," the Bagel said, "but I'd still figure we'll catch up to you in another five, six days. Sal's spending lots of money on this, so don't sleep too deep."

"Thanks," Ump said.

They hung up and Ump started walking back to the car, then changed his mind and returned to the phone. He dug in his pocket for more change and fed the slot. The phone rang four times before someone answered.

"Is she in?" Ump asked.

"Hold on," the voice answered. Ump could hear the woman walking off. A moment passed, and then a new voice was on the line.

"Frank?"

"Nan," Ump said, now truly relaxing.

"You sound tired, Frank. What's the matter?"

"I tried calling earlier but you weren't in."

"My cousins took us out for dinner," she said. "What about you? I tried calling myself."

"I'm outside," Ump said. "I can't get any privacy in there."

"Are they taking care of you?"

"I'm taking care of me," Ump said. "Who's taking care of you?"

"I'm fine," Nan said. "I miss you, though."

"Tell me about it," Ump said.

"How much longer is this going on?" Nan asked.

"Mr. Lucci isn't saying, but I'm figuring on another week, tops," Ump said. "I'm working on something to speed things up."

"Nothing dangerous, Frank," Nan said, more as a warning than a question.

"Nothing worth your worrying about," Frank offered as an answer. "Just keep tight, okay? Give my best to the kids."

"You got to go already?" Nan said.

"I'm outdoors," Frank said. "Besides, it only gets me upset, you there and me here."

"You're not cheating on me, are you?"

"Come on," Ump said. "Who would want me, anyway?"

"Me," said Nan.

Ump couldn't help smiling. "Well, Nan," he said, "if you want me, I'm yours."

EIGHTEEN

It was late morning, two days after Ump's trip to the train station, and Joseph Gratton sat at the kitchen table reading the newspaper. He paid special attention to a story about a reputed organized crime killer found dead aboard a freight train. What interested Joseph wasn't how the man had died or where he was found, but his name and picture.

The name was Gus Franco, and it matched perfectly the name on the driver's license Joseph found on the driveway.

Joseph had wondered about that license. He presumed it belonged to the same vandal who broke into the garage and blew the tires of his Dodge. He might have given it to the police if he hadn't also filed a false theft report. Now, though . . . Gus Franco, a mob killer from New York City? Someone who, just days ago, had apparently also been in Waylin? What was the connection? Who else did Joseph know from New York?

"Mind if I have some milk?" Ump asked. He stood behind Joseph, near the doorway. Joseph shifted so his body hid the newspaper.

Ump opened the refrigerator and reached for the milk carton. "I'm going to the ballpark today," he said. "If you want, I can get tickets for you and your kids."

"No thanks, I'm busy," Joseph said.

Ump washed out his glass. "You don't do much for your kids, do you?"

Joseph stared at Ump. If anyone else had said that he might have turned angry, but there wasn't anything hard in Ump's tone. He talked like someone just taking note of the obvious, not even someone interested in the answer. "Did Francine tell you to say that?"

"I'm just asking," said Ump.

"What for?"

"Freido asked me about a family favor, that's all," he said. "I haven't decided what to do."

"Yeah?" said Joseph. "Well, don't involve me in anything that helps Freido."

Ump nodded. "I'll consider that, too," he said, leaving the room.

Joseph watched the doorway until he felt absolutely certain of his privacy. Finally, he returned to the article and struggled with the same questions. Murder? Mob killer? *The garage?*

And his mind offered only one solution. One simple, logical answer for the entire mystery, and why this was all happening to him now. *Ump,* he thought, grinning, looking up and half-expecting Ump to come back in the kitchen, as if Joseph had called out his name.

He didn't, of course, but it made no difference. Pretty soon, Ump would come whenever Joseph wanted.

Darlene Maye thought back just two nights, when she had been sitting alone in her kitchen, sipping yet another solitary cup of coffee while George "worked." She was looking out the window when she happened to see the Gratton garage light flick on. This in itself was unusual, but what truly caught her attention was inside the garage: a man—a stranger—leaning against that hideous Dodge Dart and leveling a gun at Frank Brady.

Darlene knew she had to call the police. Indeed, she left her seat for the phone. But no sooner had she started dialing than she stopped. If Frank Brady was in danger, why wasn't he nervous? Why was he sitting on the car's hood, acting like a man who had nothing better to do than talk things over with an old friend? Darlene was confused. She hung up, crawled across the floor, and turned off the kitchen lights. With the security of darkness, she pressed up to the window and tried making sense of it all.

Ump moved to the side of the car and lowered out of view. With Ump gone, the stranger proceeded to bob about, ducking and rising like a man praying to the four corners of the car. A moment passed before Darlene realized what was happening: the stranger was letting air out of the tires. Darlene could see the car lowering, first the front slumping down, then the rear.

Darlene took a long breath. Now, the stranger did nothing more than admire a hedge clipper. She not only relaxed, she felt silly. Here she was, crouching in the dark, acting like a secret agent, while a couple of men spent the evening fooling with a junked car. It was idiocy and she knew it. Indeed, she was ready to quit her watch, more concerned over her own sanity than what she had seen.

But then the car overturned.

Darlene was becoming a master of the double take. She again reached for the phone; this time, she wanted to call an ambulance. She was certain someone had to be hurt and in trouble.

But perhaps not. Because if Darlene was right, why wasn't Ump worried?

Darlene could see him now, standing and brushing off his pants, doing a body stretch before examining the overturned car. Then he took a sponge off the shelf and began swabbing the floor. He did this for half a minute, then walked to a bucket and wrung the sponge.

Blood streamed from it.

Murder, she thought. She had seen it. The act was almost as amazing as Frank Brady. Watching him soak up the blood— relaxed, businesslike—was like watching a sailor swab the deck. And when he was done, he didn't rush to get rid of the body; he went back into the house for dinner.

A murder, she thought again, considering the concept more carefully. Murders, after all, simply didn't happen in Waylin and witnessing one didn't help it fit in the scheme of things. Still, she knew what was necessary. Call the police, she thought. And that was precisely what she planned to do. Indeed, she was doing it already. She lifted the phone and even started dialing the number. Then George came home.

He froze at the doorway, his eyes wide open. "The lights were out," he said. "I didn't think you were home. Jesus, if you're home, why are the lights out?"

Behind George was Darlene's boss.

Darlene hung up the phone.

George carefully closed the door, leaving Darlene's boss outside. "What is wrong with you, Darlene?" he said. "Why were you in the dark anyway?" He talked as if closing the door had also locked out any memory of his infidelity. For her part, Darlene didn't know what to say. In truth, she couldn't say anything. The evening was becoming too much for her.

George mistook Darlene's exhaustion for resignation. He went into the living room, turned on the light, and settled before the television. "Nothing happened, all right? We just happened to come home together."

Darlene was a statue . . . not leaving her post, wishing she had a gun, wishing . . . wishing she had *Ump*.

"You still haven't answered me," said George. "Why is it so dark around here?"

She remembered the murder, first the gun, then the blood. . . . None of it seemed horrible anymore. Perhaps it never did. Now it was just a lesson. A visual aid.

"Nothing," she said. "A fuse blew."

George appreciated her answer; it gave him the chance to be helpful. "Hell, I can fix that," he said. "Why didn't you tell me when I came home?"

George went to the fuse box and actually dared to kiss Darlene's forehead while crossing the kitchen. Darlene, meanwhile, thought about George, murder, and Ump. Foremost, she thought of Ump—still wondering who he was, and how he killed so easily. And who was the person he had killed? Who would come all the way out to Waylin just to be killed with a mechanic's efficiency?

They were questions that would tease her until morning. Then, after seeing the picture of Blade in the newspaper, and after reading the story about mob wars, executions, contract killings, contract *killers* . . .

"Ump," she said aloud, satisfied.

She closed the paper and wondered how much a contract cost. She also wondered if there was enough in her checking account.

"Two hundred dollars," Father Carroll said. He stared at the bills, then couldn't resist counting them again. Ten, twenty, twenty-five, forty . . .

[111]

All for tying himself to a mausoleum.

All because of that brilliant Mr. Frank Brady.

The priest thought of Ump a lot lately. At first, his thoughts hadn't been pleasant. Locked to the vault gate, literally choking to death . . . No, they hadn't been good at all. But then, while Carroll teetered near death, his elderly volunteer started working the crowd and Father Carroll could see what was going on. People stopped to see if he would live, and while they waited, they read his pamphlet. Soon, after watching this poor priest dying on his own graveyard, they also gave money. Not just change, either; they gave dollars—one, five, ten. . . .

"Please," cried the elderly volunteer, "help the dying priest? Won't you help the dying priest?"

Carroll made a show, rolling side to side, fighting like a suffocating fish. And when the rescue team arrived, he didn't stop fighting until, with a last breath, he looked up at one of the men, grinned, drooled, and fainted.

Father Carroll awoke to cheers. He waved a hand, even while he was tied to the stretcher. He was still waving when they slid him into the ambulance. As the vehicle turned, Carroll pressed his face against the side window to give the victory sign.

It was then he saw his hero, Frank Brady. It was also when he saw that other man.

"Bless you," Carroll shouted, tapping the window, hoping to get Frank Brady's attention. "Bless you, Mr. Brady!" But Frank Brady couldn't hear him. The only person listening was the orderly, who treated the priest as if he suffered from a hallucination.

It didn't matter. Frank Brady, thought Carroll, was the church's salvation. Nor did Carroll lose faith, not even when the town council obliged him to explain his behavior.

"This is not how we expect the head of a church to behave," said Matthew Farber.

"I'm sorry if I embarrassed anyone," said Carroll. "I was just trying to make a point."

"By blackmailing the rest of us?" Farber asked. To the council members, he said, "I suggest we learn from Father Carroll's indiscretion. If he wishes matters settled quickly, we ought to satisfy him."

No, things had not gone well during the council meeting. But perhaps Carroll simply had to make the council part of the issue? Or perhaps there weren't any issues at all? Perhaps there was just one problem: Matthew Farber? And perhaps, instead of removing the graveyard, it was simply a matter of removing a council president?

Father Carroll sat in a pew and mourned his problems. "Oh, Mr. Brady," he cried. "You must help me. You must stop this monster."

He was in the midst of another plea when he heard something slap the front door of the church.

Outside, on the stone landing, was the day's newspaper.

Every time Shirley Anderson opened the paper, she expected to read about her embezzlement from the town's treasury. Nor did her anxieties lessen when an auditor, as required by law, checked Waylin's revenues and expenditures. At first, she managed to keep him off track by rotating money in various accounts. Then she accidentally rotated a thousand extra dollars into the transportation account. The analyst stopped, calculated, recalculated, and finally walked into Anderson's office.

Soon, Anderson had another worry: blackmail.

The demands weren't extraordinary—a five-thousand-dollar payment and, in the event of her election, appointment as her new treasurer. But she also knew this was the tip of an iceberg. Anderson knew blackmail always started small, then grew until it became unmanageable. She couldn't stand for that, not if there were any other solution to her dilemma.

This was why she had phoned Ernesto Castagna. She wanted to talk with someone who, she had been told, was experienced with the darker sides of business. A mob boss, she had heard, a rumor that, in truth, was based solely on his Italian name.

"Mr. Castagna, I was hoping we could discuss a problem at my office. I don't think there's anyone else who can help me."

Castagna listened, not only surprised, but flattered. He hadn't heard such a line in his life, and at age 84, that was a long life. He chewed on a cigar, thought a moment, and finally agreed. Soon Mrs. Castagna was greeting the treasurer and saying, "You'll have to excuse my husband. Ernie had no brains inviting you over. He's taking a train trip tonight."

Castagna overheard the conversation and stepped out of the bedroom. "Miss Anderson," he said. "I'll be with you in a minute."

Mrs. Castagna glared at her husband. "Ernie, you're half-naked."

Castagna looked down and realized he was stripped to his underwear. Without embarrassment, he turned back in the bedroom. "Flo, ask if she's got a car," he shouted. Then, to Anderson, "You got a car, don't you? We can talk on our way to the station." Then, to his wife, "Flo, Miss Anderson will drive me."

"I can drive him," Anderson assured Mrs. Castagna.

Mrs. Castagna looked at her as if she were a complete idiot. As for Castagna, he again appeared at the bedroom door. "Flo, my zipper's stuck."

It was another twenty minutes before they were on their way to the station. With his wife at home, Castagna reached for the treasurer's leg. "So," he said, "what can I do for you, Miss Anderson?"

"I have a problem," Anderson said.

"A problem," Castagna repeated.

"It has to do with my professional future. As you probably know, I'm not only running for mayor, I'm the town treasurer."

"Town treasurer," he said.

"The truth is, Mr. Castagna, I'm having trouble with an employee. I came to you because I need advice from someone familiar with these things."

"Of course," he said.

"My problem requires a certain degree of discretion," she said. "It's a tricky problem. Something that can cause me a major embarrassment."

"A tricky problem," Castagna said.

"Yes," she said. "And I understand you have experience with these matters. Perhaps more accurately, Mr. Castagna, you have access to people who know how to quiet things before they become public."

Anderson stopped talking so Castagna could speak. Castagna, reacting, sat straighter. "You sound like a woman with troubles," he said.

"I think so," she said.

He laughed as if they had shared a joke. "I got sixty years experience behind me, so that should be good for something."

"I have two problems, really," Anderson said. "The first has to do with missing money. Someone stole funds from the treasury."

"Missing money's no good," he said.

"The second problem is at the office," she said. "Someone found out about my problem, and now he's blackmailing me."

"Playing hardball, huh?" Castagna said.

"That's why I'm talking to you. I thought . . ." She again hesitated, uncertain how to introduce criminal solutions. "I thought with your particular background, you may have encountered this kind of situation before."

"I see."

"I thought you could put me in touch with people who can help."

"I see."

Anderson slowed the car and turned into the station. "I just don't know where else to go. I don't know any—" She caught herself, at the same time glancing down. Castagna's hand was sliding up her leg. "I had heard," she said carefully, "you could provide me with certain services."

She parked, slipped free of his hand, and left the car. Castagna, with monstrous effort, pushed open his door and looked about. He was momentarily confused, then he saw the train. In an instant he remembered his trip, at the expense of retaining any memory of Anderson's discussion.

"Do you think you can help me, Mr. Castagna?" Anderson asked. "Can you put me in touch with your family?"

Castagna smacked his lips, thinking, letting Anderson lead him to the platform. "You've got some big problems," he finally said. "You should be married, you know that?"

"Mr. Castagna . . ."

"Young people don't think enough about their future. Careers are fine, but they're no substitute for kids. You'll learn when you get older."

"Sir, what I really need right now is money," she said. "I

[115]

also need a professional to help me. I don't know what you call them." Then, remembering the movies, "Do you call them enforcers?"

Castagna shrugged. "If you want to throw around technical terms . . ."

Anderson stopped walking and stared at Castagna. He stared back.

"Mr. Castagna," she said, sighing.

Castagna patted his pockets for tip money. Anderson stopped his hand.

"Mr. Castagna, is there someone else in your family I can talk to?"

But Castagna was late. Anderson watched as he excused himself and headed for the train. He turned and waved, not so much to Anderson as to the parking lot. As for Anderson, she turned away, facing the freight trains, staring at the massive silhouettes, wondering if, on impulse, she should climb aboard and ride off to nowhere. And it was while she stared out at the line of trains that she saw an odd shadow balanced on top of a coal car.

At first, Anderson didn't know what to make of it. The shadow looked almost mythical—this hulking outline of a man, this image of strength and muscle outlined against a three-quarter moon—rising above the coal car, then lifting a sacrifice to the sky. A moment later, the bundle dropped, and there was nothing but the man balancing on the rim.

Anderson stood in the dark, watching, wondering if what she had seen was real or a vision. She stared until the shadow reappeared, this time from the adjoining woods.

She stared until her myth was transformed into a person.

Brady, she thought, watching as he sneaked back to a station wagon. What was he doing out here? What had he been doing in the woods?

What had he dropped on the train?

She didn't realize these were questions that would answer themselves. All Anderson knew was that she needed a killer. Hadn't Frank Brady come close to murder during the grocery store robbery? What was he doing now?

What had he dropped on the train?

She hoped—prayed—that it had been a body. And she

prayed that if Frank Brady was a murderer, he proved as easy to blackmail as herself.

Bill Conley also had dreams of extortion.

He stared at the newspaper, put two and two together, and added up "gold mine." Like Shirley Anderson, he imagined Ump not only wiping out the opposition, but giving him all the muscle and money necessary for turning Waylin into a one-politician town. The main difference between him and the town treasurer wasn't hope, but timing.

Anderson didn't suspect Ump until she saw him at the train station; Conley suspected him even before Gus Franco was murdered.

Conley's suspicions began shortly after addressing a Chamber of Commerce luncheon. He was working a small circuit of business people when a stranger grabbed him by the shoulder and said, "I'm looking for Frank Brady."

Conley was used to being grabbed. It was the right of every local citizen to freely lock the mayor in conversation. But a stranger . . . *another* stranger, Conley thought, thinking of Ump, and not very favorably.

"Frank Brady," the man repeated. "Come on, he was in your paper."

Conley wasn't certain what to make of the man. The stranger looked like a cheap hood, even to someone who had never seen one. And the stranger kept bothering him, pushing the newspaper on the mayor and pointing to the article about the robbery. "Him," the man said, jabbing the picture. "I wanna know where he is. You should know. You're the mayor, right? You probably gave the fuck a key to the city."

Fuck! Conley thought. This little shit's talking *fuck* to me?

Conley excused himself, pushing aside the newspaper and returning to his friends. He went back to his beef ribs, squeezing more hands until, finally, with one hand on his crotch, he winked at a friend and said, "Time to open the valve." He left the party and headed for the toilet, picking a stall, unbuckling his pants, and settling on a plastic seat.

"Oh, yeah," he sighed, rolling his head back and stretching.

He looked up and saw the stranger balanced on the stall wall, one leg already swinging over the side. "What about Frank Brady?" the stranger said.

Conley reached for his pants, but the man dropped down and slapped a foot on them. Then he sat heavily on Conley's lap, opening a long razor and resting the edge at the base of Conley's penis.

"Lucky you're on a toilet, huh?" the stranger said.

Conley dared to look down. His bladder was emptying.

"Maybe you need to see his picture again." The stranger lifted the newspaper. "You remember when he did this?"

Conley's attention was fixed on the razor. The stranger followed his stare and shook his head, sympathizing. "Be tough if my hand slipped. You don't have much to lose." Then, impatient, "Come on; the sooner I find him, the sooner I can say my good-byes and get out of here."

It was the right thing to say. For the first time, Conley realized they had something in common—both wanted him out of Waylin. "He's still here," Conley said.

"Where?"

"He's staying with the Grattons," Conley said, "but you won't find him there. He's at the ballpark."

"When'll he be back?"

"This afternoon."

"And he'll be coming through town?"

Conley nodded.

"You sure?" The razor touched Conley's skin.

Conley nodded vigorously.

The stranger stared at Conley a long moment, then stood and left the stall. The moment Conley was alone he drooped forward, grabbing his crotch. He stayed curled a full minute before leaving the stall. He pulled up his pants, took one long breath, flushed, opened the door, and then caught himself.

The stranger turned from a urinal and faced him.

Conley was uncertain what to do. He waited for directions while the stranger shook off.

"What's the matter?" the man said. "You never see a guy piss before?"

Conley was too frightened to answer. He watched as the

stranger washed and headed for the door. "Fucking town," he murmured, leaving the restroom.

This time, Conley waited a full five minutes before daring to open a door. And, to his great relief, the stranger really was gone. He felt the same relief when he read about the man's death. Conley had been wondering about that odd encounter in the restroom, too afraid to mention it to the police, his imagination easily manufacturing the possible news headlines. But now it was all over. The only thing left was making sense of what had happened. How come the razor-wielding maniac was dead, and Frank Brady was alive?

"Mr. Conley?"

Conley looked up at his secretary.

"Don't forget your ten-o'clock address at the Rotary Club."

Conley grunted, waved her out of the room and returned to the article.

" 'Gus Franco, reputed organized crime killer . . .' "

Conley thought more carefully about Ump. He folded the clipping, put on his jacket, and headed for the door. Yes, he was late for his speech, but who cared? Why did it matter, when there were quicker ways to eliminate the opposition?

Mayor Conley smiled.

It was always good having a new business in town.

NINETEEN

Ump was thinking of Waylin.

He was thinking of the outdoors, the clean air, the relative peace and quiet, the friendly faces and generous gifts. . . . Of course, there had also been Blade, but that was Ump's problem, not the town. If Ump could shake free of all the Blades and settle down . . . If he could find someplace where the biggest worry was whether the leaves changed before Labor Day weekend . . . If he could leave New York . . . It wasn't a serious idea, just something to pass the time. But even as a passing thought it was a first, and as he squatted behind home plate, his mask and chest protector on, Ump wondered what his kids would think if he ever so much as suggested the idea.

"Strike one."

The batter stepped from the box and glared at Ump. Ump returned the stare, daring the batter to say a word, but the moment didn't last long—the batter broke eye contact and Ump settled into place, thinking.

What would Nan say? Would she ever consider leaving the neighborhood? She hadn't yet and Ump didn't think she ever would. Some people were rooted to New York; in Nan's case, the roots were petrified.

There was also the question of temperament. Ump wasn't blind. He knew that, at times, he could be difficult. At the same time, rules were rules, and Ump couldn't turn a blind eye to that. It wasn't in his nature. Could he be as hard-nosed in a small town as in a big town?

"Strike two."

The batter again stepped back. "That was chin high," he said.

Ump ignored him.

"I said it was chin high," the batter insisted.

Ump still didn't look up. He was being patient, something inconceivable just a week ago. But who said he couldn't change? The real question, he supposed, was whether or not Nan and he would change for the better. What good was mellowing if all you did was mellow into a potful of fat? For that matter, even after he mellowed, what would life be like so far from a real city? No food, no transportation, no occupation. Christ, no *work*. He'd go crazy living at home.

The batter stepped back in the box and Ump watched as the pitch came, the bat connected, and the ball grounded hard up the middle. He waited for the batter to safely reach first before raising his thumb. "Out," he said.

The team's manager jumped from the dugout.

"Tell me you're joking," Nolan shouted. "There wasn't even a throw to the bag. No one tagged him, no one touched the bag, no one—"

"He stepped over the line."

"Line?" said Nolan. "What line?"

Ump pointed down at the batter's box. "A batter can't step out of the box when swinging."

Nolan looked down. Most of the chalk line had been wiped clean from too many feet. "What the fuck are you talking about? The whole box is gone!"

"I remember where it was," Ump said.

Nolan rolled his eyes, waved his batter off the base and stormed back to the dugout. As for Ump, he again assumed his position, all the time thinking of the country.

Maybe he should discuss things with Nan? But even if he did, what would the kids say? What would Freido say?

The thoughts drove Ump crazy, because he hated thinking in questions. It was the easiest way in the world to waste time, especially when they were questions he couldn't answer.

"Strike," he said, the pitch hitting the inside corner.

Meanwhile, in the dugout, Nolan stared at Ump and remembered the rumors. There were stories everywhere that the league's new umpire not only had a tight strike zone, but a tight rule . . . stories of players who threw their bats, then went outside to find their windshields broken. Of a base stealer sliding into second with his spikes too high, then showing up at the hospital with a broken thumb.

No, it was not the usual balls and strikes in the stadium. Nolan knew it, the players knew it, the fans knew it. . . . And none had the guts to complain. As for Nolan, he didn't complain for another reason. He liked a physical game. He sat back, waiting for another bad call and ready when it came. Because Nolan wasn't just a manager; he was a brawler. He had been a brawler as a major-league shortstop, and he had grown worse with age. Shit flinging was part of his character, and the fans loved it. Now, after scouting the enemy, he was just waiting for the right opportunity. His next trip would set things straight. All he needed was the excuse, that was all. Not a big one, either, maybe a missed ball on one of his batters, or a missed strike for his pitcher.

He waited four innings before something happened. Then, in the ninth, came the glorious opportunity. He didn't even have to feign anger. It welled up furiously as Ump, calling the top of the ninth, watched one of Nolan's boys sail a ball over the fence for a grand slam. Then, instead of circling his hand to indicate a homer, Ump jerked a thumb. "Out," Ump shouted.

No one believed it. Not the team, not Nolan . . . certainly not the batter and runners. When the truth hit, they rushed him. It took a good half minute for Nolan just to push his way through his players.

"What are you fucking doing to my team?" Nolan jabbed a finger near Ump's face and bumped his chest. "That fucking ball cleared the fucking wall and half the fucking town!" He pushed forward, again bumping Ump's chest. Nolan was screaming full throat, his face flushed red, and every vein bulging to its limit. "You're just fucking out to screw me, aren't you? You want a fight? I'll give you a fucking fight. Is that what you want?"

"He was out," Ump said.

Nolan bumped him again, hitting harder, expecting Ump at least to fall back. Ump didn't move. It was like bumping rock. A jagged rock, because Nolan also felt something stiff hit his rib cage. When he bumped Ump a fourth time, he was still shouting, but he was also looking down at Ump's chest protector. For the first time, he noticed an odd, hard shape imprinted against it, as if there were something beneath the protector.

"You wouldn't know a fucking out if it kicked you in the ass," shouted Nolan. "You're about the worst fucking umpire I've ever seen."

"Sit down," said Ump.

"I'll sit down when you fucking give back my homer," Nolan said. "I'll sit down when you fucking make me."

But he kept staring at the protector. It reminded Nolan of his brother, a cop in Atlanta. During Thanksgivings, they would get together and his brother would brag about busting criminals. Sometimes he showed off a revolver. He'd take it out, spin it like a cowboy, then slip it back in a shoulder holster, where it stayed hidden in a jacket. He remembered how the jacket bulged, as if his brother were hiding a hard, cancerous growth below his right pectoral. Ump's bulge looked similar, maybe even identical. It made Nolan curious enough to bump Ump one last time. "*Make* me sit down, you fucker." Nolan pressed against Ump longer than necessary. "*Make* me, you . . ."

Nolan stopped. He looked down at the chest protector, then at Ump, then down again. When you looked for it, the imprint was clear.

Ump never stopped glaring at the manager. He did, however, reach for a bat. He weighed it in one hand while patting an open palm. "Would you like to know why your batter's out?"

Nolan stepped back, but Ump followed him. Without warning, Ump raised the bat over his head and swung down. Nolan covered up, certain his forehead was the target. The bat swung to the side and struck a steel railing. Ump brought it down two more times before Nolan opened his eyes. When he did, he saw the bat strike a last time and split open.

A half dozen Super Balls bounced out of its meat.

"Illegal bat," Ump said. "That's why your batter's out." He turned and walked away.

The manager took a breath before picking up the pieces.

Finally, he turned to his assistant manager, motioned toward Ump, and asked, "You see that?"

The assistant nodded.

"He would have killed me."

The assistant thought he was joking. "Why didn't he?" he said.

"Who the fuck knows?" Nolan said, then kidding, added, "Maybe he's gonna trash my car instead?"

The assistant grinned and they walked back to the locker room. It would be a half hour before Nolan went to the parking lot. He would then need another hour before going home, not so much to find his car as to identify the pieces.

To Frank Brady:

I know what you are. I also know about Gus Franco. If you do not want trouble, you will do what I want. I am not kidding. I will write again tomorrow and tell you what I want.

P.S. Don't talk to anyone or I will tell police.

Next to the note were several magazines, scissors, a blank sheet of paper, and a tub of rubber glue. With great diligence, Joseph Gratton sat at the kitchen table, trying to find all the words necessary for his letter, then cutting and pasting together sentences.

It was one of the more creative and enjoyable tasks in blackmailing; still, it didn't make it any easier finding a few of the key words to his message. Words like "kidding" and "Brady." He could, of course, try cutting out letters and squeezing them together, but all the other words were whole, and the last thing Joseph wanted was to look like an amateur, especially if Ump was half the professional he suspected. Rather than risk a bad first impression, he took full advantage of Ump's visit to the stadium, panicking only once, when Francine surprised him by coming through the back door.

"What are you doing to my magazines?" she asked.

He brushed his extra words onto his sheet of paper, but one helicoptered to the floor and Francine picked it up. " 'Police,' " she read aloud. "What is this? Why did you cut this out?"

[124]

"It's for the kids," Joseph said. "I'm pasting a list of phone numbers, in case of an emergency."

It was a wonderful excuse—it made sense, it showed concern. Francine demonstrated her approval by reaching in a cabinet for more magazines. "That word's too small," she said. "Look in these." Then she left the kitchen and walked back to her car for the groceries.

Joseph grinned, full of himself. He was better at this than he imagined. He finished collecting his work while Francine returned with the bags.

"If you're going to town later, we need to get a check to the bank," Francine said.

"We don't have to give them nothing." Joseph had his own plans for that bank debt.

"If you can't, I'll ask Frank," Francine said. "He should be back from the ballpark soon. It's too bad you couldn't go out with him."

"Oh, sure," Joseph said.

"What's so awful about spending an afternoon with your daughter?" Francine asked. "If Frank can take the time, why can't you?"

Joseph watched her more carefully. Lately, he wasn't too crazy about the direction of their conversations. There was a new slant on their relationship, one which rested heavily on Joseph, with Francine making the kind of gutsy, nagging remarks that, just a few weeks ago, would have been inconceivable. They were the kind of comments that suggested Joseph was something decidedly less than perfection.

"You think a lot of Brady, don't you?" Joseph said.

Francine shrugged and turned away. Joseph, however, didn't need to see her face.

"What do you think he does for a living, anyway?"

"He already told us," said Francine. "He works for Freido."

"And what does Freido do?"

Francine closed the refrigerator.

"Answer the question," he said.

"He's a businessman," Francine answered firmly.

"A businessman," Joseph repeated, amused. "I can do you one better than that, Francine. He's in the meat-packing business."

[125]

Francine glared at him. "What are you talking about?"

"It's just something you should know, that's all," Joseph said. "Freido's in the meat-packing business. He packs meat in boxes. The only trick is his meat wears clothes."

"I still don't know what you're talking about."

"Yeah?" said Joseph. "Then ask Freido sometime. Better yet, don't ask him. The less you know, the longer you'll live."

Francine could have spit on him. "You sound jealous."

Joseph cocked his head, curious.

"You're *jealous*, Joseph," Francine said. "You're jealous of Frank."

"And why's that?"

"Because he's a better person than you," she said. "Look at the way he takes Jennifer to the ballpark. Or helps with the shopping. Or eats with the family at dinner."

"Or works late in the garage."

"Exactly," Francine said, missing the remark. "When was the last time you cleaned the garage? And here comes a house guest who, on his own, scrubs the floor, straightens the shelves. . . ."

"I'm not jealous of Ump," Joseph said. "I do think a lot of him, though."

They both stopped talking, instead listening as a key fit in the front door lock.

"That's Frank," Francine whispered. "For once in our lives, don't embarrass me."

Joseph again didn't appreciate her tone. She sounded less like a wife and more like a sister worried about her date. "I'll work elsewhere," he said, leaving as Ump opened the door.

Joseph and Ump had a chance for only the briefest eye contact; still, it was enough for Ump to know. There was a difference between the way people looked at him when they were being personal, and when they regarded him professionally. Joseph had that second look—the kind of caution and fear the Golla brothers showed before dying.

"Frank," called Francine. She looked at Ump and smiled. "Thank goodness you're back. Do you think you can drive me to town?"

Ump couldn't object; Francine didn't give him a chance. She touched his arm and went quickly upstairs for her purse, passing Joseph, whose work was already spread out on a night table.

"I'm going to the bank," she said, her voice efficient.

"You're going with Ump?"

"With Frank, yes," Francine said. "Do you have a problem with that?"

"No, no problem," Joseph said. Then he looked up from his letter and added, "Just one favor, Francine. While you're out, have Ump pick out the steaks, all right?"

"Why?"

Joseph shrugged. "Just instinct," he said. "I've got a feeling Ump knows a few things about raw meat. That's what comes from being a butcher."

"I'm telling you it happened," the mayor insisted.

Fleming stared at Conley, then at the news clipping, then back at his friend. It wasn't the sort of story one easily accepted. In fact, there were obvious reasons not to believe him, the most fundamental being that the banking business didn't encourage confidence, at least not without a thorough background check.

Still, Fleming listened. The notion, after all, was fascinating. A professional killer in Waylin? It made no difference to Fleming, because he had no one to kill; still, the mere possibility . . . the thought that he could, if he wanted to, without anyone else knowing. . . .

"Do you have any proof?" Fleming asked.

Conley did. He had checked some outdated editions of the New York papers and dug up an article on the Lucci family. In the bottom paragraph, it ran a list of reputed members of the gang.

Fleming held the article closer to the light so he could read the name. "Frank Brady," he read aloud.

"I was thinking of telling the police," Conley said, "but it's not like he's using a false name. Besides, there isn't any physical proof he had anything to do with Gus Franco." He said this to cover his tracks, just in case Fleming turned on him, but it was an unnecessary precaution. Fleming treated inside information as a sacred confidence.

"I think you were smart," Fleming said. "You can't get

[127]

involved with these types. They're too dangerous. You're better off letting them kill each other."

"They're good at that, aren't they?" Conley said.

"Exceptional," said Fleming, thinking again, wanting to be certain no one in memory wasn't at least worth a broken leg. In truth, it wasn't that difficult. While not interested in *personal* revenge, there *were* business difficulties, in particular, bad accounts. A man like Frank Brady could go a long way in preventing final notices. Perhaps even setting up a special file in the accounts division—a little black box, filled with the names and addresses of the select few who dared not only to miss their payments, but shirked even the semblance of responsibility. "It definitely raises interesting possibilities."

"Having someone like Brady on your side could make a person very powerful."

"Bill," Fleming said, "having someone like Frank Brady on your side would be like having a cannon in your back pocket."

"Presuming, of course, you have a pocket deep enough for a cannon."

"That would be essential," Fleming agreed.

"That's one of the reasons I came to you," Conley said. "I figured between the two of us, we could manage some very deep pockets." Conley leaned forward, too excited for subtleties. "If he was in my pocket, I know just what I'd do. And you could bet your ass it wouldn't leave much doubt about who's the next mayor."

"The price would have to be right," Fleming said. "Do you have any idea why Brady's in town?"

"He's staying with Joseph Gratton. I think he's a boarder."

Fleming considered this. "Joseph Gratton," he said, sounding wistful. "I wouldn't mind breaking his legs. How much do you think Brady charges for legs?"

"Ask Joseph," Conley said. "Brady's staying at his house. Maybe that's not a coincidence. Maybe he paid Brady to come here."

Fleming looked incredulous. "Joseph Gratton hiring a killer? How could he afford it?"

"Maybe it doesn't cost as much as we think."

"It's got to cost something."

Conley shrugged. "He could charge by the bone. Or the bullet. He could have discount weeks."

Fleming shook his head. "Not Joseph," he said. "Why would Gratton bother? Who would he want killed?"

The intercom buzzed, and Fleming pressed the button.

"Mr. Fleming, Mrs. Gratton is here with her payment," said the secretary.

Fleming and Conley exchanged a look.

"Is she alone or with her husband?" Fleming asked.

"Neither," the secretary answered. "She's with someone else."

Fleming again looked at Conley, and Conley volunteered to peek outside. He needed only a glimpse to confirm his suspicion. "It's him," Conley said.

Fleming tensed. A moment ago, he had wondered if Joseph Gratton had anyone to kill; now, the question had been answered.

"He wouldn't do anything here," Conley said.

Fleming looked at his friend. Conley was trying to be helpful; at the same time, Conley wasn't the one marked for death.

"Maybe he doesn't want to do anythng at all," Conley said.

Fleming wanted to believe that. He stared at the intercom, wondering what to do, wondering why he had joined such a high-risk profession.

"Let him in," Conley said. "He wouldn't do anything in public. Not when you've got bank guards in the lobby."

Fleming listened, nodded. Conley made sense. No one killed in the middle of the day, in the middle of a crowded building. And the guards. All Fleming had to do was hit a button and a half dozen armed security men would be on Brady in seconds.

Fleming took a long, calming breath and opened the door. "Mrs. Gratton," he said. Conley winced, half-expecting a cross-fire of bullets. Instead of bullets, however, Francine offered Fleming an envelope.

"Here's your check," Francine said. "I didn't want to take any chance of your missing it."

"Of course not," Fleming said. "And hello, Mr. Brady."

"Frank's helping me with some shopping," Francine said.

[129]

Fleming glanced at Conley, hoping for support. "That's the only reason you're here, Mr. Brady?"

"I'm also expecting some people," said Ump.

"What kind of people?"

"What is it you do, Mr. Brady?" Conley asked.

"Frank's thinking about the freelance business," said Francine.

"Freelance what?" said Conley.

"It's interesting you bring that up," Ump said. "I was wondering about that earlier. I mean, freelancing in New York, that can mean one thing. But out here, in the woods, it can mean something else entirely. That's if I do something else. But I can't quite figure out what that would be."

Fleming and Conley looked to Francine for an interpretation.

"He works for my brother," Francine said. "Frank is here on a vacation."

Fleming and Conley both nodded. "You said you're looking for some friends?" Conley said.

"Friends probably isn't the right word," Ump said.

"I ask because I bumped into someone a couple of days ago," said Conley. "He was looking for you."

"Short guy?" said Ump.

"I think so."

"Kind of weird?"

"Kind of. He—"

"Carried a razor?"

Conley nodded.

Ump waved away the information. "I mean someone else."

Fleming leaned back against his desk. "We'll keep our eyes open."

"Hey, whatever you can do," said Ump. "Just no favors, please. Favors have strings, and you can choke to death on strings. That's what Nan always says."

"No favors," Fleming said, "although I'd like to discuss business with you sometime."

"Talk all you want," Ump said, turning for the door.

"I'll be back in a month with another check, Mr. Fleming," said Francine.

"Take your time, Mrs. Gratton," said Fleming. "Take all the time you need."

Francine thanked him for the courtesy and followed Ump out of the office. Alone again, Fleming and Conley relaxed.

"Think I'm safe?" Fleming asked.

Conley shook his head. "Not as long as Gratton owes you money."

Fleming nodded, knowing Conley was right.

"We need deep pockets," said Conley.

"The deepest," Fleming agreed.

Ump knew he had done something wrong. He was standing in the lobby, admiring the security system, when Francine grabbed his arm and tugged him back in the street. It was a familiar feeling to Ump; Nan had done the same thing all their married life, and always after he'd hurt her feelings. Nan would drag him off to some private place, scream at him, then wait for Ump to cajole her with hugs and kisses. In this case, however, Ump didn't know what to do.

"Is something the matter?" Ump asked. She wasn't his wife, but he still sounded just as defensive.

"Nothing," said Francine. "Nothing your wife can't make better, I'm sure."

"You're hurting my arm."

"Excuse me," she said, pushing him away. "Maybe you should phone your wife about that, too. Maybe she can give you a bandage."

"Why are you picking on Nan?" Ump asked.

"I'm not picking on anyone," she said. "You're the one who threw her in my face."

Ump was still confused. "She was on my mind, Francine. I love her."

"Well, Joseph loves me, too," she said, "but I don't go throwing that around, do I? I don't let that get in the way of things."

"Get in the way of what?" Ump said.

Francine was close to tears. She caught herself and said, "Are you really thinking of moving here?"

Ump's mind jumped tracks. One minute they were talking about Nan, and now they were on Waylin. His expression changed from one of concern to one of deep thought. "I don't know," he said. "This place is nice if you don't think about it, but if you do, then maybe it's not so good. Besides, I don't think Nan would ever go for it."

Francine hardened again at Nan's name. She stared at Ump and said, "What were you talking about in there, about a man with a razor?"

"Just shoptalk," said Ump.

"Joseph's been hinting all day about something," Francine said. "He makes it sound like he heard bad news about my brother. He keeps talking about the meat-packing business."

"I don't know a thing about packing meat," Ump said.

"What do you know?"

"I know a few things about people," he said. "And philosophers. I've read a few of them, even though they're garbage. You can take everything they say and narrow it down to a few lines." He reached in a pocket and opened his wallet. He slid out a sheet of paper and handed it to Francine.

THE RULES OF LIFE

1. Love your wife and kids.
2. Never break your word.
3. Don't be a jerk.
4. Always stop at a red light.
5. Never extinct anything.
6. Don't argue when you're wrong.
7. Count properly.
8. If you deserve shit, take it.
9. Know your left from your right.
10. Never argue with the umpire.
11. Don't bunt with two strikes.
12. Catch a ball with two hands.

"I've been studying people for years, and I can tell you now, you can learn more watching the traffic than reading a book," Ump said. "That's how I worked out this list."

" 'Don't argue when you're wrong'?" read Francine.

"Exactly," said Ump. "Common sense, right? Think of all the grief on this earth, just because people fight and argue when they know there's nothing to fight about. It's crazy. It's

[132]

like running a red light. I mean, the fucking light is staring you in the face. It's telling you to stop—no two ways about it—no one moves, but then you say what the fuck, and you break the rules, and you run it, even when the stupidest part of you says no."

" 'Know your left from your right.' "

"You know how many people have been killed because they turned left when they meant right?" he said. "How many people get lost? We're talking simple, basic crap here, Francine. It makes me furious just thinking of all the bullshit that goes on because of some lazy asshole who doesn't know his thumbs."

"I don't get the last ones," Francine said. " 'Don't bunt with two strikes,' 'catch a ball with two hands. . . .' "

"I just added those," he said. "They're still being tested."

"I like the first one best," she said.

"Yeah," said Ump, smiling. "So does Nan."

She handed him back the list. "You're a man of principle, Ump. I wish Joseph was a man of principle."

Ump stared at his rules a moment, then slipped them back in his wallet. "Yeah, well, that's another problem," he said.

"I hear about it from Freido all the time."

"Freido loves you," Ump said.

"Sometimes I wonder if Freido was right about Joseph," she said. "Sometimes I think Freido got all the brains in my family."

"Don't kid yourself," Ump said. "Just because you married a jerk doesn't mean you're one. Things work out."

"You think so?" Francine said. She leaned forward. Christ, she wanted to be kissed.

"I know people better than anything else in the world," Ump said. "I know how to protect them, how to get at them. . . . That's why I've lived this long. That's why Nan sometimes doesn't know whether to love me or hate me. Trust me, all right?" He looked down the street. "Now, if you don't mind, I'm gonna walk around some and get a better feel for this place."

Francine stepped away from him. "No problem," she said. "I'll see you at the house." She turned and walked slowly to the car.

As for Ump, he concentrated on Waylin—studying the buildings, enjoying the clean streets, sniffing the air, and ultimately, testing the town the way a person might test a new bed—for comfort, for support, for its years of good use. Finally, he stopped before a real estate office and stared at its photographs of homes. Four were large, three were small, a couple were probably just the right size for his family. All of them, however, looked like other people's homes. No matter how long he studied them, none seemed to open its doors and welcome him for a closer look. Indeed, the longer he stared, the less welcome he felt, as if the pictures tightened into a small village, closed to entry.

The image bothered Ump. Maybe he had less in common with Waylin than he imagined. And since he already thought Waylin and he had little in common, perhaps there was nothing at all?

"See anything interesting?" Darlene Maye asked.

Ump turned. Darlene was smiling at him, a warm, fresh look, so open it caught Ump off guard.

Darlene worked quickly. Like Francine, she took him by the arm; unlike Francine, instead of tugging at Ump, she pressed against him.

"I wanted to thank you again for our supper together," she said. "If you don't mind, I could use some help getting home." She pointed down the street, where a large bookcase rested near her car.

Ump was a reluctant accomplice. He saw the bookcase, and he saw the car, and he knew it was too much for her; at the same time, he wasn't that sure. "I guess," he said. "I just have to watch my gut."

"Of course," she said. "I don't want you busting your stitches. Anything you want, anything you can do. . . . I'll take what I can."

"Just so it's understood," he said, but she was already on him, pulling at him like Nan or Francine.

"I do appreciate this," she said. "My husband doesn't have time for me anymore. It's like we're living in separate worlds."

Ump listened, taking instructions as they got the bookcase on the roof and tied it down. Soon they were driving back to Darlene's house, and ten minutes later, they were bringing the bookcase indoors. The entire time, the conversation never changed. "Sometimes I don't see George for an entire week," she said. "He says he's working, but I know better. I think—no, I *know*—he's having an affair."

Ump carried the bookcase down a hallway.

"It makes for a lonely life, Ump," she said. "Ump. That's not strong enough for you. Frank is better. Do you mind if I call you Frank?"

"My wife calls me worse," Ump said.

Darlene knew exactly what Ump was doing. "You don't have to worry about your wife," she said. "Do you see me worrying about my husband?"

Darlene closed the door. Only now did Ump notice where they were—the bedroom. He stood absolutely still, holding his ground by the bureau, while Darlene began unbuttoning her blouse.

"I've been admiring you, Frank," Darlene said. "I've been watching and admiring you since the first day." She took off the blouse and let it drop to the floor. Now she was wearing only a skirt and brassiere. Ump watched as she brushed back her hair and reached behind her for the zipper. A moment later, the skirt was off.

It had been years since Ump had been seduced, and that had been at the hands of Nan. He watched this seduction with the same confusion, and Darlene didn't make it easier when she undid the clasp, letting her brassiere drop and lifting Ump's hands so they cupped her.

"You like them?" she whispered.

Ump gave her breasts a squeeze. "About right, yeah," he said.

"Your hands feel nice," she said.

His left hand probed a bit harder. "I feel a lump."

Darlene slid his hands down to her briefs. "I want to make love to you so bad," she told him.

"I can tell," he said.

She slid off her underwear and rubbed against his legs. "We've got so much to do together. So much to share."

"There are limits on everything," Ump answered.

Darlene smiled, kissed him, and finally decided to take matters over completely, reaching down and unbuckling

Ump's pants. Ump kept standing there, watching as she pulled down at the waistband and everything came off. She slid one hand against his belly, while the other wrapped about his thigh and clasped his buttocks. She was kissing the inside of his leg, working her way up, when Ump said, "This doesn't have anything to do with Gus Franco, does it?"

Darlene stopped.

"I saw you staring at me the other night when Blade had me holed up in the garage."

Darlene looked up at him. "Suppose it does?"

Ump shrugged. "Just that meaningless sex isn't so much fun if there's a meaning," he said. "And if this has anything to do with Gus, then I'm out."

"No," she said. "Not with Gus Franco."

"Good," he said. "Because that also means it has nothing to do with your husband."

Darlene pulled back. "What about my husband?"

"Just that I've got enough work already without getting myself busy turning wives into widows," he said. "That's not the secret to a happy life. Nan wouldn't be happy at all if she was a widow; she's told me that a million times."

Darlene now pulled completely free. "I'm not your wife."

"Hey, I know that," Ump said. "Nothing against you, but Nan wouldn't waste so much time stripteasing."

Darlene watched as Ump pulled up his pants and headed for the door. She was embarrassed, furious. At the same time, she desperately wanted his help. "You already owe me," she said. "I could have phoned the police, but I didn't. I saved you. You could have been thrown in jail."

"That's right," said Ump. "I'll have to consider that."

"While you're considering that, think about this, too." she slid her hand into his pants. "I'm not asking you to pull the trigger; just show me how. Tell me what to do. Tell me what I need to know."

When she pulled away, she could feel her success. It pressed against Ump's pants.

"I'll consider that, too," he said, leaving.

When Ump shut the bedroom door, Darlene sat down on a chair and reconsidered her situation. Had she gotten through

[136]

to Ump? Was he with her or not? Would he or wouldn't he teach her what to do?

No matter. She could still prepare. Within hours, she could be the most dangerous woman in Waylin. She could do all that plus make dinner and do the laundry. It was an incredible amount of work, but Darlene would manage. She always managed.

Maybe that was why George Maye had married her.

"Hey, Ump, how's it going?" said Joseph.

Ump walked past Joseph and into the living room.

"What'd you do today?" Joseph asked, following. "Anything interesting?"

Ump glanced at a clock. "Freido didn't call, did he?"

"I don't think so," Joseph said. Then, leaning toward the hallway, he shouted, "Francine—your brother call today? Hey, Francine!"

Joseph smiled, ingratiated himself with Ump, then shouted again. Francine finally appeared on the upstairs landing. "I'm not in the mood for this, Joseph. I just want to be alone."

Joseph, winking at Ump, shouted, "Ump was asking about your brother."

"He hasn't called," she said.

"What about the mail?" Joseph said. "Have you seen the mail?"

Francine didn't need this. She stormed down the steps, walked straight to the front door, bent down and picked up the mail pile. "Why can't you do this yourself, Joseph?" she said. "My God, why can't you show me a little consideration?"

"I didn't see it," he said.

She dropped the pile in his lap, glanced at Ump, and headed back upstairs. As for Joseph, he rifled through the envelopes. "For me, for me, for me. . . ." Joseph stopped. He pulled out one of the letters and said, "Wait a minute, Ump. There's something here with your name." Joseph handed him the letter. "See? 'To Frank Brady.' With my address. Kind of odd the way it's pasted together."

Ump stared at the envelope, grunted, and carried it upstairs. Joseph watched and asked, "Who knows you're staying here? Not that I mind, but if we're going to be picking up your packages . . ."

"I think I know what it is," said Ump. "I've seen this kind of thing before."

"What kind of thing?"

"Nothing," said Ump. "Junk mail."

Joseph stopped, not sure if he was being baited. He watched while Ump weighed the letter in his hand.

"This one looks a little different, though," Ump said. "There's something wrong with the envelope." He rubbed his thumb against the stamp. "No postal mark. That means it didn't go through the post office. Whoever sent this stuck the stamp on here, figuring I'd think it was mailed. Pretty stupid, huh?"

"Yeah," said Joseph. "Pretty stupid."

Joseph watched as Ump went into his bedroom and closed the door. As for Joseph, he sat on the stairs, wondering if he had fucked up royally or if Ump was just playing a game with him. Not that it made a difference. Ump would be his, anyway.

No, everything was fine. Ump would read the letter and piss in his pants. Christ, he would love to see Ump's face when he read the letter. He just bet Ump would break into a cold sweat. Maybe he was already bent over the toilet, letting it go.

Joseph couldn't resist. When he heard Ump step into the upstairs shower, he sneaked into Umps' room and looked for any sign of panic—a broken mirror, a punched pillow, open suitcases. . . . The only thing he found was a full trash can. Joseph was surprised. He wondered what went wrong, then sifted through the trash. Near the top was letter.

No wonder Ump wasn't nervous; he hadn't even opened the envelope.

Joseph was furious. He wanted to shove the letter down Ump's throat; instead, he put it back in the can and left the room. Then he went to his own bedroom, where Francine was setting her hair.

Francine saw Joseph coming, and she did her best to look loving. "I'm sorry," she said gently. "We shouldn't be fighting so much."

Joseph glared at her. "We weren't fighting at all until *he* came here."

"I like him," Francine admitted.

"Yeah, like that's a big secret," Joseph said heading down-stairs.

There was no doubt—next time, he'd have to make sure Ump read the letter. He wanted Ump wrapped about his finger and ready to finish that fucking Fleming. Joseph didn't even care how Ump did it—with a gun or bomb or a lousy sling-shot—just so long as Fleming was paid in full.

Next time, Joseph thought.

TWENTY

It was almost time for the Gollas to attack. Ump could feel it; things had been quiet too long, especially if Blade truly had been on his own, and the Gollas were busy with a more systematic search. It also meant the next time Ump was cornered, he could expect big trouble.

Still, Freido had him playing a waiting game. "Don't worry," said Freido. "Nothing's gonna happen in Waylin. Nothing *ever* happens in Waylin. Sit back and try enjoying my sister's cooking. I promise—we'll have everything figured out in another day or two, then the only thing left will be finishing Sal. All right?"

Freido waited, hoping to get Ump's approval. He waited until, finally, he tapped the mouthpiece. "Hey, Ump, you listening?"

Ump took a long breath. "You shouldn't make fun of your sister."

Freido wasn't sure he had heard Ump.

"Your sister," Ump repeated. "She has a tough enough time without your help."

"Francine?" Freido said. "Hey, Ump, I'm not her problem, Joseph is. Maybe you should think about that little family favor."

"I got other things on my mind."

"Like what?"

"Like when I'm gonna see Nan."

"You sure you're thinking of Nan and not Francine?" said Freido. "You're a married man, Ump; don't forget that."

"Maybe if you got me home, you wouldn't have to remind

me," Ump said. "Things aren't so great here. Everyone's begging for favors; no one takes care of himself."

"People peg you for a sweetheart, that's your problem," said Freido. "You haven't killed any crooks lately, have you?"

"None you don't know about," Ump said. "Find Sal, Freido."

"Okay."

"And stop bad-mouthing your sister."

"I'll do my best," Freido said, hanging up.

Ump did the same. He sat in his bedroom looking at the clock, then outside, wishing to hell Freido would come through with the information. Finally, he pulled his jacket out of the closet, headed downstairs and—

"Frank?"

Francine stopped her cleaning. She had *that* look—the one of complete infatuation—the one Ump was getting to know too well. "Frank, if you want some lunch, I can make sandwiches."

"I'll get something later," Ump said.

"It's no trouble."

Ump didn't even try answering; instead, he headed downstairs for the kitchen door.

Joseph, sitting at the kitchen table, shoveled his magazines onto his lap. "Jesus, Ump, I thought you were outside."

Francine followed Ump to the door. "Let me make you some lunch. Please, Frank."

"I just want air," Ump said.

"But I'd enjoy it."

"Let him leave," Joseph said.

"Maybe later," Ump said. He walked outside, stood briefly on the steps, and soaked in the sun. He was still looking up when he heard the tapping of glass from the neighbor's upstairs window.

Ump saw Darlene staring down at him.

Ump turned, pulled up his collar, and headed for the street. He needed to go somewhere, anywhere, just so long as he got away from all this nagging. He walked about, trying his best to play the old New York game of seeing no one and passing everyone. Utter, complete oblivion—that's what he wanted.

But when more people looked ready to collar him, he figured it was time to duck into a building.

For some foolish reason, he figured the most quiet, peaceful place to hide out was in the pews of a church.

Ump opened the door and stepped into the sanctuary. While not Catholic, Ump figured it didn't matter what fragment of God he found; the important thing was to be in a place where he could collect his thoughts, and surely He wouldn't object to that. Ump sat on a bench, lowered his head, covered his eyes. . . .

"I wanted to thank you," said Father Carroll.

Ump looked up.

"Remember?" Carroll said. "I was chained outside? You almost killed me."

"Yeah," said Ump. "How'd it go?"

"It went very well," Carroll said. "Not only did it bring in money, you might also say it helped flush out the enemy."

Ump nodded. He sat a moment, staring at the priest, trying to decide whether or not Father Carroll was good for conversation. Finally, Ump moved closer. "Father, you mind if I ask you something in complete confidence?"

Father Carroll bent as if in a confessional.

"Things haven't been going so well for me lately," Ump said.

"I expected this," Carroll said. "I thought you'd need to clear your conscience."

"It shows, huh?" Ump said. "I mean, first things got screwed up in New York, then New York spills over here, now I've got other people knocking on my door. . . ."

Carroll nodded, understanding completely.

"Father, I work for a man named Tommy Lucci. And sometimes—beween you and me—I gotta straighten out his trouble. Do you know what I mean by trouble?"

"I suppose you mean—"

"Extortion, blackmail . . . the usual garbage. Mr. Lucci has a problem, he phones my boss, my boss phones me. Sometimes I do a small job, but mostly they call me for the big jobs. You know what I mean by big jobs?"

"By big, I presume you—"

"I mean whacking people," said Ump.

The priest stared at Ump, trying to comprehend everything that had been said. "You kill people, and you're feeling guilty about it?" Carroll said.

"Not so much guilty as exhausted," said Ump. "See, when you're in my line of work . . . I don't mean to be bragging, but contract work—it's like an aphrodisiac. People pick up the scent, and soon everyone and their uncle's begging me for favors."

"You mean asking you to kill people?" Carroll said.

"It just happens," Ump said. "Whenever I spend too much time in one place and word gets out who I am . . . I once took a weekend cruise, and a half day didn't go by before people were pulling me left and right, begging me to kill their Aunt Betsy or Cousin Moe."

"And you think it's happening again?"

"Let's just say I'm being jerked around."

"And it's being jerked around that's bothering you," said the priest. "Not the killing?"

Ump looked confused.

"The idea of murdering someone," said Carroll. "That doesn't appear to bother you."

Ump shrugged, baffled by the thought. "No," he said, thinking harder, trying to fathom the priest's point. "I don't know. I mean, it can be tiring; I don't like that." He thought even harder, then looked at the priest. "What do you think? Should it?"

Carroll thought immediately of the Ten Commandments; then, almost as quickly, he thought of Matthew Farber.

"That's an interesting question," Carroll said, talking slowly. "It *is* a sin." He eyed Ump. "If you believe in that sort of thing."

"Maybe it depends who you're whacking?" Ump wondered aloud.

"There's a thought," Carroll said. "Yes, that's a definite idea." He edged even closer to Ump. "For instance, if you were to kill someone who *deserved* to be killed, I doubt anyone would object."

Ump agreed with the idea.

"The council president," Carroll said. "For instance, I don't think anyone would object to that."

Ump stared at the priest.

"Matthew Farber," Carroll explained. "The man who's destroying this church. I told you about that, didn't I? Farber is waging a war against God. He's personally sworn to bring down this church. He is, quite frankly, the most dangerous, evil-minded man I've ever met. Without a doubt, Mr. Brady, there is a throne in hell waiting for him." Father Carroll tried relaxing. While demolishing the character of Matthew Farber, he had begun sweating. "Are you sure I haven't told you about him?"

"No," said Ump, "but he sounds like a lot of people." Ump stretched and got up to leave. "Thanks for the talk, Father. I'll put five bucks in the box."

Ump reached for his wallet. Carroll, however, stopped his hand.

"You don't have to do that, Mr. Brady," said Carroll. "There are other ways to help the church."

"I don't plan to be in town much longer," Ump said.

"There are still ways," Carroll said. "People often volunteer their services."

Ump stood and walked to the door. Carroll was losing him. In another moment, he'd be gone for good.

"Your friend, for instance. He looked like a God-fearing man."

Ump turned and listened.

"A few nights ago," said Carroll. "I saw his picture in the paper. Gus Franco, the paper said. The man they found on a train."

"What about Gus?" Ump said.

"I saw the two of you together," said Carroll. "I waved from the back of an ambulance." Carroll held Ump's arm. "How about it, Mr. Brady? Can you help me? Is it asking too much for you to help the church?"

Ump was truly hating the way people grabbed him. "Actually, Father, I don't think you want what you're asking for, even if you know what you're asking."

"This is important, Mr. Brady," said Carroll. "This man—he's at war with God. And that means something. It means something to you personally. You're in God's image. You *owe* Him, Mr. Brady. We all do."

"Right now I owe someone else, thanks," Ump said.

"But you still owe Him. You owe Him from the moment you're born. And you never stop owing, Mr. Brady. It's the one debt you pay all your life."

Ump shook his head and walked down the steps.

"Think about it," Carroll called. "This town's never had anyone like you. Won't you help? Won't you save my church?"

Ump left, ready to head back to his room. Suddenly, walking through town wasn't such a great idea. Everywhere he looked now, people were staring back at him, sizing him up, picking up the scent. Ump, who made his living protecting other people, was suddenly in need of protection—if not physical, then at least something to stop the probing, the needling, the—

"Mr. Brady?"

Ump turned.

"Mr. Brady, I'm Shirley Anderson. I wonder if I could impose on you?"

Ump watched as she crooked her finger and started for a building. Did they know each other? He didn't think so, but she talked as if they did; in fact, she talked as if he were her property. "Please," she said. "My office is upstairs."

He followed her inside, up a staircase, past a secretary, and into an office. The small room was a mess of business and politics. "I don't know if you've heard, but I'm running for mayor. Have you met Bill Conley?"

"On occasion," said Ump.

"What was your impression?"

"He seemed right for this town."

"Really," said Anderson, considering his remark. "Well, Mr. Brady, some of us think different." She closed the office door. "Some of us think that after ten years, it's time for a change."

"Okay," said Ump. "I got no problems with that, either."

Anderson smiled. "You sound like a businessman."

Ump shrugged.

"I hope you're a businessman," she said, "because I'd very much like to do business."

Ump sat down and waited. Anderson sat opposite him and assumed a power position.

"Mr. Brady, I have no time for being subtle," Anderson said. "One person is trying to blackmail me, another is trying to bury me politically, and someone else is doing everything possible to keep my campaign fiscally bankrupt."

"That's an armful," said Ump.

"I hope you don't mind my intruding," she said, "but certain things have been happening around town and most of them involve you. I've been giving this a lot of thought, and I can't help wondering. . . . Mr. Brady, do you kill for a living?"

Ump stared at her.

"I'm asking, because I saw you getting rid of a body at the train station," she said. "Then I read about him yesterday. Gus Franco. Isn't that right?"

Ump kept staring at her.

"Don't misunderstand," she said. "I'm not threatening you with this information. This is purely a professional inquiry. I need to know, Mr. Brady, if your services are for hire, and if so, at what price? I'm in immediate need of such a person. And if you're not available, I'd like a referral—someone who can also provide a short-term loan."

Ump couldn't stop staring. It wasn't a threatening look—there was no anger or hatred in his eyes—but it also wasn't approving. Indeed, it was the closest Anderson had ever come to dealing with a human wall. She wondered whether Ump had heard her proposition.

Then, finally, Ump ever so slowly shook his head and said, "I got a feeling . . ."

The sentence hung and Anderson waited. Ump rested, as if unsure of his thought. At last, satisfied, he said, "I got a feeling, Miss Anderson, that sending me to Waylin wasn't one of Freido's better ideas."

He looked at Anderson as if she could understand.

"You people are blood hungry," Ump said.

Anderson refused to be put off. "Mr. Brady," she said, "I was hoping we could talk terms."

"Yeah," he said. "I know."

"I'm sorry to impose, but this is an emergency. Three people are after me. I tried talking to Mr. Castagna. Do you know Mr. Castagna? I heard he was very big in Chicago. I heard—"

Ump cut her off. "I know what you want, so let me think about it, all right?"

"But I haven't told you the whole story."

"You don't have to," he said. "Like I said, I'll think about it."

Anderson hardened. "Don't take too long," she said. "Don't forget, I saw you commit a murder."

"Right," said Ump. "You and everyone else."

"Mr. Brady, if you can't do it, then you must know someone who can. I need to know now. I—"

Ump left. He walked downstairs, looked up and down the street, reoriented himself, then turned to see Bill Conley coming at him.

"Mr. Brady," Conley called. "Frank. Frank, you weren't talking to Shirley Anderson, were you?"

Ump walked in the opposite direction.

"Frank, I'd like to talk business with you," Conley called. "Fleming and I can make a generous offer!"

Ump never broke stride.

"Frank?" Conley shouted. "Mr. Brady! Please, whatever she offered, we'll *double.*"

"It's about time you came home," said Francine.

Ump mustered a smile and closed the door behind him.

"It's almost seven o'clock. What have you been doing?"

"Walking," he said.

"Walking where?"

"First downtown, then off by some warehouses."

"You must be exhausted," she said. "You ready for supper? I've got a nice supper all ready to—"

"Not quite yet, thanks," Ump said.

He continued upstairs to his room, but Francine wouldn't let him go. She ordered Jennifer to wash the dishes and followed him to his room. "What's the matter?" she whispered. "Did I get you upset?"

"It's no one in particular," Ump said.

"Are you thinking about me? Is that it?" said Francine. "Are you afraid I might make complications?"

"I'm just starting to feel some pressure, that's all," Ump said. "It'll all be over soon."

"Is it something I can help you with?"

"No, Francine."

"Will you let me know if I can?" she said. "I want to help, Frank. I know how you feel about your wife, too. And that's okay. I just want to help."

"If something comes up, I'll let you know." Then, before Francine left, Ump said, "There is one thing, actually. During the next few nights, make sure you keep the doors locked."

"I always do," she said.

"The windows too?"

"I lock up the whole house."

"Good," Ump said. "I'm starting to get an itch. A professional instinct," he said. "Like my vacation's coming to an end."

Francine looked too concerned, so Ump spent another minute calming her down, then went into his room. He closed the door, wiped his face, sat on the bed . . . then saw the note.

It was nailed next to an open window. Ump leaned closer, tore it free, and read:

> Dear Friend,
>   I am not playing games. Enclosed is a map. Follow it and meet me tonight at midnight. I have something for you to do. Do it, and I will leave you alone. If not, I will tell the police everything. You will do what I say or else. I am not kidding. *Meet me tonight.*

Ump read the note, closed his window, read it a second time and, shaking his head, threw it in the garbage.

Yes, his vacation was definitely at an end.

TWENTY-ONE

Joseph Gratton came home wet, cold, tired, and pissed off.

For three hours, he had been outside in the night, most of that time squatting in Waylin's one dark alley. That was where Ump's map led—down North Street, then half a block east, past the barber. Joseph waited, masked by a nylon stocking and armed with a borrowed hunting rifle. His plan was to scare Ump into killing Fleming and setting fire to the bank. Now, for the second time, Ump had stood him up. Instead of dropping Freido's muscle to his knees, Joseph was left standing in the rain.

When he got home, he stuffed the nylon stocking back in Francine's bureau and threw one of his shoes against the bedroom wall. Francine rolled over and weakly opened her eyes. "What time is it?" she asked.

Joseph, wide awake, grunted and said, "Who the hell cares? I could be outside all fucking night and you wouldn't notice."

Francine rolled away from him. "Just be sure you lock the door before going to bed," she said. "Frank's worried about thieves."

"Oh, yes, ma'am," said Joseph. "If Frank wants something, I'll do it. Fancy fucking big shot from New York. So fucking smart he can't follow a stupid letter."

Joseph threw his other shoe across the room and went to close the bedroom door. He reached for the knob and—

"I heard a noise," said Ump.

Ump stood at the entrance. Joseph stared at him, too nervous to talk.

"Is the downstairs locked?" Ump asked.

Joseph nodded.

"You tired?"

Joseph again nodded.

"You going to bed now?"

"Yes, sir," Joseph said.

Ump approved the idea; then he tucked a hand under Joseph's arm and led him into the hallway. "By the way, I'm going to the ballpark tomorrow," he said. "If you want, you can come and bring your kids."

"Thanks, Ump, but I got other—"

"Think on it."

"Sure," Joseph said.

"Sure," Ump said. "Think all you want." He turned, ready to leave, but he looked at Joseph a last time. Quietly, almost confidentially, he said, "You know, I don't mean to pry—this is strictly your own business—but what am I missing about you?" Ump seemed to carefully examine his host. "I mean, you don't love your wife, you don't love your kids, you don't make money, you don't take care of your family. . . . I'm looking for something positive in this picture, Joseph. If something should happen to you—some kind of accident—what would the world lose?"

Joseph eyed Ump more carefully. He tried turning the question into a joke. "It'd lose me," he said, grinning.

Ump didn't laugh; instead, he shook his head and walked to his bedroom. "I'll take that into consideration, too," Ump said.

When Ump sensed trouble, it was rarely more than a day or two before it arrived. This time was no different, although nothing happened until the middle of the sixth inning, while he tried making up for another missed call.

He was having an awful time on the field. It wasn't just anticipating a showdown with the Gollas; his mind was flipping between so many thoughts and problems that the game itself was a distraction.

And his attitude showed in his work. His strike zone was off, his calls were late, he missed fouls, he miscalled traps. If it had been his first game, he would have had a riot on his hands. Even if it had been the second game, Ump would have been in hot water, because his reputation still hadn't spread completely through the league.

But after all the broken windshields and punctured tires, after the threats to pitchers and batters, managers and coaches, bat boys and ball girls, after enforcing the rules the only way he knew how—without mercy—and swinging a bat the only way he knew how—over his head—after changing the stadium from a place where people shouted and jeered to a place where you watched in polite quiet, no one was about to argue anything with Ump. With Ump around, there was more to worry about than just winning or losing.

Still, Ump knew he was slipping. Between thoughts, he'd remember a last call, then decide in retrospect, that—as everyone else knew—the pitch had indeed been too high, or the runner should have been given an extra base. And he stood there, wondering how he, of all people, could do such a thing. Someone who had such complete and utter respect for the rules. Someone whose decisiveness had always been natural. It was as if his time in Waylin was wearing away his judgment. Or perhaps it was the anticipation? Was Ump so busy looking for trouble that he was making it?

"I'm off today," he confessed to Doolen.

Doolen didn't answer. Ump was the one with the major-league experience, or at least that was his story. Doolen had also heard that maybe things weren't as clear as they seemed—that, far from touring the National or American Leagues, Ump was a fraud.

But Doolen knew better than to ask. Like everyone else at the stadium, he waited for someone else to ask.

Nonetheless, Ump pushed him. "What do you think?" Ump said. "Is my strike zone too high? Think I'm missing the pitches?"

Doolen had to say something. After careful consideration, he said, "It looks great, Ump."

Ump shook his head. "I don't know," he said. "Ever have one of those days where you're just absolutely sure someone's gonna try killing you?"

"It's your imagination," said Doolen.

Ump shrugged, let Doolen get back to first, then settled into position again. One pitch later, he blew another call.

"Ball," he shouted, missing a belt-high fast ball. Ump thought for a moment, realized his mistake, and corrected himself. "No," he said. "Strike."

The batter turned and stared. He stepped out of the box and waited for his manager to challenge Ump. But the manager stayed on the steps, his attention on a cup of Gatorade.

The catcher walked the ball to the mound, and Ump used the moment to scan the stadium. No wonder he had such a hard time concentrating—here he was, expecting to be hit by Sal Golla, and he was acting like it was any day. He had actually come out to the ballpark, walked onto the field, and made himself a target before thousands of people. It was ridiculous. Ump knew enough to get out of the rain, and he sure as hell knew better than to stand out in the open when someone was trying to crossmark his forehead.

The town, Ump thought. Waylin was making him weak in the brain. To hell with fresh air, he needed to get back home with his family. He needed to be checking off Nan's shopping lists.

Ump visited the mound and pulled aside the catcher. "Come on," he said. "Let's finish this."

The catcher followed Ump back to the box, settled into position, signaled, pounded his mitt, and braced for the pitch. The ball arched through the air, crossing at the chest while the batter watched. The ball struck the mitt, and the catcher froze, waiting for the call.

It never came.

"Ball or strike?" the catcher asked.

Ump wasn't even looking; instead, he stared to the right of the catcher, toward a patch of dirt.

"Ball or strike?" the catcher said again. He took a long breath, glanced to the dugout and, on his own, turned to face Ump. "You got a call?"

Ump wouldn't take his eyes off the patch. "I was trying to figure out," he said, "how that little rock moved from there to there." He pointed out a distance of about a yard. Then he pointed to the other side of the catcher and said, "And how that rock moved from there to there," indicating a larger distance.

The catcher followed Ump's finger, having no idea what he should say.

The question, however, was for himself, and Ump looked elsewhere. "Or that rock, from there to there," he said. "Or—"

This time, the dirt kicked an inch from Ump's heel. When more dirt popped between Ump and the batboy, he glanced once toward the left-field stands, then turned and headed for the home dugout. With each step, another pocket of dirt kicked in the air.

Ump pushed past the manager, striding beneath the stands and into the locker room. He went straight to the sink, where he took off his vest and looked under his shirt. His side was bleeding—a bullet had passed through the skin, entering under the ribs and exiting near his hip bone—but not enough to slow him down. It also wasn't enough to spoil his relief.

At *last*, he thought. Back to business.

He sponged the wound, washed his face, and looked in the mirror. "Nan," he said. "We're almost home."

Minutes later, he was off for the stands. He stopped only once, considering what size bat to carry. He tested the weights, making full, downward swings, wondering how the hell someone could hit a teeny, tiny ball with one of these things. Christ, it was hard enough hitting a head.

Finally, he went hunting for Golla's men. He charged off, not even thinking about dying. He was in too good a mood to die today. It was almost unfair. And an hour later, the proof was in the body count. Ump—7; Golla—0.

As for the real ballgame, Ump's disappearance had a slow but steady effect on the park. The game began a transformation, once again becoming ill-tempered. It was like pulling a finger out of a dike. The only kindness was that Ump missed seeing his game turned to ruins; instead, he was behind the rear parking lot, wiping his hands clean and finishing his talk with the last of Sal Golla's scouts.

"You want a pillow?" Ump asked.

The killer shook his head.

"I got one in my car," Ump said. "It's right over there. No problem."

"It's okay," the man said. "My spine's broke anyway. I can't feel a thing."

[153]

They were in a gutter, hidden by a hill of grass and no more than a hundred yards from the main gate. Nearby were two other bodies, and somewhere about the stadium were the rest of Sal's men, or at least their remains.

"Anything to tell me?" Ump said.

"One thing," the killer said. "Bagel said to tell you that if something like this happened, don't bother shipping back the bodies. He'll pick us up himself."

"Bagel's coming out here?"

"Only if he has to," said the killer. "And it looks like he does."

"It'd be easier if Sal told me where he was."

"That's gotta be the best-kept secret in the country." He lifted his head a last time and struggled to look about. "No wonder you were so hard to find. Hiding out in a pisshole town like this." The killer shivered and fought for his last words. "Can't wait to get back to New York," he said. "I tell you one thing—I'd rather be dead in New York than spend another five minutes here."

A half hour later, Ump was on a pay phone.

"Yeah?" Freido answered.

"It's me."

"Ump?" Freido said. "Jesus, it's about time you called."

"I got some news," Ump said. "Sal flushed me out. I think it's time to leave."

"You *think* it's time to leave," said Freido. "Ump, you don't know the half of it. I got the news of the decade. The news of the century."

"I'm only interested if it's good news," said Ump.

"Oh, it's good," said Freido. "I found him, that's all."

"Found Sal?" Ump said. "I thought no one knows where he is."

"No one except me," said Freido.

Ump waited. He could imagine Freido smiling. "So?" Ump said. "If you know where he is, tell me. When am I getting back to the city?"

"If you want Sal, you don't come back to the city."

"And what's that mean?"

"Let's put it this way," said Freido. "Have you ever been mountain climbing?"

PART III

MÁNO-A-MÁNO

TWENTY-TWO

Sal couldn't take credit for his mountaintop compound. It was first built in the 1920s by Spike Cutter, a railroad magnate who, fearing the growth of unions, sought all the security that a 40-grade incline and a payload of explosives could provide. He spent millions of 1920s dollars on his personal security, creating the ultimate fortress, or prison, depending on the perspective.

As for the mountain itself, while not especially high—no more than fifteen hundred feet—what made it impenetrable was Spike's use of the space. Along the entire thirty-mile base of the mountain, he installed an electric fence. Behind the fence, working its way up the mountain, he varied layers of attack dogs, armed guards, trip wires, and explosive mines. All of this ended at the compound itself, which was accessed by gyrocopter, and only then through steel reinforced doors.

Years later, a team of investors sought to convert his maniac vision into a ski resort. They opened holes in the fences, bulldozed a road to the mansion, stripped down ski slopes, added lifts, and built a lodging wing at the main house. The investors, however, never managed to find all the mines. After one skier tripped on an undiscovered explosive, the mountain was closed, sold, sold again, and finally bought by a drug dealer. The dealer restored the mountain to its initial purpose, not only rebuilding the fences and bringing back the dogs, but also adding night lights, security cameras, heat sensors, and a score of additional devices.

It was Sal's good fortune to be friends with the dealer. As a favor, Sal was given the keys to the mansion and, consequently, use of its defenses. While Ump stayed hidden in Waylin, Sal spent much of his time on Spike's Mountain, masterminding a two-front war.

The first front was against Tommy Lucci's business. With Bagel coordinating, Sal struck throughout the city. Uptown, downtown, the Bronx, Manhattan, Yonkers, Jersey . . . Sometimes it was just a few shots at a car, other times an explosion in a restaurant or doorway. It didn't make a difference to Sal, so long as it kept Tommy off balance. Sal's boys would pop into a Lucci bar, smash the bottles, shatter the glasses, pepper the walls with bullets, maybe take out a couple of the waiters. Always, they left the place a casserole of destruction, and always, they left Tommy Lucci with one message: hand over Frank Brady.

Which was the second part of Sal's attack. Because even if he spared Tommy Lucci—even if, after all this back and forth, Sal cooled enough to agree that *maybe* Tommy could live, and *maybe* they could work out a deal—even if Sal toyed with the idea of peace, there was still the bottom line.

Frank "Ump" Brady had to die.

Slowly.

Painfully.

This was nonnegotiable, and this was how Sal kept half his men busy—searching for Ump, all with the sole purpose of administering Golla justice.

"I want everything checked," Sal said. "Where he lives, where he drinks, where he plays, Lucci safehouses, friends, family, people who owe him favors, people who are scared of him . . . Trace his checks, his credit-card slips. Everything, you got it? *Everything.*"

Plus Sal wanted hourly reports. He wanted a round-the-clock search, and he wanted one as thorough as the most exhaustive federal investigation. Even his closest associates thought he had gone overboard, that he had turned obsessive, more worried about one man than his whole organization. But then, most people misunderstood Sal's rage. They thought he was driven by revenge. In fact, this was only a small part of the picture.

Of course, Sal wasn't thrilled at having his family massacred; at the same time, he was a businessman. In a year, maybe

[158]

two or three, he could get over the loss. And maybe if Tommy Lucci offered the right price—say, half a million per brother—Sal could get over it sooner.

But there was one thing he couldn't get over: the Look.

Sal would remember that forever—lying on the porch floor, shards of glass in his arms and legs, listening to gunfire inside while outside, by the front gate . . . Outside, staring at him, so smug after killing his brothers and making a shambles of the Golla mansion . . .

That Look. Not only stuffing it in Sal's face, but letting him know that he'd be back.

Of all the humiliations, it was the Look that did Sal in, the sight of that face moments after Ump had escaped. Sal could never forgive and forget that. Screw Tommy Lucci, screw his brothers, screw the whole goddamn world. There would be no peace until Sal personally wiped that expression off Brady's face.

If only it wasn't so hard finding him. Well, give Tommy Lucci credit. He caught on quick to Sal's obsession. Why else hide a hit man, except to drain Sal's resources, making the Gollas weaker, more vulnerable, more susceptible to openings and mistakes. Very, very clever, and there was nothing Sal could do about it, because even though he knew all this, he *still* wanted to find Ump, which made Sal a royal sucker. All he could do was spend more time and money and hope to get it all finished soon.

On the other hand, he had never thought it would be this difficult finding Brady. He had never anticipated Tommy virtually erasing Ump from existence.

Bagel constantly reassured Sal they were doing their best. "We know he's out of the city," Bagel said, "and we think he's out of the state."

"Wonderful," said Sal. "That only leaves forty-nine more."

"Right," said Bagel, missing the sarcasm. "Figuring, of course, that he's in the U.S."

Sal cursed Bagel to hell. What Bagel really meant was that they had searched everywhere—every direction on the compass—and found nothing. They couldn't even find his family. A discipline problem, Sal thought. He was thinking that, maybe, it was time to take Bagel to the woodshed. Or someone

[159]

else—maybe chop a few heads. But then Frank Brady went ahead and did it for him.

Gus Franco, dead in Pittsburgh. It was insult added to injury, no matter how Bagel tried to reassure him.

"This wasn't meant to piss you, Mr. Golla. I think he's just being professional."

"Really?" Sal said. "And since when did you write the book on Brady?"

"I haven't. It's just that after I talked to him, he didn't sound—"

"*Talked* to him?"

"That's how we knew where to find Blade," Bagel explained.

"Talked on the phone?"

"Long distance, I think," said Bagel. "It wasn't a great connection."

"He had the balls to call up and tell us where to find one of our own guys?"

"I would've done the same," said Bagel. "Really, Mr. Golla, I don't think this is a personal thing with him."

Again, Sal cursed him to hell. It was impossible. His own people were being jerked around, and they didn't even know it. If he had to spend another week listening to excuses and phone calls . . . But the fortune changed. After all the clues had dried out, they were saved by Gus Franco's funeral.

Since Gus had been found in Pittsburgh, Bagel figured Ump was somewhere in the vicinity. He began calling in favors, never thinking that Blade had only ended up in Pittsburgh after a long train ride. And when it did occur to him, he faced another problem: how to narrow the search so that he wouldn't spend a lifetime searching every town that lay within dumping distance of a thousand-mile railroad track.

It seemed an impossible job until Gus himself provided the answer. As always, Bagel was given the job of making the funeral arrangements. Since he knew Gus had a mother, he stopped by Gus's apartment to search for her phone number.

Bagel found more than the number; he also found the article that Mrs. Franco had clipped—the piece about a certain Lucci hit man who had single-handedly saved a grocery store.

Bagel went straight to the phone. "Mr. Golla?" he said. "I think I'm onto something."

Within hours, they had a scout driving west into the back woods, settling in a motel, and beginning the search for Ump. A day later, Ump was tracked down. "He's here," the scout told Bagel, standing by a pay phone, staring down a gun scope and training the cross on Ump's forehead. "Want me to take a shot at him?"

"No," said Bagel. "For Chrissake, wait. He doesn't know you're there, does he?"

"He shouldn't."

"Then definitely wait," said Bagel. "He's not going anywhere. I'll send six more guys out, then we'll pull the trigger."

"It only takes one guy to pull a trigger," said the scout, insulted.

"Look, trust me," Bagel said. "You haven't seen him in action. I want more manpower. The way things have worked out so far, if we even clip this guy, we'll be lucky."

So the scout waited, and a few days later the Gollas took their best shot—in fact, took several of them.

And now, that was also water under the bridge, and Ump had moved again. Would it be another waiting game? Because Sal couldn't spend a lifetime on this. For the umpteenth time, he dragged Bagel into his office and shouted, "I don't care how you find him, understand? Dig him up. Send him a letter. Send flowers to Tommy Lucci. Tell the son of a bitch that if he's got any guts, he'll show his goddamn face."

"Mr. Golla, that may not be the smartest—"

"*Fuck* smart," said Sal. "If it works, send him my address. I just want him now, all right? I want us to have it out, man to man. Just him, just me. Anywhere he wants it, anytime he wants, any—"

A light on the phone blinked and Sal pressed a button.

"Yeah?" he said.

"Mr. Golla," said the guard. "I'm calling from the front gate."

"So what?"

"There's someone here to see you. He says you're expecting him."

"What's his name?"

[161]

"He won't give it."

"What's he look like?"

"Kind of tall, heavyset," said the guard. "He says he works for Tommy Lucci."

Sal caught his breath. "Ask him . . ." Sal glanced at Bagel, then said, "Ask him if his name is Frank Brady."

There was a moment of muffled talk, then the guard returned to the phone. "He said his friends call him Ump."

Sal stiffened and crouched over the phone. "Listen carefully," he ordered the guard. "Don't say another thing. Take out your gun. Take it out and shoot the fuck between the eyes."

"But—"

"*Do* it," Sal said. He slammed a table and shouted, "*Kill the fuck!*" Then to Bagel, "He's at the gate! Get someone down there and take care of him!" Then, to the phone, "Shoot him, understand? Don't keep talking. *Shoot. Shoot!*" Sal waited for an answer, listened for words, a gun shot. . . . "You hear me? Hey, you understand? Hello? Hello?"

"Mr. Golla?"

Sal shut up. It was a different voice—one he hadn't heard in weeks.

"Mr. Golla," Ump said. "I think we have some unfinished business."

TWENTY-THREE

When Freido visited Waylin to pick up Ump, he slapped the
seat beside him and said, "Ump, get in. Relax. Take a load off
your feet."

Ump stepped off the road and into the limousine. The
moment he was in the car, Freido ruffled his hair.

"You're looking great," Freido said. "I think getting you
out here was the best idea I ever had. Don't worry about your
bags; I sent Teddy over there to do the packing. Can't have you
standing around like a target, right? Not when the action's
coming down." Freido tapped the driver's partition. "Hey,
Benny, let's see if you can break a few speed limits going home,
all right? You drove out here like it was rush hour." Then, to
Ump, "Everything's a hurry. I can't even say hi to my sister."
He opened a small refrigerator. "Want lunch? Got your favorite
here—triple-layer roast beef, two slices Swiss, cole slaw. . . .
How was it out here, anyway? You like the country?"

"I could have trimmed a few days," said Ump.

"Yeah," said Freido. "People say it's good for you, but you
never hear that from anyone who's eaten real food."

"Things were getting too familiar in town," Ump said.

"Familiar how?" asked Freido.

"Familiar like at Tommy's cousin's wedding," Ump said.

Freido looked at Ump, wide-eyed. "You're kidding? People
been bugging you for work?"

Ump nodded.

"So, you do any freelancing?"

"No, but I've been thinking about it."

"Jesus," Freido said, laughing again. "What about Joseph?"

"I'm thinking about him, too."

Freido turned sincere, his voice grateful, hopeful. "Thanks, Ump. I appreciate it. If Joseph had a little accident, it would be the best thing that could happen to Francine." Freido relaxed and said, "How is Francine?"

"She's all right."

"I don't mean to get personal, Ump, but you sounded a little itchy on the phone. You two haven't gotten involved, have you?"

"No," said Ump.

"Not that I'd mind," Freido said, "but you're married and Nan's a sweetheart."

"Nan's the best," said Ump.

"So's Francine," said Freido. "And I don't want her hurt. I know her. I mean, after living with Joseph all these years, and then having someone like you around the house . . . Putting you there may not have been the best idea."

"Nothing happened," Ump said. "And stop talking about your sister like she can't take care of herself. She's done pretty well so far."

"What's that mean?"

"It means what it means," said Ump. "Your sister as good as lives alone. No one's given her a break. Not you, not Joseph . . . She's gotten more than she deserves."

Freido was trying to make sense of what Ump said. "Is that why you're thinking about doing Joseph?"

Ump didn't need to answer. They spent the better part of the trip riding quietly back toward the city. Near the end, Ump started sniffing the air. "Christ," he said. "They call this oxygen?"

Freido ignored the remark, instead turning on a small television. He flipped to a cop show and settled back, but Ump reached forward and turned off the sound. "Open your ears a little," Ump told Freido. "There's already too much noise on these roads."

Freido looked annoyed. "You turned into a real country boy."

Ump stared out the window at the skyline. "Look at that pollution. You can see the haze."

"Well, on behalf of New York, let me apologize," said Freido.

"I'm serious," said Ump. "We breathe that shit."

"Don't let it bother you too much," said Freido. "We're not going over the river; we're heading north. I want you to meet someone."

Freido opened the seat partition, made sure the driver had the right directions, and settled back in his seat. He again reached for the TV dial, then after glancing at Ump, plugged in an ear jack. For the rest of the ride, Ump stared out the window while Freido watched TV.

They reached Freido's house a half hour later. Freido lived by the George Washington Bridge in a house large enough to keep Freido happy, but not large enough to call extravagant. It had a den, three bedrooms, a finished basement, a tiled kitchen and a brick exterior. Its best feature, however, was a two-car garage. The garage made it possible to get things in and out of the car without anyone seeing. In this case, the thing was Ump; just a day ago, however, the thing had been one of Sal's boys.

"Come on," said Freido. "He's downstairs."

The garage door closed and Freido hopped out of the car, walking quickly to the side door, switching off the alarm and leading Ump inside.

"Don't worry, it's me," Freido shouted ahead. "I got a surprise."

Freido waved to a man at the bottom of the stairs. The guard had a rifle over one shoulder and a gun in his hand. He looked up the stairs, then said, "Ump?" He looked closer and grinned. "Hey, Ump, that you?"

"Leon?" Ump said.

Leon couldn't stop grinning. He tucked away the gun and shook Ump's hand. "About time you came back," Leon said. "Is it true what happened to Blade?"

Ump shrugged, which meant yes. Leon kept grinning, his face close to worship.

"I wish I'd been there," Leon said. "The Blade . . . Man, pretty soon all the old psychos will be gone."

"Show Ump our guest," Freido said.

Leon nodded, leading Ump through the basement. "You must've gone crazy out in Wayburg."

"Waylin," Ump corrected.

"Well, we didn't forget you, I can promise that. Me and Freido and everyone's been trying for weeks to find Sal. We didn't know what to do; then Max tripped on this."

He unlocked a closet and swung open the door. Inside, gagged and tied, was a small, balding man, shoeless and stripped to his underwear.

"Recognize him?"

Ump shook his head.

"Danny Matz," said Leon.

"Sal's accountant," said Freido. He wiggled off the gag, and Matz caught his breath. "Matz, say hi to Ump."

Matz looked up at Ump. "Hi," he said.

Ump squatted next to him. He said to Freido, "What are you going to do with him? Kill him?"

"Naw," said Freido. "Matz wants to be here. He says Sal's crazy. All Sal does is talk about killing you."

"I've heard a lot about you, Mr. Brady," Matz said. "According to Mr. Golla, you're a dead man."

Freido patted Ump's shoulder. "You're wondering why he's in the closet, right? That's just in case something fucks up. Until we kill Sal, Matz wants to be kidnapped. Once Sal's out of the way, Matz can work for us."

"If I were you, I'd get in the closet too," Matz told Ump.

Ump looked at Freido. "I don't get Sal," he said. "What's his beef? If he hadn't stuck his brother behind his own desk, none of this would be a problem."

"Sal doesn't see it that way," said Leon. "He thinks you're the pain in the ass."

"Matz," said Freido, "tell Ump where he is."

"Telling him isn't the problem," said Matz. "The problem's getting there."

"Getting where?" said Ump.

"Spike's Mountain," said Matz. "That's where he's hiding out."

"He's not coming down, either," Leon said. "We've had guys staking out the base. Now and then a chopper touches down, but even then he doesn't get on. He's playing it tight. You gotta go there."

"Either that, or we gotta hide you again," said Freido.

Ump looked at each of them, then walked off to a chair and sat down. Freido followed.

"You want to know more about the mountain?" Freido asked. "Matz worked there. He can tell you all the details."

Ump raised his hand, waving off the help.

"You might want to listen, Mr. Brady," said Matz. "I don't know if you've ever seen Spike's, but it's really a remarkable—"

"I just need to know two things," Ump said.

"Name it," said Freido.

"Can we get there today?" he asked. "And before I go, can I talk with Mr. Lucci?"

"Tommy's on his way now," Freido said.

Ump nodded, then stood up and left the basement. He waited alone in the living room until Tommy showed up. When Tommy finally arrived, the mob boss extended both hands and reached out for Ump. "Frank," Tommy said. "It's been too long."

"I've thought the same thing, Mr. Lucci," Ump said.

"But it's almost over. You'll be glad to know your family's fine. I've had them watched twenty-four hours."

"I appreciate that very much, sir."

"Taking care of your wife and kids is nothing compared to what you've done to Sal. The guy's turned into a nut case. A complete idiot."

"Somehow I think that, between Sal and me, he's not the idiot."

"Look, just because you killed his brothers . . ."

"It's not just that," said Ump. "Letting you and Freido ship me out of town . . . Letting you separate me from my family . . ."

Freido appeared at the doorway. "Hey," he said, "that was all necessary, Ump."

"No debt is worth that much, I don't care what I owe," Ump said. "You got me behaving like your brother-in-law, Freido. You had me running around hiding, dealing with lunatics, and all the time you had me breaking my number one rule. The *number one rule*."

Freido didn't even want to hear the rule; all he cared about was Tommy Lucci. It was never good barking at the boss, and he didn't know if Tommy could take it.

Tommy, however, showed the same patience he'd managed during his last meeting with Ump. Like Freido, he had learned that, with Ump, you bent some ground rules.

"What is it you want, Ump," said Tommy. "An apology? I apologize. I was trying to save your family, not wreck it."

"I don't want an apology," said Ump. "I want out."

"Ump . . ."

"I've been thinking about this a lot, Freido," Ump said. "You really screwed me this time."

"Ump, you don't have to quit," Freido said. "Mr. Lucci apologized. I apologize. Things like this happen once in a lifetime. After Sal's out of the way—"

"Don't start," said Ump. "Just get me to the fucking mountain and let's get this over with."

Tommy and Freido waited a moment, but Ump had nothing else to say. Finally, Tommy nodded to Freido, and Freido led Ump back to the garage, where a minivan was parked.

"I'll follow you to the mountain base," said Freido. "After that, you'll be on your own."

"Right," said Ump.

"I put a bunch of weapons in the back," said Freido. "I didn't really know what you'd need, so I kind of overdid it. Guns, bombs, rifles, knives, axes . . ."

Ump didn't even look.

"I know you don't care," Freido said, "but at least listen, all right? It's about two thousand feet from the base to the top. There's an electric fence around the bottom, with armed guards protecting the fence, and land mines protecting the incline. If you make it up the side, you'll have to get by trip wires, security cameras, more guards, more mines. And if you get to the top, you'll still have to figure out a way into the compound and then at Sal, because there're no windows on the ground level, and the doors are made of reinforced steel. You got that?"

Ump nodded.

"Now, I want you to think while you're here," Freido said.

"Is there anything you need? Is there any way that I can help you? Is there anything any of us can do?"

Ump thought a moment. "Just one thing," he said. "Make sure the Gollas aren't quadruplets."

"I swear, this is the last one," said Freido. "How about while you're doing the job? You mind if I wait at the base to take you home?"

"It's better than taking the bus," said Ump.

"Fine," said Freido. "I'll wait as long as you want. You tell me—how much time will you need to kill Sal?"

Ump thought again. "Two thousand feet to the top?"

Freido nodded.

"Guards? Land mines?"

"Yeah," said Freido.

"Dogs, too? And choppers?"

"The works," said Freido.

Ump thought harder, then finally shrugged. "I don't know," he said. "An hour too long?"

TWENTY-FOUR

Ump wondered why more people didn't use the front door. Not that it always got you in, but it was still a good place to start. It worked the last time he visited Sal Golla, so Ump had every reason to expect it would work again.

"Please," Ump told the guard. "I think he'll want to see me."

The guard eyed Ump, not recognizing or believing him. In all the time he'd been assigned to the front gate, no one had used the road. It was as if the road to the mountaintop were a decoy. "Who should I say is here?"

"Tell him I'm from Tommy Lucci," Ump said.

The guard went to the phone while Ump assessed the situation. The guard was armed, but that wasn't too important: Ump knew how to take bullets. More important was that the guard stationed himself behind the fence. Ump was also being watched by a second man, who sat in a cement-based booth. All things considered, it wasn't perfect security, but Ump sure wasn't going to break down the fence with his car and still be able to drive up the mountain—which, Ump supposed, was the point of the fence and cement barrier: not a final defense, but the first step toward stripping away the attacker.

The guard covered the mouthpiece and shouted, "Hey, are you Frank Brady?"

Ump climbed back into the van and settled behind the steering wheel. "My friends call me Ump."

The guard nodded and uncovered the mouthpiece so he could again talk to Sal Golla. Ump watched as the guard's demeanor changed. One minute he was confused, the next embarrassed, and, finally, alert.

But by then, Ump had pulled on his rubber gloves, tightened his seat belt, and shifted gears. while the guard reached for his gun, Ump headed full force into the gate.

The first thing to go was the fence. It was full of juice and could have sent Ump through the roof, if not for his precautions; instead, thanks to his insulation, Ump was simply treated to an electric light show. He kept his foot on the pedal, and the mesh steel collapsed against his momentum. Still going top speed, he tilted the van, banking up the booth. The front of the van climbed the cement and shattered hard against the plexiglass walls.

Ump shook off the impact and unbuckled. Nearby were the guards, both on the ground. He stepped over the wreckage, considered going back to the van for a weapon, but instead saw the dangling phone. He picked it up and listened.

"You hear me?" Sal shouted. "Hey, you understand? Hello? Hello?"

"Mr. Golla," Ump said. "I think we have some unfinished business."

Sal pulled his temper under control. "Frank Brady," Sal said. "You bet we have unfinished business."

"I'm coming up now," Ump said. "Since we may not get the chance to talk again, I just wanted to tell you I'm sorry about your brothers. I was trying to kill you, not them."

"I'll keep that in mind when I'm cutting off your balls," said Sal.

"Just so you know," said Ump, hanging up. It was a good time to stop talking. When he turned toward the van, hoping to dig out some manner of weapon, a line of bullets cut into the nearby trees. Ump covered his head and jumped behind his wreck. He ducked low while, on the other side, someone kept firing from the back of a jeep. The gunman was hunched behind a machine gun, and he fired endlessly, without aim, without reason, as if there were something to gain from punching holes in a wrecked automobile. This, actually, was according to instructions from Bagel, who had said when it came to Ump, they were better off shooting first and asking questions later.

Still, even Bagel might have thought twice about wasting

so many bullets. The jeep bounced through the woods, the gunner never taking his finger off the trigger, puncturing the van with a thousand 8-mm holes. Nor would it have stopped, except that Freido had been true to his word. Instead of simply supplying Ump with weapons, he had overloaded him. Freido was thinking that the only way for Ump to do his job was to drive up the mountain, slowly and steadily, like the commander of a heavily armed tank.

The gunner struck a brick of explosives, and the van balled into an explosive fire. Even Sal, way up on his mountaintop, could see the burst of metal and smoke.

"Bagel!" Sal shouted. "Bagel, did they get him? Is Brady dead?"

Bagel finished with the walkie-talkie, then turned to answer Sal. "It's hard to tell," he said. "The jeep was too close to the explosion. No one down there has the legs for checking."

Sal kicked at his desk, frustrated, as another of his men came running in. "We got someone tracked in the north woods."

Sal followed the man to a bank of monitors, each monitor hooked to a different camera. Sal watched as the various views shifted, the cameras rotating in search of the intruder. "Jesus," said one of the men, "look at that." He was pointing at monitor twelve, which showed one of the attack dogs on its side. It had either been throttled or drugged. "I don't believe it."

"How many dogs we got?" someone asked.

"It depends which side of the mountain you go up," the man answered. "Ten on that side, I think."

"So where are the others?"

Sal was the one to point. "There," he said, staring at monitor four. The remaining dogs had crouched behind a fallen log, howling and yammering. Nearby, Ump crawled about on his knees, searching the ground. "Look at those fucking mutts."

"They're smart," said Bagel. "I told you not to underestimate him. Ump's about the best Tommy Lucci's got. Real headstrong. If you ask me, your best bet is—"

"Keep it to yourself, Bagel," Sal said.

Bagel quieted.

"What's he doing?" someone asked.

"I don't know," the first man said. They all watched. Ump looked like he was one of the dogs—pawing at the dirt, then gently brushing at the top soil. "Maybe he's gonna mark his territory."

"He's digging," said Bagel.

"That helps a lot," Sal said.

"The land mines," Bagel said. "Aren't there a few scattered in that section?"

Now everyone watched more carefully, paying attention while Ump dug down and pulled out a heavy steel disk. Ump examined it briefly, turning it in all directions, then tucked the disk under an arm. Without even glancing at the dogs, he walked another few steps and started digging again. Soon he had a second disk under his arms.

"Christ," said Sal. "What's he planning to do, blow up the whole fucking mountain?"

Ump brushed himself clean and started walking straight at the monitor.

"What's he doing now?" Sal asked. "Where's he going?"

The camera was mounted on a tree, and the moment Ump reached the tree's base, he ducked out of view. Still, they all knew he was there. The view on the monitor began swaying. It was like looking out the porthole of a ship caught in a storm; the view dipped back and forth, left and right, sometimes pointing to the sky, sometimes straight at the ground. "This is making me sick," someone said.

With one last surge, the camera swayed all the way forward, tilting into the grass and leaving them in a blur. No one said a thing. They were mesmerized, as if they were out there at Ump's mercy, rather than the camera. Together they felt their lives on the line; then Ump jerked free the camera and stared into the lens.

Nan was probably the only other person to get this close to Ump. The monitor was full of him, and it made everyone lean away. Then Ump turned the camera, and the view was again blurred.

An instant later, the monitor went dead.

"I think he pulled the plug," someone said.

Bagel took a long breath. "We better get ready," he said.

[173]

The men looked to Sal for directions, but Sal still had his attention on the screens.

"He's nothing special," Sal said. "I want us to track him down. I want us to—"

Sal watched as the rest of the monitors went dead.

There was a much-needed moment of quiet. Finally, one of the men cleared his throat and said, "I think this time he shorted the system."

They all kept staring at the black screens. "That's the problem with these old systems," someone else said. "You can't short the new ones; but these old ones—you touch two of the wrong wires . . ."

"It doesn't matter," Sal insisted. "Bagel, how soon until we can get more people on his side of the mountain?"

"I sent orders the moment Ump broke through," said Bagel. "It's just tricky, that's all. With all those land mines . . ."

"How many people we got in the house?"

"Twelve."

Sal thought a moment, remembering his last encounter with Ump.

"You think we're okay?" he asked.

Bagel stared at Sal. A few minutes ago, eighteen men seemed more than enough. But now, after the van and the dogs and the mines . . .

"Maybe I should call back some of the men," said Bagel.

Sal nodded, then left the security room in favor of his roof. He stood on top of an observation deck, staring in the direction where Ump had last been, searching for signs of gunfire, and hoping for war. In fact, it was already happening all around him. Maybe it was the wind, or maybe the mountain carried an echo, but from his rooftop, it was as if Ump were charging from all sides. Sal heard gunfire from the woods behind him, then screaming from in front. One moment there was firing from the east, then, seconds later, he heard trees collapsing somewhere on the west ridge. Only over time did he begin to sense a pattern to the activity. All of the fighting—all the gunfire and smoke and shouting and confusion—was actually converging. They were meeting near a ridge, everyone coming in from the various sides, and for a few precious minutes, Sal actually believed that Ump wouldn't reach the compound. If his impression was right, his men had surrounded Ump and were now pressing together—all of them at once—into a tight circle, ready for the capture or the kill.

Bagel joined Sal on the roof.

"They got him," Sal said. "Over there, to the west. They're all together. Another second, they'll be on top of him."

Bagel followed the direction of Sal's finger. "You mean everyone's over there?"

"You bet," Sal said. "No chance he's gonna escape."

"Every last one?"

Sal looked at Bagel, wondering why he sounded so worried. "What's your problem?" said Sal.

Bagel wasn't sure he should say anything. "I was just thinking, that's all," he said.

"Thinking about what?" said Sal.

"Well, see, if I was Ump," said Bagel, "and I could fool everyone into getting together, and if I had a land mine . . ."

Sal thought. Sal understood.

He watched as the circle got tighter.

"Shit," Sal said, stunned to a whisper.

The explosion echoed off the mountain, and then the smoke and noise softened, stretching in the wind. Soon, they were back to the peace and quiet of the countryside.

Bagel relaxed. At least there would be no more fighting in the woods.

"I can't stand this," Sal said. "Is he human? You really think twelve men can't handle him? You really think he can take me?"

Bagel considered what to say. "I think," he finally said, "we better get ready."

TWENTY-FIVE

Ump was running late.

Ump had told Freido he'd be off the mountain in an hour, but here it was, almost half his time gone, and he still hadn't reached the house. This bothered him, because he hated breaking promises. Once you let one go, then everything tumbled on your head—killing Sal's brothers was proof of that. Besides, he had no idea whether Freido would wait the extra half hour. If Ump didn't speed things up, he could be left in the woods without a ride home.

The idea made him uncomfortable, as did the exercise. Freido had spent so much time warning Ump about dogs and land mines, he had forgotten to ask whether Ump had ever walked a mile uphill. Ump hadn't done this kind of exercise in a decade. He had forgotten how much it worked the upper thighs, and during his last hundred or so meters, he could feel the strain.

But at last he was near the top. When the ridge exploded, he was actually in sight of the compound. Now the only problem was getting into the building.

For Ump, it was like staring at one of his kids' books, with the knights and the queens, and in particular the old stone castles. On the ground level, just as Freido had said, there were no windows, only a few doors that could have been stolen off a bank vault. The second level had windows, but even these were recessed and shuttered, guarding against intruders.

As for the third level, Ump didn't concern himself with the particulars. He could see an outdoor stairwell leading to a heliport, but who cared? He was on the ground, which meant his problem was at eye level. He could try the front door once again, but it was hard to tell which side *was* the front. Guards stood at all the entrances, their rifles lowered, each expecting trouble and no one wanting it.

Ump thought a moment, then tucked his spare land mine under an arm. He settled on one of the unguarded walls of the compound—unguarded because it was nothing but flat brick and mortar. No doors, no windows, just a solid, rock-hard dam, sealing in Sal and keeping out Ump.

Ump leaned his mine against the wall, flipped the safety, stepped back, and began throwing stones. Each toss was aimed at the detonator and each toss missed, until he remembered those pitching instructions about balancing on the toes instead of the heels.

Within seconds, he had a hole in the wall the size of a truck.

The moment the wall collapsed, he moved in, climbing over the fallen brick and into what was left of a conference room. It proved to be a lucky hit. Five of Sal's guards had been in the room for lunch; now, they were buried—all except one, whom Ump lifted by the collar. "Hey," Ump said. "Hey, which way's Sal?"

The man pointed to a doorway and Ump followed the directions, picking up a gun and a piece of concrete before turning about the corner. He made it as far as a staircase before four more men started firing down from a balcony. Ump ducked quickly beneath the landing and fired back, pumping bullets into the mezzanine floor. He could hear the men moving higher up the stairs.

For a moment there was quiet, and Ump used the break to lean out. "Is Sal up there?" he shouted.

Ump could hear the men whispering. Finally, one of them shouted back, "We're not allowed to say."

Ump considered this. "Well if he is, can you tell him Frank Brady's here to see him?"

Ump could hear them talking, and then the scramble of someone running down a hall. Ump, meanwhile, figured he'd spent too much time in one place. He looked for a light switch, found one near the doorway, and began banging his broken cinder block against the wall. The men on the upstairs landing heard him hammering away, but no one dared lean over for a look. Instead, someone called, "Hey, you the guy who aced Blade?"

"That's me," Ump said, still pounding the wall, chipping at the plaster.

He heard them talk this over, then the same man said, "They call you Ump?"

"That's me again."

Ump, meanwhile, broke away a last piece of wall and examined his find. It was a long aluminum tube with a joint for wires. While one wire hooked up to the overhead light, the main ones seemed to keep going to the upper floors.

Ump reached in a pocket for his rubber gloves, then grabbed hold of the tube.

"What you did to Blade," the man said. "Are you planning to do the same to us?"

"I'm just here for Sal."

"Does it have to be Sal?" the man said. "Can it be someone else? We could give you someone else."

"Sorry," said Ump.

The man agreed. "Sorry, nothing; if it was someone else, we could throw him down. But if it's Sal, then you gotta get through us."

"Too bad," Ump said.

"I'm not looking forward to this," the man said.

Ump tested his grip a last time. Satisfied, he pulled the tube out of the wall and broke the hallway circuit. Then he looked inside the tube and began crossing wires.

The next thing everyone knew, half the house lights flicked off.

"Hey! Ump? Ump, what're you doing?"

It wasn't complete darkness, but it was damn close. There were no windows on the ground floor, and all the windows on the second and third had been shuttered tight. The one source of light was the hole Ump had blown through the conference wall, and that was nothing. Ump made his way up part of the stairs, and while the guards on the second floor fired blindly, Ump flexed his muscles, powering his way forward and evening the odds by three more men.

"Sal?" Ump shouted. "Sal, why don't you come out here? You're making this expensive."

"Fuck you, Brady," Sal shouted back.

Ump followed Sal's voice. "Come on," Ump said. "We're making a mess and this isn't even your place." Ump felt a doorknob, grabbed it, and swung open the door.

He was answered by a hundred rounds of gunfire.

For half a minute, it was as if someone had lit a flare. The white flash of the guns sparked the air, and Sal watched, screaming almost hysterically, thoroughly pleased to see his army finish the enemy.

Or at least Sal thought they had.

When the firing stopped, one of the gunmen walked cautiously into the hallway, groping in the dark, searching for the body. "I don't think we hit him," he said.

"Don't be stupid," said Sal. "Someone turn on a light. Open the curtains, for Chrissake."

The man kept feeling the ground. "There isn't anything here." He was joined by another of the gunmen.

"All I feel is glass," the second man said.

"That's because you shot a mirror."

"That's because we *what*?" the man said.

Ump didn't repeat himself. Instead, he slammed them into the wall.

"What was that noise?" Sal shouted. "Someone tell me what happened?"

Sal pulled back the curtain and watched his remaining men dive for cover. They were running from Ump, who had lifted a coffee table and heaved it into the room. Then Ump took out his own gun and pointed it at Sal. The mob boss stood at the window, utterly defenseless.

"Sal," Ump said, satisfied with himself.

Sal froze, uncertain what to do.

"You're looking good," Ump said. "Anything you wanna do before I finish business?"

Sal looked to his men, but none moved. Ump had his weapon aimed dead at Sal's head. If they flinched, he died.

"Come on," said Ump. "I gotta be down the hill in five minutes."

[179]

Sal knotted his fingers on the curtain cord. "You know something, Ump?" he said. "It's too bright in here."

And with that, Sal again cut the light. Ump listened as Sal fumbled through the darkness and out a side door. Ump loyally chased after him. It reminded him of the last time, with Sal slamming shut the partitions while Ump kept closing the distance. Once again, it ended with Ump bursting through the last barrier.

This time, however, there was one big difference; someone had anticipated Sal's end run. The moment Ump crashed through the door, a beam of light flashed in his eyes and a rifle leveled at his forehead.

"Don't move."

Ump obeyed.

"Throw away your gun, drop on your knees, and tuck your hands beneath your legs."

Ump tossed aside his weapon and squatted on his hands.

Sal slowly rose off the floor, just beginning to comprehend what had happened. "Yeah," Sal said. "This is good. This is just what I want." Sal, more confident, took a closer look at Ump. "I got him, don't I? This time I got him."

Ump kept staring into the light. Finally, the man tilted the beam so Ump could see him.

"Bagel," Ump said. He couldn't help grinning.

Bagel smiled back. "This'll be one to tell the kids," he said. "The day their daddy caught Frank Brady."

TWENTY-SIX

"Keep him here," ordered Sal. "Keep a gun on him while I figure out what to do."

"Yes, sir, Mr. Golla," said Bagel. Then, the moment Sal went out of the room, Bagel looked down at Ump and said, "Promise not to do anything?"

"Promise," said Ump.

And with that, Bagel put away his gun. As for Ump, he got off the floor, stretched his back and sat on a chair.

"Why didn't you phone before leaving Waylin?" Bagel asked. "Maybe I could have arranged something between you and Sal."

Ump shrugged. "Things started happening too fast," he said.

Bagel nodded. "I can't stand it when that happens."

"I must've had half the town begging me for work."

"That's awful," said Bagel.

"Yeah, well, I don't want to bog you down with sob stories. I'm just kind of sick of it, is all." Ump shook his head. "I don't know. . . . How many people you figure you've whacked, Bagel?"

Bagel shrugged. "I don't know." He thought, trying to count, but not able to rest on a figure. "Things have been busy lately, with this Lucci thing, but over a career?" He also shook his head, "Why count? It's been years since I had to worry about quotas."

"Of course," said Ump. "You don't know, I don't know. . . . I mean, why count? A job's a job. That's why I'm here for Sal. That's why you'd be here."

"I don't know about that," said Bagel. "I think you're on your own with this one, Ump."

"Hey, you'd be here," said Ump. "Any real pro would. The main point is that when we do our jobs, it's for a purpose. But the rest of this fucking world . . . First, they want to kill each other over a sneeze, then they don't have the guts to do it themselves. It's like governments, what with hiring soldiers and sending them out to kill, or hiring terrorists to kidnap people. I swear, Bagel, sometimes I think we're the only ones left with any integrity."

"Maybe we are," said Bagel.

Ump looked disgusted. "They talk about legalizing dope. It's us they oughtta legalize. It'd make for a hell of a simpler world."

"No way," Bagel said. "If they won't legalize pay sex, they sure as hell won't legalize pay death."

Sal reappeared at the doorway, this time with three of his hired guns. He looked in, saw Ump sitting on the chair, and nearly lost it.

"Relax," Bagel told him. "Ump's not going anywhere."

Sal eyed Bagel, then ordered the men to stand guard. Sal left to make one last arrangement, and the men stared at Ump, uncertain what to do until Bagel waved them closer and said, "Say hello to a legend."

One by one, they shook Ump's hand.

"Look," Bagel told Ump, "before Sal kills you, tell everyone how you got Tony and Joey, okay? You can't let a good story die."

Ump tried waving off the history, but soon they were all insisting, and Ump was obliged to give out the details. When he finished, Bagel patted Ump on the shoulder and said, "You're one in a million, Ump. There'll never be another like you." Then he stood up as Sal again appeared at the doorway.

"All right," Sal said, "help me get him downstairs. I've got it all figured."

But Bagel excused himself and walked up to Sal, so they could talk discreetly. "Mr. Golla," he whispered, "if you don't mind, I'd strongly suggest you take care of business now, up here." He leaned closer. "While we're still in control."

"Control?"

"You saw how he made it up the mountain," Bagel said. "Why take chances? Let's put a gun to his head, pull the trigger, and get done with it."

"Kill him quick," said Sal. "Is that what you think?"

Bagel nodded.

"And that's supposed to make me happy?" said Sal. "That would even things for my brothers?"

"I don't mean that," said Bagel. "I just mean you don't get too many chances like this. Let me do it now. I'll get him telling another story, I'll sit beside him, then when he's busy, I'll pull the trigger. He won't even know what hit him."

"Yeah," said Sal. "He wouldn't. And that's exactly the problem." He left Bagel and stood in front of Ump. "Come on and get up."

Ump obliged, and Sal's men stepped back.

"Just keep your guns on him," Sal warned his men. "Brady, you keep your hands on your head, right? I don't want to see a flinch."

"Mr. Golla, you don't have to worry," Bagel said. "He's promised. He's not gonna—"

"Cut with the bullshit," Sal said. "Get him downstairs. And keep next to him, Bagel. Don't give him a chance to sneak off."

Bagel obeyed, leading Ump out of the room and down the stairs. He walked step for step with Ump, and when they were far enough from Sal, Bagel bent slightly so he could again whisper; this time, however, he talked with his "prisoner."

"Sal's making a big mistake not killing you," he said.

Ump nodded.

"Look," Bagel said, "if this doesn't work out for Sal—and I don't think it will—you mind if I give you a call? There's gonna be a lot of people looking for work once he's dead, and I'd appreciate some kind of referral."

"I'll leave a message with Freido," said Ump. "Tommy'll need you, anyway. After this, I'm quitting."

"You quitting? Come on. . . ."

"It's just not worth the grief," said Ump. "You know the last time I saw my kids?"

"It's just this Golla-Lucci thing," said Bagel. "Once that blows over, we'll—"

[183]

Sal pushed in. "What did you say? What are you talking about?"

Bagel glanced back at Sal. "We were talking about Ump's kids."

Sal looked wary. "Well, break my heart," he said. "I wouldn't worry too much about them, Brady. I'm gonna kill them too."

"If you don't mind my saying so," said Ump, "you take things too personal, Mr. Golla."

"Somehow, I think that's more your concern than mine," said Sal.

It was still dark on the ground floor, but two of Sal's men began opening the steel doors and letting in more light. Sal pointed toward one of the doorways, then walked within inches of Ump's face. He pressed a gun under his chin and said, "You know what I'm gonna do? I'm gonna take you back to my place. Then I'm gonna dig a hole in the backyard. I'm gonna dig until we find the septic tank. Then we're gonna torch open a hole and drop you in with a little food and maybe a vent for air. And then . . . *then* . . . we're gonna close the top and pile the dirt back on." Sal grabbed Ump by the hair. "And that's where you're gonna die. Wallowing in my piss and shit until it kills you. And I'm gonna be eating and drinking lots in the next few days. I'm gonna be celebrating the fact that you're at the bottom of my pipes rolling in shit. I might even throw a party. That would really get things busy down there, wouldn't it?"

Sal glanced toward the doorway, which led to a garage. Then he nodded Ump inside. Ump walked to the entrance, turned, faced Bagel, and said, "Promise off, okay?"

Bagel looked at Sal, showed his disappointment, then said, "Promise off."

Ump nodded, then let Sal push him all the way into the garage.

It was a large garage, made more for working on cars than storing them. Three cars were parked inside—a sports car, a limo, and a Rolls-Royce. Whoever was there last had been doing some wheel work on the Rolls, and it was seated on a hydraulic lift.

"Someone open the door," Sal said. "Bagel, get in here. Help me find rope."

"I think I'm needed upstairs, Mr. Golla," Bagel said.

"Bullshit," said Sal. "I need you here, Bagel. Help me find a—"

"I'm needed upstairs," Bagel said, turning and leaving. Sal stared at Bagel, wondering where Bagel got the nerve to treat him like that.

For now, though, he kept his mind on Ump.

"I found rope," said one of Sal's men.

"Tie him."

The man did, a slipknot that twisted around Ump's hands and finished at his throat. If Ump struggled, he would choke himself to death.

"What now?" the man said. "Should I get the car?"

Sal stared at Ump. Ump looked back, not revealing a thing.

"Did you check him for weapons?"

"Twice."

Sal kept staring, suspicious of Ump, wondering why he didn't look nervous. "Check him again."

Ump was patted down a third time, and Sal supervised every inch of the search. When his men finished, he covered the spots they had overlooked: the inside of Ump's mouth, the space behind his crotch. . . .

"Put some chains on him," Sal said.

His men hesitated. "But we've already got him tied up with the rope. He can't—"

"I want chains also," Sal said. "Twice around. And make them tight."

No one argued. Someone found a tire chain, and they used it to bind Ump's arms. Ump made it easy for them, letting them turn him about, never looking at anyone, not even Sal. They could just as easily be fitting him for a suit.

"That's it," said one of the men. "That's the last of the chain."

"Good," said Sal. "Now break his wrists."

Ump stopped looking at the walls.

Sal knew he had Ump's attention. He also saw his men hesitate. "Go on," Sal said. "I told you to break his wrists."

While one of the men held a gun to Ump's head, the other

went behind Ump, rested a crowbar across his wrists, then smacked down with a tire iron.

Ump winced, the pain briefly showing on his face.

"Okay," said the man. "Wrists broken."

Sal and Ump kept staring at each other.

"All right," said Sal. "Now one of his legs."

Ump looked angry. "You already got my wrists."

"I know," Sal said. "That's why I only want one of your legs."

The men waited, but Sal glared at them, and they took their positions.

"This isn't right, Sal," said Ump. "This is not a professional way to—"

Ump grunted, wincing again, then fell hard on the garage floor.

"Leg's broke," Sal was told.

Ump lay on his side, not only fighting the pain, but also for his breath. The fall had shifted his weight, pulling the rope and tightening the grip around his throat.

"Anything else?" one of Sal's men asked.

"I don't know," said Sal. "I'm thinking about his eyes, but I want him to see the tank before he gets in."

Another of his men opened the garage. "I could use some help out here. I think someone's coming up the road."

Sal kept his attention on Ump.

"It's some of Tommy Lucci's people," another said. "You might want to take a look."

Sal was still reluctant to leave. "I don't trust him," he said, staring at Ump. Then he saw the Rolls-Royce—a mammoth, fortified car, with a half-ton engine and a two-ton body. The car gave Sal an idea. "Roll him over here," he said.

They kicked Ump until he was lying flat alongside the Rolls-Royce.

"All right," Sal said, "now get him underneath."

They again kicked him, not stopping until Ump was under the chassis.

"Good," Sal said. "Now lower it."

The button for the lift was on the floor, and one of Sal's men used his toe to push it. Slowly, the car sank onto Ump's chest. When the lift stopped, Sal rested a hand against the door panel and bent down. "Ump," he said. "Hey, Ump, you okay?"

Sal wanted an answer, but all he heard was a strained breath.

"Ump, don't die on me. Not yet."

Sal listened closer and heard something else. A soft, wet gasp, another difficult breath, a deep swallow . . .

Sal understood. He was crying. Frank "Ump" Brady was crying.

The man by the door called for Sal. "I can see something now," he said. "They got guns."

Sal glanced at his men. "You guys handle it. That's why you're paid."

"What about—"

"Don't worry about Brady," Sal said. "I'll take care of him."

They still hesitated, but Sal told them to leave. "I've got nothing to worry about," he said. "The man's tied in a choke knot, he's wrapped in chains, and he's got two broken wrists, one broken leg, and two-and-a-half tons of steel sitting on his chest." Sal waved them away. "You really don't think I can handle this?"

The men, one by one, walked out the door. Sal, meanwhile, squatted next to the car. He waited until he was alone, then said to Ump, "In case you're wondering, I'm enjoying this. I'm enjoying this a lot."

Ump kept crying. The light was poor and Sal couldn't see too well beneath the car, but he could hear Ump jerking with each of his tears. Sal heard the ropes rubbing and the chains scratching against the car's underbelly.

"What can I get you?" Sal said. "You want a tissue?"

Ump still couldn't answer, but it didn't bother Sal. It wasn't the first time he'd left a man blubbering. "Don't worry. Soon we'll get you to my house. Then we'll wash you down with a few quarts of piss."

"Time?" Ump whispered.

Sal bent closer, surprised to hear Ump talking. "What was that, Brady? You want something?"

It took almost a minute before Ump managed a sentence. "What time is it?" he said.

Sal glanced at his watch. "Why?" Sal said. "What are you late for, dinner?"

Sal was still grinning when Ump reached out and pressed his arm over Sal's wrist. Sal tried pulling free, but couldn't. And then, slowly, the Rolls-Royce began tilting. Sal looked up and watched as the car balanced on its hubs, hesitated, then flipped over on its side.

While Sal lay still under the car, Ump took his toe off the button controlling the hydraulic jack and began shaking free of the rope and chain. He leaned heavily on the overturned car, then hobbled about to the rear, so he could look underneath.

"Sal?" Ump said. "Hey, Sal?"

Sal looked up. The weight of the car had crushed his body. Blood poured from his mouth and showed no signs of slowing.

"It was a good idea, Sal, but you should have moved the jack."

Ump wasn't rubbing it in; he was just talking. Sal, however, took it wrong. He shook his head, his eyes burning with hatred, his mouth trying to form a word. All he managed to do, though, was bubble blood.

Ump bent closer. "What's that?" he said. "Something I can do?"

The blood kept bubbling.

"Better talk now," Ump said. "You only got about fifteen seconds."

Ump was wrong by five. Sal bubbled a last time, then his head drooped to the side.

Ump looked around, then hobbled for the garage door. There wasn't any more time to waste. Sal's watch said three o'clock, and if Ump didn't get down quick, Freido would leave without him.

He only stopped worrying when he saw Freido driving up to meet him.

"Hey," Ump called. "Hey, Freido."

Freido took a shot at Sal's men, glanced at Ump, waved, then kept firing. Ump watched the battle, not in great shape and not sure what to do. Finally, he hobbled back into the house and found Bagel.

Bagel looked up from a magazine. "Ump," he said, "you look like shit."

"I'd rather look like shit than be in shit," Ump said.

Bagel examined Ump's wrists and leg. "You need a doctor."

Ump nodded toward the door. "First see if you can put a cork on Sal's boys," he said. "They don't know when to stop."

Bagel walked to the entrance and saw the gunfight. "Fucking jerks," he murmured. Then, to Ump. "Look, sit down and relax. I'll stop this nonsense or kill the pricks myself, okay?"

Ump found his way to a bar and reached for a bottle of soda. "Don't be too tough," Ump said. "They're just doing their jobs."

TWENTY-SEVEN

"Frank," cried Nan. "Oh, my God, Frank, who did this to you?"

Nan pushed past Freido and grabbed her husband. Ump sat on the edge of the hospital bed with his wrists and leg in casts. "For Chrissake, Nan, I did it myself."

Ump waited, expecting a hug, braced for the knockdown rush; but Nan stopped short. The last time she had seen her husband, he was lying in bed with a bleeding gut. Now she came home to find him without the use of his hands and a leg. She looked hard at Freido and said, "You said you'd take care of him. I'll take care of you, you piece of—"

"Will you leave him alone?" Ump said. "Just give me a hug. I've been missing them."

Nan turned back to Ump and gently, gingerly gave him his squeezes. "No more of this," she said. "It's too dangerous. I've had enough."

Ump ran his hands through her hair. "How are the kids?" he said. "Why didn't you bring them?"

Freido said, "Mr. Lucci has them at his house. He thought until we checked out your house, they'd be safest with him. Unless you mind, we thought your wife should stay there, too."

Ump nodded, appreciative. "Freido, you mind leaving me and Nan alone?"

Freido headed for the door. "You two enjoy yourselves," he said. "I'll wait outside with Leon."

Freido left, and the moment they were alone, Ump waved Nan closer. "So what were things like at your sister's?"

"Miserable," she said.

"Miss me?"

"What do you think?"

"I don't know," he said. "You sounded pretty busy over there."

"Not that busy," she answered. Ump kissed her and, despite broken wrists, reached for the buttons of her blouse. Nan watched and said, "What the hell are you doing?"

"Looking," he said.

"This is a hospital," she said. "Get your fingers off me or your wrists won't be the only thing broken."

Ump, grinning, took his hands off the blouse. Instead, he gently pulled her down on the bed. They cuddled against each other, tired, enjoying the closeness.

"I feel like I haven't slept in weeks," he said.

"Me, too," Nan said, closing her eyes.

Moments later, they were asleep.

Tommy Lucci showed up the next morning. "Ump?" he said, carrying flowers. "Ump, you awake?"

Ump was more than awake, he was off the bed and already changed. Freido stood nearby, holding his crutches.

"Sorry I couldn't come by yesterday, but there were a few loose ends I had to tie," Tommy said.

"Thanks for taking care of Nan," Ump said.

"No problem," Tommy said. "Besides, I'm the one who should be doing the thanking." Tommy pulled up a chair. "Are you serious about quitting?"

Ump turned so he wouldn't have to answer.

"I mean, if it's money," said Tommy, "let me know. Let's talk." He said to Freido. "He didn't get a better offer elsewhere, did he?"

Freido shrugged.

"Look," Tommy continued, now back to Ump. "If you did, then let me know what it was. I'll match it. I'll double it. I'll—"

"Please," said Ump. "I've got a lot to think about, all right, so let's not do this."

Tommy pulled back, insulted. "Of course not," he said. "Don't let me waste your time. If you've got other things on your mind . . ."

Ump didn't react, and Tommy got suspicious.

"You do have other business, don't you?" Tommy looked concerned. "Are you working for someone else, Ump?"

Ump didn't know what to say. "Not really," he said. "I don't know; I haven't made up my mind."

Tommy looked at Freido for an explanation. Freido tensed, knowing he was on the hot seat. "I think what Ump's talking about," Freido said, "is a little personal favor for me. Nothing that affects you, Mr. Lucci, just some family business."

Tommy hardened. "Freido, you, of all people, know better than to mix my people with personal problems. I don't care what you two have been talking about." Tommy looked to Ump. "I don't care what he asked you, Ump; you're not doing it. Freido is way, *way* out of line."

Freido looked worried. "I'm sorry, Mr. Lucci. I wasn't thinking that way. I was thinking that—"

"*Shut up*, Freido," said Tommy. "You don't ask favors of my people."

Ump saved him. "Except he didn't," Ump said. "I mean, if I'm not working for you anymore, I'm not your people."

Tommy and Freido faced Ump. Ump stared at Tommy Lucci.

"I think," Ump said, "I'm going back to Waylin."

Tommy focused so hard on Ump that he missed Freido's smile.

"It'll just be for the night," Ump said. "We can talk again tomorrow, if you want."

Tommy didn't know what to think. Finally, he relaxed enough to say, "This isn't dangerous, is it?"

Ump shook his head.

"Will you need help?" Tommy said. "You got busted hands, a busted leg. . . ."

"I wouldn't go if I didn't think I could do it," Ump said. "Just take care of my family one more night. I'd appreciate that."

Tommy nodded.

"And Freido, get me a car and driver," he said. "If Mr. Lucci doesn't mind."

Tommy gave the okay, and Freido agreed. Ump handed Freido a list.

"I'll also need these things."

Freido looked at the list. He read it once, did a doubletake, then handed the list to Tommy, who read it stone-faced.

"This list," Tommy said, "is pretty heavy-duty."

Ump didn't say a word. He waited for Tommy to approve it, which he did by handing the list back to Freido.

Freido looked it over again and said, "Sure thing, Ump."

"Thanks," Ump said.

With that, Tommy and Freido left, Tommy to go home, Freido to start taking care of Ump's arrangements.

"That's one fucking list," Tommy said to Freido. "Think you'll have any trouble filling it?"

"I'll check storage," Freido said.

They walked down the hall to an elevator. They were both quiet until Tommy, grinning, turned to Freido and said, "You know, I like him. I like the son of a bitch. But I'll be fucking damned if I understand him."

Freido glanced at him and said, "You and me and everyone else," he said. "I used to think he was the crazy one. Now I'm not so sure."

"What changed your mind?" said Tommy.

"History."

"History?"

Freido nodded. "He's alive," he said. "Most of the rest are dead."

Two days had gone by, and Bill Conley was getting nervous.

In less than a week, there would be an election he was certain to lose. He needed help. He needed it now, quick as possible, and he needed it in the shape of an exterminator.

In short, he wanted—he *needed*—Ump.

He talked every few hours to Fleming, not only for emotional support, but for information on Ump's whereabouts. Conley had heard about Ump's quick and mysterious exit from the ballpark. Rumor was Ump had been stricken with a heart attack or epileptic fit, that he had actually hit the dirt and rolled about until he tumbled into the locker room. It sounded reasonable, but it didn't explain why Ump had so thoroughly disappeared, why he hadn't shown up at a hospital.

No, Conley believed Ump had manufactured some elaborate scene so he could leave town without explanation. It was a way, Conley thought, for Frank Brady to escape before Conley could begin obliging him to favors.

But Conley wasn't about to be easily dismissed. He knew Frank Brady had committed murder. Fleming knew, too. Together, they'd get the police into the picture, tell them what they suspected, then set him up. It might not win him the election, but at least Conley would know that, while he was selling real estate, Brady would be spending the next two dozen years poking ass in prison.

"Fleming?" he said, again on the phone.

Fleming knew exactly why Conley was calling. "I still haven't heard a thing."

"I was just thinking," Conley said. "Maybe Gratton really did nail down a deal. Maybe Brady's just out of town temporarily."

"You give Joseph too much credit," Fleming said.

"But maybe—"

"Joseph's at the bar," Fleming said. "He spent all last night drinking beer and bitching about Frank Brady."

"That's what he *says*," said Conley. "But suppose it's just a cover? He could just want us to—"

"Joseph doesn't know a thing," Fleming again said. "Brady's gone, Bill. He's back to New York."

"How do you know?"

"I know. That's where he works. The day he disappeared, another limousine passed through town. It probably stopped and picked him up."

"But the election . . ."

"There's nothing we can do," said Fleming.

"He can't do this," said Conley. "I won't let him."

"You're talking about a killer, Bill," said Fleming. "You don't get into a street fight with a killer."

Conley's secretary knocked on the door. "Mr. Conley?"

He covered the mouthpiece and looked up.

"Sir, there's a gentleman to see you."

Conley waited as his visitor walked into the office. Immediately, Conley whispered an apology to Fleming, hung up, and stood to extend a hand. "Mr. Brady," he said, his voice trembling.

Ump used his crutches to swing into the room.

Conley, looking past him, said to the secretary, "I think we'd like to be alone." She closed the door, and Conley began registering Ump's condition. Ump returned the attention, watching Conley's anticipation slip to disappointment, watching as all of Conley's hopes crushed under the weight of Ump's three casts.

Ump stopped the free-fall. "Don't worry," he said. "I can still do a job."

Conley stared at Ump, still insecure, not at all certain whether the time had come to stop being elusive. After all, regardless of what Conley wanted, the wrong conversation, with the wrong person, and asking for the wrong things . . .

"Do you want to sit?" Conley said.

Ump shook his head. "It doesn't hurt anymore. It hurt when they did the break, but not now. You ever have someone break your bones with a tire iron?"

Conley shook his head.

"You're lucky. The thing is, people always make the same mistake. They think a person's strength comes from their muscle and bones. But there's only two ways to get a person— shoot him in the vitals or break his heart. Sal didn't do either."

"Sal?" Conley repeated, struggling to recognize the name.

"Don't worry yourself," said Ump. "He's dead, anyway."

Conley stared at Ump.

"So are his brothers," Ump said. "Excuse me if I sound like I'm bragging, but you do enough of this stuff . . ."

"No need to apologize, Mr. Brady," said Conley. "I'm just glad you're back in town."

"I thought you would be," said Ump. "I did read the signals right? You got someone you want dead?"

Conley hesitated only a moment. "Yes," he finally admitted. "If you don't mind."

"Mind? Me?" said Ump. "I live for these moments. Can't get enough."

"You don't look in very good shape."

"Don't let it bother you," said Ump. "Sal's last laugh, that's all. Look, I think I know who you got in mind. That woman running for mayor, right?"

Conley nodded.

"Good," said Ump. "No problem. But you really got to want the job done."

"Oh, that's not an issue," said Conley. "I—"

"I mean it's not gonna be cheap," said Ump. "For the sort of thing you have in mind, I normally get paid ten grand. But in this case, with the extra distance, and since you're not a client, I'm charging triple that."

"Triple?" said Conley, more stunned than he let on.

"Plus expenses," said Ump, "which will probably mean another thousand at least."

Conley hedged. "That's an awful lot of money," he said. "I hope you're not thinking that, because I'm mayor, I make a large salary."

"I really don't care what you make," said Ump. "You could be shoveling horseshit and my price would stay the same." Ump leaned forward and dropped a piece of paper on Conley's desk. "If you want the job done, meet me at this place tonight at midnight."

Conley picked up the paper and stared at the address.

"And if your banker friend wants in on this, tell him to come, too."

"You mean Fleming," said Conley.

"Whatever," said Ump. He winked at Conley and headed for the door. He was almost out when a thought crossed his mind. He turned back to the mayor. "Incidentally, I was wondering: whatever happened to the law in this town?"

Conley was confused.

"Police," said Ump. "A sheriff. Anything. I've seen a lot of crap around here, but I don't think I've seen one badge."

"We have a sheriff," Conley assured him. "He's just not very busy."

"Not busy?" Ump said.

"Not busy," Conley said. "Waylin is a quiet town, Mr. Brady. People just go about their business. Normally, I mean."

Ump considered this, had another thought, then gave up on it. Instead, he again headed out the door. "Don't forget," he warned Conley. "Midnight."

"Midnight," Conley assured him, watching as Ump left.

The second Ump closed the door, Conley was back on the phone with Fleming.

"He's back," said Conley.

"Frank Brady?" Fleming said.

"And that's not all." Conley could barely contain his excitement. "He stopped by my office," he said. "He wants to do business."

Ump hated playing Marlon Brando. At the same time, he knew that people expected it, and anything else would make Ump seem less than authentic. It made no difference that, by pretending to be something he actually was, he was taking part in some paper-thin irony. It couldn't be helped, not if he hoped to close matters in a day.

So Ump left the mayor, used his crutches to swing down the street, practiced his Brando voice, and stopped before Shirley Anderson's building. He wished she didn't work at the top of a flight of stairs. Ump stood at the bottom, wondering if he should have her come down, but thought this would be a sign of weakness. Instead he took the steps, one by one, until he reached the second-floor landing. With a moment's hesitation, he began swinging toward the back office until, with a last weight shift, he let his cast kick open Shirley Anderson's door.

Anderson looked up from her meeting, clearly startled. So were her colleagues, but only Anderson appreciated the consequence of Ump's arrival.

"Will all of you leave, please?" Anderson told her co-workers.

She waited until they had privacy; then, as always direct, she circled him, stared at his broken body, and said, "What good are you?"

"Don't worry," he began. "I can still do a job."

Anderson rested against her desk. "Anyone can do one job," she said. "I want to know if you can do three."

"You're that sure you want me to do my stuff?"

"Mr. Brady," she said, "I'm surer than sure."

Ump watched to see if she was just bluffing. But she was tough, maybe tougher than Freido. No—this was someone who didn't need testing.

Fifteen minutes later, Ump left her office and swung toward the church.

This would be one of the longer walks of the day. He hobbled along the sidewalk, taking it slow, but also never breaking pace, the way a gunfighter stalks a small Western town. It was a good image, considering how people gave Ump an extrawide berth. It was as if the stories at the ballpark had drifted out of the grandstands and into Waylin. Almost everyone seemed to have heard something, and those who hadn't were being pulled away by those who had.

Well, that was fine, too. It added to the mystery, which, with a busted body, was important for Ump. Indeed, his walk was meant to encourage it. Leon, after all—sitting in Freido's car and ready to drive Ump anywhere—could easily have taken him around town. But Ump didn't want that. He—

"Bang!"

Ump looked down. The scream came from a seven-year-old dressed like a toy soldier. The mother, of course, was paralyzed, never expecting her child to communicate with Ump, and now hoping the moment would pass unnoticed. Ump spared her any panic, ignoring the child, swaying off the curb . . . and coming close to being killed.

A car swept past a red light and banked an inch from his bad leg. No, not just a car . . . a taxi. *The* taxi. Ump watched it swerve around another corner and disappear. He stood still, fighting a gut instinct to give chase, waiting for the anger to settle enough so he could keep his mind on business. Then, with the memory safely stored, he crossed the street. He kept up the momentum until he reached the church.

"Father," Ump shouted, banging at the studded wood, yelling as if he was at a friend's house. "Father?"

Carroll, however, was outside. Ump found him sitting on a bare patch of grass, no more than a yard from a bulldozer. There was no one digging today, but the tractor had already excavated at least one of the grave sites. Father Carroll sat beside the excavation, his body heavy against the remnants of a crypt.

Ump leaned against a tombstone. "What a mess," he said.

Father Carroll shook his head, stunned. "Can you believe what they've done?" He never stopped staring at the hole.

Ump also stared at the hole. Finally, he shrugged. "So

what?" he said. "Who the hell cares where you're buried, anyway?"

Carroll sighed, and Ump rested a hand on his shoulder.

"I know guys who ended up in saltwater," Ump said. "Does that mean they're any less comfortable than the guys who ended up in the dirt or the cement or anywhere else? Dead's dead."

"This is different," Carroll said. "These were my neighbors. This was my land. . . . Now it's all gone. All the property, from the back to the sidewalk." Carroll turned so he could see Ump. "Hardee's," he said. "I'm going to be neighbors with a square hamburger."

Ump didn't answer.

"I want revenge, Mr. Brady."

"No, you don't," Ump said. "I came here thinking you did, but you don't."

"I do," Carroll said. "I want you to get him. I want you to get Farber."

"No, you don't."

"I *do*," Carroll said. "It's more than the cemetery; he wants the church, too. He's not going to be happy until he has every inch of ground. It's him against me, Mr. Brady, and about the only thing I have that he doesn't is you."

"What makes you think you got me?"

"Because you're here," Carroll said. "And you're a man of God. And, most of all, you know what will happen if you don't help."

"What will happen?" Ump said.

Father Carrol dared to grab him. "Don't forget what I saw," he said. "And don't forget what you told me. You told me you're a killer."

"What I told you was private."

"It's only private if you're in confession," said Carroll. He sounded pleased that Ump had missed this loophole.

"Father," said Ump, "do you know what my business associates do when someone tries blackmailing them?"

"I don't care," said Carroll. "You are asking me to choose between the anger of a gangster or the anger of God. Who do you think I fear most?"

"I'd give careful consideration to both," said Ump.

"But this isn't your home." Carroll tightened his grip. "Do it, Mr. Brady. Do it or I'll see you sitting on the electric chair."

Ump stared at Carroll, trying to decide if he had given the priest enough outs. Finally, he reached in a pocket and pulled out another slip of paper. "Here's an address," Ump said. "If you mean it, be there by midnight tonight."

Father Carroll took the paper. "But—"

"You want to play hardball," said Ump, "this is how we do it."

Without another word, Ump left. He headed back to the street, this time waving down his car. Despite the best of intentions, his arms and legs were finally getting too sore for movement. Leon jumped out of the driver's seat and opened the front door. "You sure you don't want the back, Ump?" Leon said. "You got more room in the back. The back's also got the TV and the phone and the—"

"I'll sit with you," Ump said, swinging in his leg. It took a half minute before he had sidled into the seat. Leon slammed the door shut, then jogged back to his post behind the steering wheel. "Thanks, Leon. I had to get away for a minute. There're some things I can't figure."

"Things like what?" Leon asked.

"Things like what the hell's happening to us? What's going on when a town full of people have the balls to go asking an absolute stranger for favors—favors you wouldn't even ask a best friend?"

"They're chicken," Leon said.

"It's more than that," said Ump. "It's instant satisfaction. It's wanting to block out everyone's problems but your own. It's never thinking that in order to solve your own problems, you're also making problems for ten other people."

Leon shrugged. "That goes with our job, Ump," he said. "If people worried about making problems every time they wanted someone dead, we'd never work."

"Maybe that wouldn't be so bad," said Ump. "Right now, I got so much work, I could open a franchise."

It was four o'clock by the time he reached the Gratton's house. Leon parked slightly out of view, so Ump would first have the chance to visit Darlene.

[200]

"Frank?" Darlene said; then, like everyone else, she stared at his injuries. "Oh, my goodness, Frank. What on earth—"

"You mind if I come in?"

Darlene stepped aside and Ump swung into the room.

"Now close the door," Ump said.

Darlene obeyed.

"Now strip."

Darlene stared at him.

"Come on," Ump said. "Strip naked."

Darlene hesitated, then reached for her top blouse button. She lowered her eyes, raised them, undid a button, turned slightly, undid another button, smiled gently. . . .

Ump would have none of it. While Darlene played her games, he limped to the liquor cabinet. Darlene waited, wanting Ump's attention, but as soon as he sat on a stool, he looked back at her and said, "Did I tell you to stop?"

Darlene no longer smiled. She was waiting for Ump's passion, still pretending this was a seduction. "I thought you might like to help me," she said, fingering her clasp.

"You got it on, you take it off," he said.

Darlene gave a small, nervous laugh as if they had shared a joke. Ump remained a rock. As far as she could tell, this was nothing to him.

"Panties, too," he ordered, heading for the kitchen.

Darlene obeyed. When she was completely naked, she pressed the clothes against her chest and followed him into the kitchen. "What are you looking for?" she said.

"A broomstick. You got one?"

She nodded.

"I could also use some oil or jelly or something," Ump said. "That's more for you than me. I don't care so much about that. Mostly I want the broomstick."

Darlene didn't move. Ump saw how she had frozen. He stopped his search and faced her. "What's the matter?" he said. "You want me to kill your husband, right?"

"Yes," she managed.

"And you like me, right?" Ump said. "That's the impression I got."

"I like you."

[201]

"I mean *really* like me," Ump said. "Like, in doing anything. Provided, of course, I took care of your husband."

"Provided . . ." she managed.

Ump leaned closer, confused. "What's that?"

"Provided you took care of him," she finished, her voice barely audible.

Ump glared at her, then, satisfied, nodded. "Good," he said. "Then we have a business understanding. You do what I want, I do what you want."

"Yes," she said. "That's the agreement."

"Fine," he said, continuing his search. "And what I want requires a broom."

Darlene took a deep breath, then slowly, uncertainly, began helping his search.

"Actually, I don't need the whole broom," said Ump. "Just the stick."

"The stick," she murmured.

"About two feet."

She went through the motions of looking. "I don't suppose something smaller would—"

"No," Ump said. "But maybe I can do something with this. . . ."

He reached in a closet and pulled out a vacuum.

"Where's the nozzle?"

She pointed toward a closet.

"Fine," Ump said. "You take the machine upstairs, and I'll get the nozzle buttered up. Meanwhile, Leon can get ready."

"Leon?"

"The guy in the car," said Ump. "Leon and me do everything together."

Darlene held her clothes tighter.

"Do you have a problem with this?" said Ump. "If you do, I can—"

Darlene shook her head. "No problem," she said. "I thought it was just you and me, that's all."

"No way," Ump said. "Leon and me split everything. I don't care about you, Darlene, understand? Leon and me are just gonna have a little fun, then go out and kill your husband."

Darlene looked sick.

"Hey," said Ump, "if you're not ready, I'll just leave and—"

"It's okay," she said. "I just wasn't expecting someone else." She caught her breath and, calming, said, "It's fine."

Ump gave her a hard look, giving her every chance in the world to change her mind, giving her the time to scream and throw him out the door.

"You go get your friend," she said. "I'll take the machine upstairs."

And she turned and headed up the staircase.

Ump stood there a moment, amazed at Darlene, wondering why on earth, if life was this miserable, she even needed his help. What was so tough about firing a gun? Still, Darlene, like the others, had passed the test. Ump tested their resolve, and each proved they not only wanted Ump's services, but were prepared to do whatever was necessary to guarantee them. It was sad, it was funny . . . but it was also dangerous. Ump didn't trust people who wanted something that badly. This, above all else, was why he had to weed out those who were serious and those who were playing a game. And this was also why he had to resolve matters today, before anyone's passions had time to brew.

Ump went to the door and called for Leon.

"What's up?" Leon asked.

Ump reached in his pocket and pulled out a slip of paper. "Do me a favor, okay?" he said. "Go upstairs and tell Darlene I gotta run. Also, give her this note. Tell her to meet me there about midnight."

"Sure," said Leon. He took the paper and headed up to the bedroom. Ump waited, listening as Leon made a right, then a left. Ump couldn't hear the conversation, but it didn't matter. In another minute, he was back downstairs.

Leon stared at Ump, confused. "I gave her the message," he said.

"Good," said Ump.

Together, they walked out of the house and across the grass toward the Gratton's. Ump waited. He could feel Leon thinking.

"She was naked," Leon finally said.

"I know."

They reached the walkway and headed for the front steps.

"She asked me if I wanted the vacuum or if it was for you."

[203]

"What did you tell her?"

"I told her to clean her own fucking house," said Leon.

Ump considered Leon's answer. "Good," he said. Then he balanced against the railing while Leon rang the bell. They waited only briefly before the door opened.

"Ump?" said Joseph.

Joseph had the slowest reaction of them all. He stared at Ump, not quite believing what he saw. Then he looked at Leon, grinned, and wagged a finger at both of them. "Ump," he said again. "Ump, I thought you were gone."

Leon put a hand against Joseph and pushed him back. Ump entered the living room.

"Where's Francine?"

"In the kitchen," Joseph said. "Shit, I could've sworn you'd taken off. Freido called. He said you had a job to do. He said—"

"Get your wife, Joseph."

"Of course," Joseph said. He winked, then moved toward the kitchen door. "Sweetheart," he shouted. "Francine, get your ass out here. You got a guest."

Ump watched the kitchen entrance, while Joseph watched Ump, and Leon watched Joseph. Leon was the most confused of the three. He just couldn't figure out this town. Naked women with vacuums, drunken scum who looked ready to give up their wives. . . .

"Hi, Frank," said Francine.

She stayed by the kitchen doorway, almost hiding from view.

Ump walked up to her. "We have to talk."

"I don't want to," she said.

"This is important," he said. "This has to do with your family."

"I don't care," she said. "I wasn't expecting you. I thought Freido said you were gone."

Ump took a closer look at her. He wondered why she was making this so difficult, then just as quickly understood. She was hiding, keeping her face shaded. Ump could guess the problem—some of Joseph's frustration escaping as a little wife beating.

"Why are you staring?" she said. "Why do you keep looking at me?"

"Sorry," he said.

"Don't just say sorry," Francine said. "If you want your room, you can have it. Jennifer moved back in, but I can move her out."

"It's okay," he said. "I just came to talk to you. To see if you wanted me to do something."

Francine softened. "I'm sorry," she said. Then, tenderly, "I want you to stay, if you can."

"I'm just in town for the night."

With a glance at the door—a careful check for Joseph—she whispered, "That's okay, too."

Ump shook his head. "You know something, Francine?"

Francine waited.

"When it comes to shit, you get more than your fair share."

"Most people do," she said.

"You think so?" said Ump. "Lately, I've been thinking most people don't get half what they deserve." He shook his head, then headed back into the living room.

"Where are you going?" Francine asked.

"Out."

"I thought you wanted to ask something."

"You already answered me," he said.

"I did?"

"Practically shouted in my ear," he said, leaving the kitchen. He nodded Leon back to the car and turned to Joseph. Joseph grinned back.

"You're looking good, Ump," Joseph started again. "You want to go to town? I thought we could talk over a few things. I thought—"

"Let's go to the garage," said Ump.

Joseph glanced past Ump to Francine. She watched both of them. Joseph, uncertain, said, "Sure," and followed Ump outside and to the walkway.

"It really is good seeing you, Ump," said Joseph.

Ump waited until Joseph lifted the garage door and turned on the light. "Don't bother closing it," Ump said. "I just wanted us to have a few minutes alone."

"Alone?"

"I got some letters while I was staying in your house," said Ump. "I thought you might know about them."

Joseph shook his head, as if to say, me? He was too nervous, unable to say anything.

"Maybe not," said Ump, shrugging. "But if you do, tell the person who sent them I'm ready to talk business. If he's interested, he can meet me at this address around midnight." Ump gave him a slip of paper. "Tell him not to show up unless he's absolutely certain he wants to do business. Understand?"

Joseph nodded, and Ump forced the paper into his palm.

"Understand?" Ump said again.

"Yeah, I guess," said Joseph. "I'm not sure, but I think I do."

"I think you do, too," said Ump, turning and leaving. Ump headed for his car, where Leon had already turned on the ignition. Ump sat next to Leon and slammed the door shut. He glanced only once out the side window. Across the street, watching, were Francine, Joseph, and Darlene, each tucked in the shadows, each waiting for Ump's next move.

So was Leon.

"What next?" Leon asked.

Ump turned his attention away from the street and to the back seat. On the floor of the car were two cardboard boxes. "We've got a few hours to kill," Ump said. "Want dinner?"

"Why not?" said Leon. "Tommy gave me his credit card. We can go anywhere you want. You particular?"

"Not me," said Ump. "Just so long as we eat light. I hate to work on a full stomach."

TWENTY-EIGHT

Ump stood by the warehouse door, impatient and knowing he shouldn't be. After all, it was ridiculous to expect someone like Joseph to be on time. In fact, there wasn't even a guarantee he'd show. There were no obligations. They were the extortionists, not Ump; Ump was merely trying to simplify matters.

Still, restraint wasn't one of Joseph's qualities. This was also what Joseph had been begging for—a chance to meet Ump professionally—so there wasn't any doubt about Joseph; the only question was whether he could find the address.

He wouldn't be the only person to find it difficult. Shirley Anderson had been late, as had Bill Conley. The timing was almost awkward, but Ump took care of both quickly. As for now, Ump reminded himself that he still had most of the night. There wasn't any need for losing his temper.

Minutes later, he looked up as the last of the cars turned off the highway and onto the quarter-mile dirt road.

It was a good location. Ump had checked several during his walk outside Waylin. He had finally settled on this one, a mile outside town, without a neighbor nearby to hear the gunshots. They were tucked deep in the woods to have privacy, but close enough to Waylin so his "guests" would feel at home.

Ump watched as Joseph finished the drive and came to a skidding stop. Joseph flicked off the headlights, cursed the goddamn night, and threw open the door. He virtually charged at Ump and shouted, "All right, enough of these games. You know it's me, and I know all about you. Right?"

Ump didn't answer, but it didn't matter. Joseph was drunk, which meant he didn't need conversation, just someone to hear him. He poked Ump in the chest and said, "Now, here's the deal. I want you to take care of one or two people for me, and if you do, I won't snitch about that other guy. But if you don't, then I will. Simple enough?"

"Sounds like I expected," said Ump.

"And you better do what I say, because Freido's my brother-in-law, and Freido's your boss. You double-cross me, and you're gonna be in deep shit."

"Freido is interested in you," Ump said.

"That's right," said Joseph. "It's one big family, Ump. You cross me and you cross—"

Ump stopped him. "Let's go inside," he said. "You're already late." Ump turned and headed for the warehouse door. Joseph stood his ground, at least until Ump opened the door and pointed him inside. "Come on," Ump said.

Joseph followed Ump into the warehouse.

It was a single room, about a hundred yards in length and fifty yards wide, with corrugated sheet-metal walls and ceilings. There were no windows in the shelter, and from what Joseph could see, only one other door—a sliding panel, which was locked shut with a quarter-inch chain and padlock. The structure could easily be a hangar for a small fleet of airplanes, if only Waylin had an airport. Now, however, it was nothing more than an empty warehouse.

Except, of course, for Ump's guests—bound, gagged, and stretched against the left wall.

Joseph took a closer look. At first he thought they were dead, but then he saw the eyes. They were watching him with a mix of fear, anger, and frustration. When Joseph turned to Ump for an explanation, Ump threw him a rope.

"Do me a favor, Joseph," said Ump. "Tie up your own feet."

Joseph caught the rope, but didn't move. He was now watching one of Ump's hands. There was a cast that went from the elbow and then webbed about his palm; however, fitted in the palm was one of the deadliest-looking guns Joseph had ever seen.

"Go ahead," Ump said. "Don't worry. You're Freido's brother, remember?"

Joseph obeyed, sitting alongside the other bodies. When he

had finished, Ump ordered him to roll onto his stomach. Joseph obeyed, completely submissive to Ump, not even considering a struggle. In this respect, he was the same as the others—terrified, docile, behaving like a pet dog that offers its belly.

"What's this about, Ump?" Joseph said. "I thought we were friends. Jesus Christ, what do you think you're doing? What's Freido going to say? What's . . ." Joseph stopped. He realized that the person next to him was the one man he hated most in the world—Walter Fleming. And beside him was someone else Joseph hated—Bill Conley. and beside him was the treasurer, and beside her were Joseph's neighbors, and beside them . . .

"I'm gonna kill you," Joseph told Fleming. He turned furious, completely forgetting his fear. "Me and Ump. We're gonna teach you about bleeding poor people."

Ump, meanwhile, took off the other gags.

"Oh, God," moaned Matthew Farber, stretching his mouth.

"What is this?" Shirley Anderson demanded. "If you're trying to embarrass me, or extort from me—"

"Frank," Conley shouted. "Ump? Ump, I told you I had the money. We thought that was the idea. We thought—"

"Mr. Brady, what is this about?" asked Father Carroll.

"Mr. Brady?" said Fleming. "Mr. Brady, we can get you all the money you want. Just don't hurt us. Please? All you have to do is—"

"Sir?" a voice murmured.

Ump turned and faced Anderson's blackmailer.

"Excuse me," the man said again, "but what happens next?"

Ump moved closer. "Your name's Earl, right?"

The commotion quieted. Earl cleared his throat and said, "Yes, sir." Tears were running down his face and he was struggling to wipe his eyes with his shoulder—not easy to do, since Ump had everyone's arms twisted behind their backs.

"Earl, you're here as a favor to Miss Anderson," Ump said. "And Mr. Farber, you're here as a favor to Father Carroll."

"Favor?" said Farber. "I wouldn't piss on a wall for him."

Ump stepped back from his guests, tucked his gun in a back pocket, and turned his attention to the boxes. Leon had carried them in hours ago, but Ump waited until now to open their lids. He started with the first box, breaking the tape with a razor, then reaching in, pulling out the packing paper, and toppling out the contents.

Ump's guests found themselves staring at a small mound of cheap handguns.

Ump wasn't into dramatics. He wasted no time getting to the second box, again cutting the tape, and again dropping the contents on the floor.

This time, they stared at a pile of knives, blackjacks, and clubs.

No one said a word; they simply watched as Ump, without hesitation, began tossing the various weapons about the room, some as far as the most distant corner, others only steps from their feet. They watched as the weapons clattered against the metal wall, then dropped to the cement floor. Once a gun went off and they heard a bullet ricochet. Instinctively, the crowd winced, some shutting their eyes, others pressing to the floor. Only Ump ignored the ricochet. But then again, Ump was the professional.

"Earl asked what happens next," Ump said. "What happens next is pretty simple. There're nine people in this room, and seven of you want to hire me, and that's too much. The other two, Earl and Mr. Farber, don't know me too well, but they kind of invited themselves."

"Invited ourselves to what?" said Farber.

"We call it Gilley's roulette," Ump said. With the boxes emptied, Ump reached in a pocket and pulled out a packet of razor blades. He walked down his line of hostages and dropped one razor at each of their feet. "Whoever's left won't have a thing to worry about. I'll clean up the entire mess."

"Excuse me," said Fleming. "What do you mean when you say whoever's left?"

Ump shrugged. "Isn't that clear?" he said.

At first, no one said a thing; then George Maye interrupted the quiet. "Why the hell are my wife and I here? Who asked us to show up?"

Ump didn't answer, which only proved more irritating to George. He looked to his sides and said, "Which one of you is it?" Then, to Darlene, "Who is it honey? You have any idea?"

Darlene also didn't answer; all her concentration was on the razor blade.

Ump turned and began the walk back to the door. This started an onslaught of questions which didn't stop until he reached the doorway. Ump faced them a last time and said, "Look, no one's telling you to do anything, understand? I'm leaving here, and I'll be back in about four or five hours. If you don't want to do anything, that's fine. Don't. Just sit here. But if anyone does, that's okay also. I'll make sure nothing gets discovered. Think of it as Christmas. I mean, how many people get a chance to kill someone without having to worry about it?"

There was a long quiet. Finally, Farber said, "We aren't murderers, Mr. Brady. Even Father Carroll isn't angry enough to kill someone."

"If that's true," said Ump, "maybe both of you will be around when I come back."

Farber turned indignant. "What do you mean by that? What the hell is that supposed to—"

Ump left. They watched as the door slammed shut, and then heard him slide across a bolt, locking it from the outside.

Farber wanted to finish his thought. He turned to George Maye and, in a quieter voice, said, "What's that supposed to mean?"

George shook his head. So far none of them had moved, probably because no one yet believed what had happened.

"The police will show up," said Conley. "The police will come, and we'll get free, and then we'll see what happens."

"The first thing to do is get free," said Father Carroll.

"Exactly," said Conley. "Hell, he gave us the razors. Once we cut the ropes, we'll figure a way out."

"That's what we need to do; cut the ropes," said George Maye. "Darlene . . . Sweetheart, reach down by your feet for the razor. Then you can cut my rope, and I'll cut yours."

Darlene still wouldn't talk to her husband.

"Darlene?" he said.

Farber, meanwhile, turned to the priest and said, "I don't suppose you'd mind a short truce, just until we're free of this place? You cut my ropes, I'll cut yours?"

"Perhaps," said Carroll.

"Perhaps?"

"Perhaps," said Carroll, "if you cut mine first."

Next to Carroll, Earl turned to the town treasurer, trying to offer his wrists. "Miss Anderson?" he pleaded.

Anderson didn't even look at him. "Fuck off, Earl," she said.

Conley was smarter. He leaned next to Fleming and said, "I'll cut yours if you cut mine."

Fleming nodded, and both men began wriggling for the razors. They only then saw Joseph, who, on his own, had picked up a blade and was working at his rope.

Fleming became worried. "Hey," Fleming said to the others. "Hey, someone stop him. Someone take his razor!"

Conley tried kicking at Joseph, but Joseph rolled away. "You're just too fucking late," Joseph said. "Another second and I'm free. Then we'll see about Christmas."

"*Stop* him," Fleming shouted.

George wriggled closer to Joseph. Rather than fight, however, he extended his wrists. "Me, too."

"Joseph," called Farber. He didn't know the man, but he tried sounding like an old friend. "Joseph, free all of us and we can get out of here."

It was all premature, because even with the razor, Joseph had a lot of rope to cut. Joseph realized this himself when, in the midst of gloating, he lost his grip and the razor slipped. Suddenly he was scraping the floor just like Conley and Fleming.

"Just a second," Joseph said. "I can see it, I can see it. . . ."

Then, just as quickly, he couldn't see it. No one could.

Ump killed the lights.

There was a fresh quiet. No one moved—afraid of another surprise, needing a moment to readjust to the darkness. Waiting, however, didn't improve anyone's eyesight. Without windows, and with the doors bolted shut, the room was as close to total darkness as any of them had experienced.

George Maye leaned toward the vicinity of his wife and whispered, "What the hell's going on? Why'd he turn off the lights?"

Darlene whispered back, "To make it easier for us."

"Shit, don't talk stupid," George said. "How does this make anything easier?"

Darlene understood completely. "None of us can kill if we

see who we're killing," she said. "That's why we talked to him in the first place."

"We?" George said.

Darlene ignored him, thinking aloud. "I didn't get it at first, but now I understand," she said. "In here, with the lights out . . . I think I could do it here. In the dark, it's not like you're killing at all. No blood . . . You don't have to see a thing."

"You also don't know who the hell you're killing," George said.

Darlene thought a moment, then said, "Who cares, if you're the only one left?"

George considered everything Darlene had said, shocked less by what Frank Brady had set up than his wife's reasoning. "You don't sound good, Darlene." He inched closer to comfort her. "You're making this sound like it's real. It's not, okay? Killing isn't right and everyone here knows it. We're just going to sit still until it's over. You hear me? We're just going to wait it out and—"

George stopped inching over. Unless he was mistaken, he had inched clear to where Darlene had been sitting.

"Darlene?" he called. "Darlene?"

And then he heard her. . . . Near his feet, struggling in the dirt, breathing hard as if she had no time.

And cutting . . .

Cutting . . .

"I still don't get it," Leon said. "Wouldn't it be easier just letting things go?"

"These people don't know how to let things go," said Ump. He made himself comfortable in the car.

Leon shook his head, unconvinced. "Gilley's roulette," he said. "I haven't heard about that since Terry used it on the Mancusos about five years ago."

"The Mancusos?" Ump said.

"Well, not Alf or Fred Mancuso, but Vinny and Burt and all the guys underneath," said Leon. "After Alf and Fred died, all their number twos started fighting, trying to figure out who was the new top dog. So Freido and Mr. Lucci, they asked Terry to straighten them out. Terry gave them the Gilley's treatment.

He stuck Vinny and the rest of them in a basement, dropped a couple of guns, and said he'd be back in the morning."

"So that's how Vinny took charge."

"Vinny's good," said Leon. "He would've gotten it anyway, but this definitely quickened things. The point, Ump, is that maybe it works with guys used to pulling triggers, but these people here, they aren't like you and me. I mean, look at where the hell we are. We are, honest to God, out in the middle of nowhere, sitting in a fucking cornfield a hundred miles from home. This makes no sense."

"What I'm doing's already done," said Ump. "Besides, I've got other business. Want to do me a favor and take me back to the house?"

Leon turned the car around and headed for town. Once they were on the highway, Leon glanced at Ump, grinned, and said, "Don't you want to know how he did it?"

Ump didn't understand.

"How he did it," repeated Leon. "How Vinnie survived."

"By killing everyone else," Ump said.

"Not exactly," Leon said. "See, up until the last second, it looked like Soup had won it, but that was because Vinnie spent the whole fight hiding in a small corner of the basement. Soup must have figured everyone was dead, because the moment I opened the basement door, Soup came strutting up the stairs, his hand open like I was going to give him a trophy. Just before he reached the top step, Vinnie popped him."

Ten minutes later, Leon pulled in front of the Gratton house. "Thanks," said Ump. "Meet me back at the warehouse about breakfast time."

"Anything you want, Ump; that's why I'm here."

Ump double-checked the time, then sent Leon on his way. He still had his keys to the Gratton house, and he used them to get inside, figuring at this hour Francine would be asleep.

He was surprised when she turned on the light.

"Joseph?" she called.

Ump stopped at the front door and stared up at the landing. Francine was in a bathrobe. She should have been surprised at seeing Ump; instead, she thought first of her bruise, again covering her cheek.

Ump said, "I've seen it. Don't worry, I've seen worse."

Francine lowered her hand. "How long are you staying?"

"Just a few hours," Ump said. "Long enough to finish a few things."

"Finish what?"

"It's not worth explaining," he said.

"Except that it involves Joseph," she said.

"I'd say Joseph involved himself," Ump said. He excused himself and hobbled to the telephone. He dialed, waited. . . . After two rings, a voice answered and Ump said, "Freido? . . . Yeah, wake up. . . . I don't know yet. He's playing Gilley's with a bunch of other people. . . . No . . . Four, five hours, until morning . . . That's what I figured. In the meantime, you should make arrangements." He glanced at Francine. "Yeah, I think so. If she isn't, she isn't. This isn't between them, anyway. . . . Freido, like I said; this wasn't a favor. If he loses, fine; if he wins, the same rules apply to him as for everyone else. . . . I don't know. Hold on, I'll ask." Ump cupped the mouthpiece and asked Francine, "You want to talk with your brother?"

Francine walked to the phone, not sure why Ump was talking to her brother. "Freido, what's going on?" she asked.

While she listened to Freido, Ump limped off to the kitchen.

"No, Freido, I don't understand at all," she said. "What are you talking about, and how does this involve Joseph?" She strained to keep Ump in view. "Money? You've already paid me for Frank's room. Why should you give me more? . . . No, he's in the kitchen. . . . All right, stop it. You're at the apartment? I can call you after I talk with Frank."

Francine hung up and looked for Ump. She found him on a kitchen stool, leafing through the phone book. "Frank?"

Ump found what he wanted, marked it, and looked up at Francine. "You mind if I ask you a question?"

"Not if you'll answer mine," she said.

Ump considered this. "All right, he said. "My question is, how would you feel if Joseph came in the door right now and went upstairs to bed?"

Francine thought a moment. "Honest answer?"

Ump nodded.

Francine looked down. "I don't know," she said. "I can't answer."

"Nothing at all?" Ump said.

"Nothing good," she answered. The question bothered her. "If you want something more . . ."

"I want the truth," said Ump.

"Then you got it," she said. "Don't expect me to make up emotions. Joseph and I aren't that close right now."

Ump accepted this. "All right," he said. "Now tell me how you'd feel if Joseph didn't come through that door? Suppose he never came home?"

Francine froze. It was a look of absolute fear. "Did Joseph get hurt?"

"Maybe," said Ump. "Maybe not."

She sat beside Ump. "What's Freido up to?"

"Nothing."

"Don't lie to me. I'm not completely stupid. I've been doing a little checking on my own and I've got a fair idea of how Freido makes a living. That also means I can make a good guess about you."

"I'm still not lying," said Ump. "If you know what Freido does, fine. If you know what I do, even better. But what's going on with Joseph is between him and me. Your husband and half this town have been trying to twist my one good leg for favors."

"So?"

"So, they all wanted to play a game, I'm letting them play," said Ump. "The point, Francine, is you've got a choice— you can either hang around here for the final score, or your brother'll put you and the kids up at a hotel until things settle. Then you can decide what to do with yourself."

Francine stared at him. Ump wasn't sure if he saw gratitude or anger. "You're telling me that you and Freido may have killed Joseph?"

"That's what Freido would tell you," said Ump. "I wouldn't put it that way."

"And what would you tell me?" she said. "It sure as hell better be good, Frank, because I might just kill you myself. If Freido would dare stick his nose in my affairs . . . If he would pretend to hurt Joseph as a favor to me . . ."

"Look, I know you don't need Freido," said Ump. "You

don't need me either. You're tougher than Joseph, I don't care how much he bruises you. You're as tough as my wife."

Francine was surprised by the mention of Ump's wife. It softened her.

"I still don't get it, Frank," she said quietly.

"I'm not too hot on explaining things," Ump said. "The simplest way to put it is that, three, four times, Joseph egged me for business. I ignored him, but he kept pushing, just like the others. So now I'm giving him a chance to take care of it himself."

Francine simply shook her head.

"Personally, I think he's gonna do okay," said Ump. "Joseph's a fuck. Fucks tend to live longer than other people. But whatever happens to him doesn't necessarily have to change your situation. Joseph walked away from the house tonight and so can you. Freido's ready to help. No matter what happens to Joseph, you can have complete control over your life."

"That's easy for you to say," she said. "You'll be home with your wife tomorrow."

"It's easy to say because I'm staring at a woman with a black eye."

Francine reached to cover her face again, and Ump pulled down her hand. She turned and looked at Ump, thinking, for a moment, they were going to kiss . . . that Ump would hold her tight and kiss her and carry her upstairs, and that would be the end. No more Joseph, no more Freido . . .

"I just can't, Francine," he said.

She wished hard for another answer.

"See," Ump said, "I'm happy. You're hatesick. Me, I'm lovesick."

Francine thought a moment, then freed her hand and walked to the kitchen door. "I'm going upstairs to think it over," she said. She looked over her shoulder and smiled sadly. "If you want to join me, feel free."

"I'm gonna try like hell not to," Ump said.

Francine continued upstairs. As for Ump, he scanned the phone directory again. The number rang maybe twelve times before someone answered. "Waylin Cabs," a voice said.

"Yeah, I want a taxi," said Ump. "I want one bad."

"What's your address?"

Ump gave the dispatcher a location.

"Fine, Mr. . . ."

"Brady," Ump said.

"We can have a car there in twenty minutes."

"That's almost fine," he said, "except I want a particular cab. You got a car with the license plate HC-344?"

The dispatcher put him on hold, checked the number, and said, "That's one of ours."

"Then that's the cab I want," Ump said. "Send *him*. Tell him to come in an hour, and tell him it's the guy with the cast. Also, tell him to come ready."

"Ready?" the dispatcher said.

"He should understand," Ump said, hanging up.

He picked up his crutches, left the kitchen, and headed for the front door. He had a distance to walk, but it was all right, he had the time.

More important, he had a job.

It had been coming since the day Ump arrived.

Rule after rule broken . . . A complete disregard for common sense . . . A challenge to everything Ump valued.

And it didn't come from Joseph, or Bill Conley, or Fleming, or Shirley Anderson, or Father Carroll, or anyone else in the warehouse. No, the gauntlet was thrown by someone Ump had yet to meet—an anonymous hack who liked running red lights and swerving inches from Ump, just to speed away. The others were also important, but this was truly his unfinished business—making certain that no one, no matter who they were or where they lived, dared take the rules for granted. Certainly not with the flaunting disregard the cabbie had shown. If he allowed it . . . If he stayed in New York and let the rules be broken one by one, first in Waylin, then in the county, then the state . . .

But he wouldn't. That was why he had returned, and why, at two in the morning, he stood in the center of a dark alley, waiting, knowing that, when the time came, he would have to overcome his handicaps. Because this was no ordinary cabbie; this was a killer. Ump could sense it in a man, and he had felt the tingling every time the cab veered near him. It was like dealing with another Blade, except this one didn't carry a razor, he drove a six-cylinder engine and carried no-fault insurance. Well, why not? Who said a killer always needs a hand weapon?

So Ump stood in the alley, balanced on his crutches, brick walls on either side, streets at either end of the alley. He was waiting when, from behind, there came the grind of an engine and the first touch of headlights.

Ump used his crutches to pivot. He turned in time to see the lights sweep into the alley. Ump didn't move. The car was no more than fifty yards away, a yellow death machine. And beyond the headlights, still tucked behind his steering wheel, Ump could see the dark outline of a man. It could have been all of Ump's villains rolled into one, everyone who had dropped eleven items on a ten-item express line, or had broken a speed limit, or had run a red light, or had miscounted change, or had mistaken left for right, or had stopped loving his family, or had argued with an umpire. . . . There he was, idling the engine, waiting for Ump to lift an arm and call a cab.

"Hey," the cabby shouted. "Frank Brady."

Ump leaned into the headlights. "Who is it?"

The cabbie laughed. "I used to live in New York. I lived about two blocks from your house."

Ump still didn't follow.

"You remember," the cabbie said. "I was driving a livery. I was in business until I clipped a kid on his bike. Then you got pissed and beat the shit out of me."

Ump thought he remembered, but couldn't come up with a name.

"My wife left," the cabbie said. "I also lost my New York license, but that didn't matter, because you totaled my car."

Ump still couldn't remember.

"Come on," the driver said. "You threw my TV out the window. Then my stereo and the sofa and the bed. . . ."

"Albert Rifka," said Ump. "You lived on Elmont Street."

"*Piney Avenue,*" said Rifka. "Jesus Christ, what's with you? You do this sort of thing every day of your life?"

Ump didn't answer.

"It's because of you I ended up in this shithole," the cabbie said. "Please, tell me you still want a cab."

"I still want a cab," said Ump.

"Good," Rifka said, revving the engine. "Then all you have to do is whistle."

Ump relaxed, taking stock of his body, concentrating on the target. He had made a point of finding a place where they would be locked in battle, something that would eliminate any of the confusion of a warehouse. And he had found it. He had to wonder briefly if, maybe, he had tilted the odds a bit too heavily in the cabbie's favor.

Then he threw aside the crutches, brought his fingers to his lips, and whistled.

Instantly, the cabbie shifted into gear.

Ump reached behind his back, tugged his gun free, and leveled the sight. He aimed for the windshield, but then came the surprise. The car was roaring at him, clocking up from zero to sixty, less than fifteen yards away, and just when Ump had a line on the cabbie's head, he was blinded by the high beams. Ump winced, unable to see the driver, and not even able to make out the car. It was only seconds to impact, and he had to make a decision to jump left or right. There would be a chance for only one guess.

Ump threw his weight to the left.

The side mirror whipped against his wrist and he landed hard, breaking his right wrist cast. Still, it could have been worse, especially if the cabbie had veered with him. Now his biggest worry was finding the gun. When the car had struck his hand, the gun had flicked away. Ump knew it was somewhere in the alley—the car couldn't have carried it far—but after first being in the dark, and then staring into blinding light, and then again ending up in darkness . . . There was only one thing he could make out clearly: the car, as it exited onto the street, had made a U-turn and was heading back into the alley.

Ump leaned against the wall and pulled himself up. It was just like before, except now he didn't have a weapon. The car bore down on him, this time the high beams staying on from start to finish. Ump used the light to look about quickly for his gun. All he could make out were the garbage cans, and beside the cans, a small pile of broken cinder blocks.

Ump hopped over to the cinder blocks. When the cabbie was again on top of him, he lifted one, heaved it at the grille and threw himself on top of the cans.

The cinder block landed in front of the car, but when the cabbie ran over it, the car jacked into the air. The rear fishtailed into the cans and Ump again found himself on the ground, watching as the cab finished its escape on the opposite street.

But the car was wounded. On its way out, Ump could see the sparks underneath its chassis—a busted muffler dragging across the pavement. There was also smoke coming from the hood, and it made Ump think that maybe Albert Rifka was also hurt. And if he was hurt too badly, maybe he'd take off, and they'd have to settle for a future rematch.

But Ump was underestimating Rifka. Sure, Ump wanted the cabbie, but the cabbie also wanted him. Ump should have caught on when Rifka turned the car around. "I'm going to get you, Brady," he shouted. "This time, you're dragging under my car."

Ump again took his position, with one difference; this time, when the cabbie gunned the engine, Ump stood in the center of the alley, his legs separated, with a cinder block already raised above his head. And he didn't move, not when the car began accelerating, not when Rifka screamed and slammed his car horn.

Ump should have jumped. It was down to a rock versus a four-foot steel grille, with the grille barreling at him at amazing speed. He was going to lose. He had to lose.

But Ump was too busy for second thoughts. He reared back and heaved the block at the car.

The cabbie covered his face. The brick came down like a meteor, shattering the windshield, making a crater in the dashboard, and leaving the cabby fighting for control of his car. He slammed on the brakes and careened against the alley walls before stopping. Then the cabbie caught his breath and tried figuring out what had happened. One minute he was on top of Brady, the next he was under attack. And it was all real—the windshield was gone, the cinder block was still wedged in the dashboard. . . . The only thing missing was the enemy.

The only thing missing was Ump.

"Brady?" the cabbie shouted.

There was nothing. In front was the empty alley; behind, he could see clear to the street.

"Brady, where the fuck are you?"

Nervous, he tried opening his door, but it was jammed. All the wall slamming had twisted it shut, he figured. Then he heard something. Rather than push at the door, he rolled down the window and looked down.

Ump was alongside the car, his sleeve caught on the door handle, his body stretched on the street.

"Brady," Rifka said, pleased.

The cabbie knew better than to get out and fight. He rolled up the window, shifted, and again hit the accelerator. With Ump hanging on, the cabbie turned toward the garbage cans. He sliced against the cans, smashing Brady into the garbage. Then he had a better idea and veered for the alley wall. He pressed even harder on the accelerator, then gave a quick twist to the steering wheel. A second later, Ump was ground against the wall. Rifka hit against the bricks so hard that the shape of Ump pressed in the side of the car. By the time he reached the end of the alley, Ump's entire body was imprinted into the paneling.

Rifka reached the end of the alley and spun the car against a lamppost. The cabbie rolled down the window, expecting to see nothing but a splatter of blood, or at best the tips of a few fingers knotted on the door handle.

But he was still there. In fact, he even had a hand on the door handle.

This was too much for Rifka. He told Ump to die, then took a final trip down the alley. The cabbie careened left and right, smashed the car into both walls, did his best to turn his car into a heap and Ump into a corpse. Nothing could survive this beating. By the time he finished the alley, the door was bending into his lap. Rifka stopped, catching his breath, looking out his window to enjoy his victory.

And Ump was still hanging on. One hand was still on the car, and the other held a broad strip of wood. "I grabbed it when you ran me into the cans," said Ump, "When I lift it up, I can skid right off the walls."

Rifka looked down, amazed.

Then Ump reached in and wrapped an arm about Rifka's throat.

"You also got to let your bones bounce," Ump said. "Think about soft things, like warm butter."

The cabbie tried to pull free, but it didn't make any difference. Ump was too strong. The cabbie could only do one thing: hit the accelerator and take them both out. And if that was how Frank Brady wanted it, that's how it would be. "Soft bones, my ass," the cabbie said. He floored the pedal, shot out of the alley, and headed for the nearest building. "Fuck you and your mother," Rifka said. Then the car lurched over the sidewalk and smashed into a plate-glass window.

It didn't stop until they struck a checkout counter; then the car came to such a hard stop the cabbie was thrown forward, his body breaking through what was left of his shattered windshield. He landed in a rack of magazines, his body covered in glass.

"Oh, God," he cried. "Oh, Christ, I think I broke my neck."

Meanwhile, outside, Ump picked himself up off the sidewalk, the door handle dangling from his sleeve, and limped to the edge of the disaster. When the cabbie saw him, he forgot his pain and tried reaching for Ump. "You fucking, fucking moron," Rifka shouted. "What's it take to kill you? What in God's name does it take?"

Ump stared a moment, then realized he was in a clothes store. He found a new shirt and jacket, then limped away from the scene. In part, he wanted to disappear before the police came; however, he was also escaping the question.

Why wasn't he dead? After being shot, stabbed, crushed beneath cars, slammed into walls, dragged through alleys . . . why was he breathing? How could his lungs work, or his joints bend, or his head think, or his legs balance?

Was he really that good, or was he just that lucky?

Or was it something else—was there something more important going on? Was Ump a little bit more than human?

Was Ump a little bit of a miracle?

He stood at the corner and looked up at the sky. Thank goodness Nan wasn't around; the last thing he wanted was her seeing him turn religious. But it seemed the right thing to do for now. He looked up and, almost in a whisper, said, "Why are you doing this? Why are you letting me live?"

He never expected an answer, but he was given one. Indeed, he was given an answer as soon as the question was asked.

While Ump watched, the corner light changed from red to

[223]

green. Ump stared a moment, then obeyed, crossing the street and stopping at the opposite corner.

The instant his foot touched the curb, the light turned red.

That was his answer.

The rules, he thought. That was why he lived.

That's why he would always live.

Ump was satisfied with the answer. Whether it came from God or someone else or from himself, it didn't matter. He was at peace. He left the cabbie and the corner, hummed quietly, and searched for a phone so he could buy a ride back to the warehouse.

TWENTY-NINE

"Where to?"

Ump reached over the seat and gave the address. He was in a second cab and just now checking the time. Four-thirty—four hours since he had locked the warehouse doors.

"You're sure about this?" the cabbie said. "This is nowhere."

"I'm sure," Ump said.

The cabbie shrugged, and while he drove them out of town, Ump used the time to change clothes. In ten minutes, the cab was off the highway and at the warehouse. He parked by a turnaround and Ump handed him twenty dollars.

"I can't change this," said the driver.

"Then don't," said Ump, leaving the cab and limping to Leon's car. He could see Leon stretched in the back seat, his feet perched on an open window and his arms dangling out another. Leon could have been mistaken for a corpse—he had that rolled-carpet look, like someone who was too stiff for folding, but could be bent a little at the ends. Ump walked up to the car, tapped Leon's feet, and said, "Wake up."

Leon raised his head. "Ump?" He rubbed his eyes and tried reading his wristwatch. "What time is it? I haven't been sleeping long, I don't think. When did you get here? What time is it?"

Ump relaxed, satisfied with himself, knowing that, at most, all he had left to do was a little late-night housekeeping. With Leon's help, Ump figured they could be gone in less than an hour.

"Ump, you want a doughnut?"

Leon was up now, stretching, yawning, reaching to the floor of the car for a cardboard box.

"What kind?" Ump said, looking for a jelly.

"I got here an hour ago," said Leon. "How'd things go in town?"

Ump chewed and nodded. "I think well."

Leon, his mouth full with a cruller, gave Ump the once-over and said, "You look a mess."

"I'm a little sore."

Leon watched Ump, then took another bite. "I haven't heard a peep from them," he said, nodding at the warehouse.

"Maybe it's finished. Maybe we can go in early."

Leon shrugged. "Your call," he said. "We do what you want to do. That's why I'm here."

Ump walked to the warehouse door, listened, heard nothing, looked at Leon, and shrugged.

"I bet they're all dead," Leon said.

Ump glanced at his watch and realized they were only twenty minutes early. "Let's peek," he said. Leon agreed, and while Ump dug in his pocket for the key, Leon walked to the side of the warehouse for the circuit breaker. Ump opened the padlock, pulled the chain free, slid open the door, and shouted, "Hey—who's it gonna be?"

Nothing. Ump waited for anyone to come forward, but no one did. He didn't know if they really had all been popped, or if too many people were playing Vinnie's game—sitting back and waiting to pick off whoever ran for the door. He whistled, clapped his hands. . . . Nobody moved until Leon threw the switch; then, in the light, it was like watching the dead slowly rise.

They were scattered about the room—someone caught in the firing position, another in the midst of crawling for freedom, another belly down. There seemed no strategy to what they were doing, until Ump realized that somehow, in the darkness, Conley and Fleming had found each other and were braced back-to-back, ready to defend from all directions. Elsewhere, George Maye had hidden behind an oil drum, while Darlene was no more than a yard from Ump, squatting by the door, the gun cradled in her hands, so lost in thought she didn't even look at the opened door.

Leon stood next to Ump and surveyed the scene. "Jeez. I'm beginning to understand why they wanted you. They probably can't shit without directions."

Leon pointed out Father Carroll, who had his gun aimed at the back of Shirley Anderson, who had hers aimed at no one. As with Darlene, even with the lights on, no one moved—Anderson because she still expected trouble, and Carroll because he looked terrified at his own behavior.

"They aren't even bleeding," said Leon. "They might as well have spent the night in bed."

Ump looked at a far corner of the room where there was a small sign of activity. The council president Matthew Farber and Shirley Anderson's blackmailer were in a deathfight, both gripping each other's throat, with the balance hanging on a struggle for Farber's knife.

Leon walked over to break it up. "All right, all right," he said. "You had your chance. Time's up."

It wasn't enough. The fight didn't stop until Leon booted them. "What, are you guys hard of hearing?"

"He came after me," said Farber. "He snuck up from behind and—" Farber jerked the knife free. The blackmailer fell back and Farber began poking the air. Then Leon kicked them again, and the knife slipped from Farber's hand. Soon both men turned to Leon for help.

"I said it's over," Leon repeated. "Now stand up and head for the door."

They caught their breath, brushed themselves off and, looking down, embarrassed, joined the others in a slow walk for the door.

"Hey," Leon shouted at everyone. "Hey, don't be slobs. Clean up after yourselves. Pick up those razors."

Ump stood at the entrance, where he made certain the weapons were dropped in their boxes. With each of the revolvers, he checked the chambers and emptied them. As for Leon, he cursed everyone in the group, then walked about with a plastic garbage sack, picking up the loose rope and litter. "Say, Ump," Leon shouted. "How clean do you want this place? I got a pile of shit in one corner and some puke by the drum."

Ump told him not to bother, and Leon finished his work. As for Ump, he did a second count of his guests, then limped into the warehouse, looking for Joseph. For a minute, he couldn't find him. He even suspected Joseph had manufactured an escape, which would have at least proved that Francine's husband could be resourceful.

Joseph, however, was only in the midst of a botched escape. Ump found him working at one of the sheet-metal walls, his fingers caught under the metal.

"I unlocked the door," Ump told him. "You can go out the easy way."

Joseph looked over his shoulder. He shook his head and said, "You're gonna kill me."

Ump looked perplexed.

"You hate me," Joseph said. "That's what this is all about, so you could get one of them to kill me. But they didn't, and now you're gonna."

Ump didn't know what to say. Rather than discuss matters, he bent over and took Joseph's gun.

"Well, if you want the door, it's there," said Ump, turning and walking away.

Outside, Leon was sliding the boxes onto the back seat. As for Ump's guests, they stood in a line and waited. No one said a word, no one ran away. . . . They only wanted Ump. They needed someone to put a shape to the evening, to explain what had happened, and let them know everything was all right.

Ump walked out of the warehouse, stared at them all, and said, "Anyone hungry? Leon's got doughnuts."

Still no one answered. Leon shook his head for the last time and decided to wait for Ump in the car.

Ump was also through. He left the box of doughnuts on the road and opened the passenger door. He was ready to leave, when Father Carroll stepped forward and called, "Mr. Brady?"

Ump turned and Father Carroll walked closer. His eyes were glazed, and he slumped with each step until shuffling to a stop.

"Mr. Brady, do you know what we've been through?"

"I got a fair idea," Ump said.

"And this was your idea of help?" He glanced at Matthew Farber, then leaned forward and whispered, "Nothing's changed."

"That's not my fault," Ump said.

[228]

Darlene also moved closer. "My husband is still alive."

Now Anderson joined them. "They're all alive," she said to Ump. "I don't know what we did tonight."

"I'm getting a divorce," Darlene said.

"I'm getting a lawyer," said Anderson.

"I don't know what I'm supposed to do," said Carroll.

"Excuse me," said Conley. "What are you all talking about? Should I be hearing any of this?"

Ump hushed them, but their tongues were loosened. What was the point? they asked. What did we get? What did we gain?

Ump finally had enough. He told Leon to turn on the engine, then said to them, "You know what you got out of this? You really want to know?"

They quieted.

Ump held his temper in check long enough to answer. "You got to live," he said. "Where I come from, that makes for a good night's work." He slammed the door shut and rolled down the window. "You decide. Either you all won or all lost. No matter what, you don't need me anymore."

"I need you," said Carroll.

"None of you do," Ump said. "You can always come back to the warehouse, right?"

Ump looked past Father Carroll to Joseph. Joseph had appeared at the warehouse door, and now he shouted, "What about Francine?" Joseph stumbled up to the car. "You saw her while I was in there, didn't you? First you play me for the jerk and then you poke her."

Ump wished he weren't so tired; he might have taken Joseph back into the warehouse and, with just the two of them, locked the door.

"What'd you do with her?" Joseph shouted. "Where's my family?"

Ump stared at him. "The honest-to-God truth, Joseph—I don't know. I could find out if I wanted to, but I got my own life. You follow that? I ask, because it seems to be the one point none of you understand."

Ump tapped Leon's arm, and Leon turned them around and out for the road. When they reached the intersection, Leon asked, "Where now?"

"Home," said Ump.

"Straight into the sun, huh?" Leon asked, grinning. Ump looked almost asleep. Leon, however, was wide awake; he had eaten too many doughnuts. "What a bunch of fucks," he said. "Not one of them dead. They weren't even cut. No marks, no blood . . ."

"They got lucky," said Ump tiredly.

"Luck, bullshit," said Leon. "None of them had any balls."

"I don't know about that," said Ump. "You didn't see the guns. Two were used up and one had only three bullets."

Leon glanced at Ump, thinking he was kidding, but Ump didn't change his story. Leon grinned, started chuckling, then slapped Ump on the arm. "Come on," he said, laughing.

Ump looked at Leon and said, "Do me a favor and find a phone."

Leon, still enjoying the joke, nodded and pulled off by a phone booth. It was six in the morning when Ump tried calling home. "Nan?"

"Frank," said Nan. "Frank, I was just making breakfast."

"You were supposed to spend the night at Tommy Lucci's," Ump said.

"I got sick and tired of being at other people's homes."

"I thought you would," said Ump.

"You take care of your business?"

"Got it all done," he said.

"It's all finished?" she said. "You're ready to come home?"

"I'm ready," said Ump. "Provided you still want me."

"I want you," she said. "Stop wasting time. If you're here in two hours, you got breakfast. Think you can make it?"

"I better," said Ump.

"Then get home."

"You bet."

"I love you, Frank."

"That's what keeps me going, Nan." He hung up and walked back to the car.

Ump climbed into the passenger seat, and Leon said, "What's she making?"

"I think pancakes," Ump said.

"Really?" Leon said. "Pancakes? How long will she hold them?"

"Two hours," said Ump.

[230]

Leon thought a moment. "I can do that. I bet I can."

"Then do it," said Ump. "Just watch the speed limit. And don't run the lights."

Leon signaled and headed for the interstate.

As for Ump, he closed his eyes again. The sun was over the horizon and he was basking in the early light.

It was going to be a warm day.

As warm as a hot gun.

As warm as pancakes.